Wherever We Step
the Land is Mined

Wherever We Step the Land is Mined

NATALIE SCOTT

JONATHAN CAPE
THIRTY BEDFORD SQUARE LONDON

First published 1980
Copyright © Natalie Scott 1980
Jonathan Cape Ltd, 30 Bedford Square, London WC1

British Library Cataloguing in Publication Data

Scott, Natalie
Wherever we step the land is mined.
I. Title
823'.9'IF   PR9619.3.S/
ISBN 0–224–01736–5

The author and publishers are grateful for permission to
reproduce lines from the song 'By the light of the silvery
moon', lyric by Ed Madden, music by Gus Edwards: ©
1909 Warner Bros Inc., copyright renewed, all rights re-
served; also used by permission of B. Feldman & Co. Ltd,
138–140 Charing Cross Road, London WC2H 0LD.

Printed in Great Britain by The Anchor Press Ltd
and bound by Wm Brendon & Son Ltd
both of Tiptree, Essex

For Andy

'He who has a why to live can bear with almost any how.'

Nietzsche

Chapter One

She closes the door after her, of course she doesn't slam it, and the lock clicks. It always does with a grudging reluctance as it sets her outside the handsome house; dark, warm, full of furniture and clothes.

'I must have some time to myself,' murmurs Jonquil Jamieson, middle-aged now, but never, apart from a few baby years, able to cope successfully with that name, chosen by Betty and Fred Spring forty-seven years ago.

Forty-seven years ago!

'She's not going to suffer like me,' Betty Spring had vowed, dimpling the tiny cheek, aglow with the achievement of birth safely negotiated. And did not tempt fate to try again. 'My little girl's not going to be named ordinary.'

'Might be lumbering her a bit,' suggested young Fred Spring tentatively; round-faced, pink, naive and almost as innocent as his new baby daughter, but dead within seven years, worn and frayed, unable to meet the attack presented by life, by Betty Spring and a liver disease.

The night air is cool, silky. It is silent, heavily loaded with moonlight, and she crosses the precise pattern of the paving to lift the latch on the solid, protective gate which she must have opened and closed twelve thousand times in the last twelve years.

'Unseasonable,' she tells herself and means the weather.

It is August and a coldness should be seeping through her sweater, the wool-mix spencer, skirt and medium-gauge panty hose wrapped over scarlet briefs. Her feet are tight in her shoes. Walking fast in high heels, she realises, gets more difficult with the years. She hadn't thought to change them.

Jonquil Jamieson, known as Jon from the day she became aware a name could be abbreviated to become acceptable, is of average height; five feet five in bare feet. She weighs nine and a half stone on the scales in the bathroom tiled in pink and grey, and where once skinny, now is slimmish with a tendency to pillowed hips which will inflate without exercise. Her face is oval and bland, sandy hair cut sensibly just to cover the ears. She has learned to choose the colour of her clothes with care otherwise her skin looks livery. Her expression is usually sweet, two half moons of a circle folding into either side of her mouth, there to stay in sickness and in health, in pleasure and repose. Brown eyes her lucky ticket in the lottery of looks, with absolute directness and absence of guile, they reach out from deep sockets and remain memorable in a face that could otherwise be forgotten.

Jonquil Jamieson is the wife of Gilbert. She has borne two children, Ruth and Paul.

It is surprisingly quiet in this built-up area of well-established, well-maintained suburbia, within four kilometres of the rattle of the city whose Harbour gives it prominence in geography texts in some parts of the world. Tourists and its own citizens when sending obligatory postcards and calendars overseas certainly include Kodachrome reproductions of the Bridge and the Opera House for which Sydney claims a small fame.

She is walking briskly now, through slanted starlight and twisted shade, having passed familiar gates and gardens ... the Sampsons where he, Timothy, has just taken silk, she, Sonya, a third lover along with her Higher School Certificate. Sonya is very energetic; their Afghan named Bobo.

The Gillets: he, Keith, an accountant, she, Gloria, a school librarian, so knows what every child should read. Little Tracy Gillet wears thick glasses.

The Maloneys: Agnes and Brian, fervent week-end gardeners when released from the chain of butcher's shops where each of their sons manages a branch. As they diligently dig, weed, mow and rake, their faces seem to have caught the red glare of meat and she has wondered, occasionally, whether they're compensating purposefully, as they plant and nourish, for so much dismembering that brings them wealth.

The Melis: whose large family determinedly leave house and garden unkempt, Giorgio and Lena unconcerned. There's a drawn tightness to her heart. Paul was often to be found there.

The moon rises higher, swells. She's unaware of how long she's been walking, how far she's gone. She walks on and on, at a slower pace, a regular pace.

Where is she going? It doesn't matter, but squinting for a landmark, is surprised. There's a brief flare-up of hostilities within her … is it stomach, bowels or heart? It doesn't matter. Momentarily she's shrivelled; a scrawny old tobacco-chewing ancient of a primitive tribe, stumps for teeth, claws for hands. It passes.

Cold, the air seeps into the cashmere sweater; she flails arms like two propellers and moves faster. The headlights of an approaching car lance the night and she's caught foolishly in their glare. Does the driver question this middle-aged propelling woman, well-cut and sensible clothes defined in the lights, but not the scarlet briefs?

She rounds a corner and the roadway widens. Trees precede her at regulated intervals, knobbled trunks forced into beds of concrete which the council decrees they must not crack.

'Off with your head if you grow too fast,' she tells them, 'off with your head, off with your head, off with your head,' and her feet march to this tune.

Taller trees flank her left; towering blocks of flats divided by gardens in which few children are permitted to play. The severity of outline is more apparent at night with no colour of green grass shearing to brown soil; where flowers and shrubs stand regimented, uniformly inky. An odd irradiated glow is cast on a few by lighting from the street and the outdoor lamps of the buildings themselves. These growing things take on the sterility of the tinsel tree Gilbert bought years ago, and still in use at Christmas.

'Breathe,' she defies a waterspout covered in metallic ivy. 'Breathe,' and she gulps at the night air savagely before shaking herself into order like a dog wet from a swim. She subsides into a normal breathing pattern and goes on. She burrows to remember which civilisation stacked their dead as we stack our living. Lights burn in some of the windows, others snap erratically, but most are black voids and she feels alone in an unpeopled world.

'Shauveen,' she reads and crosses a driveway; then Clareville, Buckley Towers, Shalimar, Bellevue, Huntley. Huntley's balconies curve with iron railings, each corner topped by a pot neat in the shape of an urn.

She approaches an illuminated hoarding, streamers of plastic hanging raggedly. Though an August night no wind stirs them to fairground gaiety.

'Here', declares the hoarding on this building under construction, and her eyes steal over the words, 'is a unique opportunity to purchase and become owner of superior residences with City and Harbour glimpses. Northern aspect, very quiet and peaceful. Three bedrooms, master bedroom en suite, spacious living areas, dream kitchen. Laundry, L.U. garage, storeroom. Exceptional value in this Dress Circle Area.'

This citadel is named too. Green Briars.

Chapter Two

Green Briars. Nothing was wasted there. Not quite a mean little semi, an adequate little semi-detached. A narrow path ran the length of the house where damp marked brown and the fishbone flourished.

Betty had determined she should own property when it became obvious that Fred Spring's condition was terminal. His protest was mild, prompted only by debilitation. The process of moving, let alone moving house, was almost beyond him.

Live is movement and I am nearly out of life, he thought, searching for words in which to frame such a thought.

'Bet,' he said, a young man, shrunken and old, 'couldn't it be done ... well ... you know, afterwards?' If there was a shadow of a plea in his voice he preferred it undetected. It was not a thing for the present.

Betty, her face a puzzle, was ogling the print of 'Homes, Home Sites and Property for Sale', one foot patting, fingers drumming the lino of the kitchen table, scarred, but not battle-scarred as it would be should she be thwarted. If Betty knew she was behaving badly she couldn't stop. Aware of a restriction in her throat, even had she wanted to answer it would have been difficult.

'Hmmm,' she murmured, deaf to all but the inner voice which spoke above Fred's, and a great deal more temptingly ...

'Vacant possession, unique opportunity. Four large rooms, two with quality carpet. Half-tiled bathroom with gas heater. Enclosed verandah. Kitchen with dining alcove. Laundry fitted with gas copper. Sound investment.'

'Bet ... '

'What?'

There was a long pause and the kitchen clock ticked.

'If it's best for Jonnie ... '

Her animosity evaporated, the muscles in her throat relaxed, the fingers on the lino quietened. Scraping the chair back she turned to face the wraith that was her husband and vowed to honour his memory always.

'You know I'm only thinking of her. The security ... '

Fred's body, once so large and substantial, was a billowing sail folded to a skeletal mast before a rising storm. His toes were two sharp points under the blankets of the bed Betty had decided must be brought to one end of the kitchen. She couldn't be running up and down the narrow stairway night and day.

'It'll be more company.' She had lulled misgivings when he'd protested, mildly of course. Fred had never slammed a door in his life but had yearned for a door between himself and his wife these last three months. If she'd had a scrap of love left for him couldn't she have allowed him a door?

Emaciated, his head which inclined towards her rocked back on the pivot of his neck to the indent of the pillows. Life was closing in on him and the scuffles of everyone destined to live on were barely his concern.

'Jonnie ... ' Words were difficult as though his throat was filled with glue. 'Jonnie ... '

'Must you call her Jonnie?' The habit she'd been trying to eradicate for seven years rasped her tone.

'I ... I ... well, does it matter? Now?'

It still mattered to her, but she understood as a good wife should. 'It's just that I want her to have a better chance,' she relented.

But too late. Fred had only seconds left of life. A breeze

fretted one net curtain with lazy-daisy embossed border, though the window was barely open, the other tied for some reason at the top in a knot. With a supreme effort, some dart of will, he defied her for the last time.

'Jonnie ... '

'Jon ... QUIL.'

The strain of nursing Fred, or the impatience harboured towards him for most of their married life, gave the two syllables of their daughter's name a querulous twist. She wished things would change and didn't realise for another twenty minutes as she continued, assiduously, to scan the columns for the appropriate possibility – the bargain – that things had changed. The quietness of the room stretched out and she began to hear the tap in the sink drip, drip, drip.

She had been freed to the singular duty of child-raising. She hadn't willed Fred's death, and there was nothing with which she would reproach herself over the next few weeks or future years. She had done her duty.

'I did my duty by your father. I never failed him. I married him, and I stuck with him,' was something Jonquil would hear, and try to bear, regularly.

Upstairs in the smaller of the two small rooms where the wallpaper had faded to a uniform beige, Jonquil was asleep. Apart from the bed, a cupboard with an animal-print curtain held her clothes. There was also an enamelled chair, the pink Fred had painted it chipped where the tipped heels of her shoes knocked against it on wet afternoons colouring-in. The books with bending soft covers were never steady when she propped them on the bed, squared to rainbow the pages. The child liked to colour-in but rarely would the crayons stay within the outlines of circus tents and flower pots. What she liked more was to let the crayons stray, it gave her a funny feeling, on plain sheets of paper. Faces with three eyes, bodies whose arms stretched as far as the sun, telegraph poles sparking into stars, mice with a mass of whiskers, frogs who sat in buses, their skins never green.

'Not very neat,' her mother would say with a sniff, and after much practice she was to learn to be neat, not to stray.

As the breeze fretted the curtain at the kitchen window, Jonquil started in her sleep, limbs jerking out from the covering bed-clothes, stick-like and tense.

'Daddy,' she sighed and in a dream her arms folded and engaged about her father's neck, warm like the blankets. Her little hands explored his stubbly hair, lovingly slid to the skin that bumped at his hairline, fingers circling happily as latterly she had seldom been able to do.

'Your father needs rest,' she was told, but at every opportunity presented, she tried to gum herself to his side, reluctant to let him out of sight. But ... 'Go out and play in the garden, Jonquil.'

The garden, which neighbouring mothers with the same area called a yard, was small, a criss-crossed green rectangle. Once Fred had wanted to keep chickens but Betty, not keen, had been discouraging.

'They'd peck it all bare,' she warned, and of course was right, 'and wouldn't lay all year. So what's the use? Anyway it's rented.'

But he'd planted out vegetables; spinach which grew easily, carrots, cabbages and tomatoes though he'd had to watch the blight. He'd given strawberries a try, but they hadn't taken. Edges clipped, the patch of lawn nourished, then, painstakingly, he'd built the birdcage.

'Love-birds,' his wife had snorted at the first pair, but Fred had built large enough for a dozen birds.

On her fifth birthday he'd given Jonquil two Melanesian pygmies and on her sixth, a pair of rosy-faced short-tails.

There were no more birds when she turned seven. With her mother she'd gone to the hospital, necessary to allow over an hour to get there. Missing the connection meant three buses and quite a walk. Once inside the swinging doors the passages smelt sharply of soap. There were shiny sofas to sit on if ever early.

From the steel cupboard which held his belongings by the

bed in the ward where voices were muted exchanging platitudes or jokes, where the few flowers in cheap vases seemed too bright, Fred had carefully extracted a parcel for his little girl.

'What is it, Fred?' Betty asked over their daughter's head and hoped it hadn't been rashly extravagant. 'When did you get it?'

Fred watched as Jonquil drew off the ribbon and tore at the wrapping. No reply, her question ignored, Betty bent to retrieve the ribbon from the floor, measured its length, then wound it systematically over closed fingers before tucking it into her handbag. She began to smooth at the Cellophane which crackled in resistance.

'"*Birds of Australia*! 160 colour plates from the lith ... lithographs ... of John Gould." Hardly a book for a child of seven.' Betty bridled.

'Why not?' Fred snapped who had never snapped, not once that she could remember in all their married life.

Betty, about to adopt a haughty attitude, thought twice about it. What she felt, she supposed in a flash of self-pity, was a matter of indifference to everyone here.

A nurse with flawless skin glided to Fred's bedside to take up a proprietary stand. Commissioned to buy the book during off-duty hours, she was curious to see the child's reaction. It had cost so much she thought Fred mad, but he was adamant.

'She likes it,' the nurse whispered conspiratorially, and though Betty clicked her tongue it passed unnoticed.

Jonquil was absorbed. She turned from a cassowary to a brolga to a pelican, or rather the book turned itself, her hands too tiny to control the pages.

Her parents exchanged their small news in the way patients and family do, somehow paralysed by the atmosphere of the hospital, an institution where so much is unknown, so many doors closed.

'And what else did my birthday girl get?'

Jonquil pulled at the skirt of her dress. 'Mummy made this, and ... '

'Stand up. Turn around so your father can see,' Betty

commanded, pleased with the child in spotted voile, but unreasonably piqued that Jonquil hadn't yet told of the miniature sewing machine. 'And ... '

Jonquil had resettled herself as close as she could to Fred, their sandy heads bent to the Prince Albert Lyrebird.

'"These are timid birds which run away when alarmed with their tails erect,"' Fred read slowly, '"or fly to the nearest tree where, with great hops in and out of the branches, they seek a safe place."'

'And?' Betty would not be overlooked.

The child raised glowing eyes, her little white teeth gleamed. Mystified, she drew up her left shoulder, bit her lower lip and looked to Fred, who gently prompted:

'And what else did you get today?'

Jonquil bent again to the lyrebirds, the male lushly plumed, the tail feathers formed to the lyre, softer in colour. The female gave him a beady eye and the child looked straight to her mother and said:

'Sewing sheen.'

'And ... ' but she'd lost her attention and wondered if it was entirely tactful to mention *The Illustrated Child's Book of Prayer*, inscribed by Auntie Doris in bold hand: 'To dear Jonquil who will need all our prayers in her eighth year.'

The bell rang signifying visiting hour was over. With unnecessary haste some of the figures at some of the bedsides rose, eager to be out and away, almost apologetic for good health in such a place.

Smiles pasted on the adult faces, after they'd kissed him Fred watched them nibble out, Jonquil bent to one side with the book she refused to let Betty touch. She turned to wave but her mother had her fastened by the other hand and all the child was able to do was twist and shake her head jerkily in his direction. His outstretched hand, a papery white, trembled.

When what had occurred in her kitchen was apparent to Betty and she knew positively her husband was dead, flooding relief was her first response. There had been time to accommodate to Fred's approaching death. Why should she feel otherwise? She had condemned Fred long ago. It wasn't his fault he lacked the drive and ambition she'd falsely endowed him with when first they'd met. No, it wasn't his fault, it would have been the same with whoever she'd married. First, in marriage, she sought protection from a savage world, then a great change and a new life, which, in all fairness, she would have helped him construct. She'd kept buoyant, but bitterness had crept in with the realisation that Fred didn't, as she put it, 'want to go places'. Fred would have liked a brood of children, it could have been managed, but how could they properly afford them? She wouldn't be crushed by never-ending nappies and time-payments that expired only in old age. Dutiful, nevertheless she was an outlaw, and if she held the gun to her own head, Fred, too, was a casualty. She'd urged him to seek promotion and though he would have been pleased to please her, however he juggled his life it sprawled and sagged like baggy, once-good clothes which he didn't see how to discard.

Fred, content to sit with a cup of tea in his hand, Betty didn't covet champagne, didn't cry for the moon of material possessions, but was driven, not by ambition, but some energetic force demanding she expend that energy. 'I want to go up not down,' she'd tried to explain.

Why shouldn't she feel relief?

Nevertheless she kept a good front when neighbours, relatives and friends crowded into the front room after the drabness of the funeral. With them they brought cakes baked in haste and in sympathy. There were endless brews of tea in the pewter pot with the pansy-shaped lid which long ago had been presented to Fred's father on retirement. The E.P.N.S. spoons and forks Fred's workmates had clubbed together to give on his marriage were taken from the velvet-lined boxes and put into use too.

Discreetly the mourners enquired what Betty intended to do, how she would manage? And with a little girl, who wandered eyes wide from one to the other of them, dressed in sober maroon, a distant relative forgetting himself for the moment to lift her high and swing her among their heads.

Though her plans were laid Betty was not ready to divulge them. Not yet. The cost of the funeral had to be calculated before she could be certain, as well as the amount of Fred's insurance plus bonuses. Betty, contrary to what everyone present assumed, was not fearful of the future. She sliced marble cake and chocolate logs. Offering buns and piped biscuits from the assorted crockery on which they'd arrived under protective throw-overs, her hands were steady, did not tremble. She was not yet thirty, capable, resilient, and if in the dark reaches of the night any dream was troubled, she shrugged off the absurdity of it following her into daylight hours.

'She's so brave,' was murmured time and time again, and if she heard she made no reply.

Jonquil, bundled out of her bed by a neighbour, had rubbed uncomprehendingly at sleepy eyes, and when later, solemnly but directly, Betty had told her her father was now in heaven, her bewilderment was complete. She didn't understand but did sense in some disquieting way that things would be different. Why was this so? What would happen next? Years later she would remember, or believe she did, few details of Fred's face, body, but a sensation, a part of herself going away, a drawn-out receding that was strange and made her feel sick and afraid. As if pierced by an arrow she set up an uncharacter-istic howl such as her mother could not recall. The child's breath came in gasps and the tears, squeezed from her eyes, became a torrent.

Further bewildered by all the kissing and stroking of the next few days, not only from Betty but any adult who came near, her weeping grew more spasmodic. Betty, rarely given to crooning or cuddling the child, which she considered a coddling activity, embraced her again and again. The lashes of Jonquil's eyes glued into tight little bunches of brooms against the pallor of her cheeks, she blinked perplexedly at the black armbands and solemn expressions of the faces which bent solicitously down to hers.

A month later she became a gipsy of the roads.

'Get your shoes on,' or, 'Bring me your hairbrush and a ribbon,' Betty Spring would call; could it be gaily? They would breakfast early ... 'Eat your porridge; every scrap, Jonquil. It's to line your stomach and keep you going.'

With a sheaf of papers under one arm; notebook, pencil, local directory as well as sandwiches, Thermos and bananas which blackened, Betty organised her strategy with near-military precision.

'Fetch your cardigan,' and it too was stuffed into the string bag. 'Could be cold by the time we're back.'

Not once after Fred's funeral were the rented premises referred to as 'home'.

On one of the early excursions Jonquil had insisted with terrier determination, on taking *Birds of Australia*. It proved too heavy to take again. And while the little girl talked a great deal to herself when alone, she could be silent for hours. When Betty conversed with her, often she couldn't find answers, though she tried to catch the tune and follow.

Despite the fact that she was in a hurry, Betty, true to her generation, was bred to a time when it was usual to suffer delay. Jonquil straggling, they crossed and criss-crossed areas acceptable either by neighbourhood or price, and many a morning agonised into afternoon, the hours dense and solid for the child, before the right property was brought to light.

'This is IT,' Betty trumpeted at last, and sabbath bells in the locality of narrow streets where the palings of dividing fences stood like old, grey soldiers ready for pensioning announced the evening service. Somewhere a whistle wailed.

'This is IT!'

'What is, what is?' Jonquil, tired at the bus stop, little shoulders hunched, right foot drawn over the instep of the left, inexplicably sensed some joy in the air. 'What, what?' but her mother's reply seemed unsatisfactory so there must be more to it than she was told. And it must be a joke; Betty smiled and smiled.

Dusk began to smear the sky and a wind with a gritty edge to it rose as they bumped along on a No. 25, a sticky bull's-eye slipped into her mouth, Betty humming, smiling still, indulgent. What was the cause for celebration? Jonquil tried to sit straight and put a proper expression on her face.

Green Briars.

'Who'd have thought it,' Betty was to say twice before they reached their stop and descended, the length of the street deserted, rain threatening, Betty bubbling like a hot poker plunged into water. 'Who'd have thought it! That this is it!'

Funny, of all the advertisements, the properties inspected, that this should be it!

'Semi, comprising two-and-a-half bedrooms, kitchen, bath, inside W.C., rear access, very handy position.'

What had made it her choice? The price, of course, well, it was time for a change of luck, but the inside W.C., the two-and-a-half bedrooms had equally urged her to make the offer.

Calculatingly she slipped in her recent status — widow of barely three months — to the agent ignorant it made a paper house of a marriage which had collapsed before death intervened. As she discussed terms Betty expanded, free of the tinge of distress periodically felt that her daughter was so thin, the little face as pale as the banana she was given to peel. Somehow it made the bargaining easier, less intimidating, and as the cat's cradle of conditions wove above the child's head, her mother, if not in her element, was far from edgy.

From the picket gate at the front to the corrugated roof that covered the rooms at the back, the tiles somehow petering out half way, Betty had found what she wanted. For the moment. During the period of time it took for legalities to be sifted, sorted and finalised, she absorbed hours allocating each of the five-and-a-half rooms. Drawing the plans a dozen times, she'd stop to pull at her lower lip, grip it in her teeth thoughtfully, then redraw the plans, fusing them with colours from Jonquil's crayons, watched gravely by the child. The pains of selection became a daily concern, every aspect under severe scrutiny, and far from lonely in the bed shared with Fred before he had to be taken to the kitchen, his young widow paced the empty rooms of her new acquisition, concerned not with the furniture to fill them, but the profits which would result.

The half bedroom, more boxroom than bedroom but saved from waste by the high shuttered window, was allocated at first to her daughter.

'After all,' her tone light-hearted, 'she IS small for her age. Half a person you might say,' and Betty trilled a few notes, the mantel wireless affording cool-as-cucumber certainty as Bing Crosby crooned ... 'blue room, tea for two room, and every day's a holiday ... ' Betty, of course, didn't approve holidays apart from necessary convalescence or the dictates of Christmas and Easter.

Reconsidering, reordering, she returned to the original plan of distribution. The front room, with high, fixed panes alternating green and plum above the bay window, was where she'd receive the customers; here the fittings would be done. It was spacious. Twelve neat indentations on the carpeted floor declared the three-piece suite of the former owners and unshadowed rectangles of wallpaper revealed they'd owned large pictures. If gum arabic failed to blend the shades she'd be forced to find something tasteful in large frames too. The window seat she'd overlay in velvety grey, and though uncomfortable the tightly buttoned sofa would lend tone, along with the china cabinet, a nest of tables and the cheval mirror which would rock and tilt to her customers' reflections. Later they would be known as clients.

Down the hall, the lino runner patterned dove grey, green and white, scuffed and patchy in parts but serviceable still, was the room she'd share with Jonquil. Time enough to move her to the half room when the child was fully grown.

The second bedroom would be let to a respectable business gentleman of quiet habits, no doubts crossing her mind she'd locate one. Betty did not intend to forgo respectability. The dining room was to be her workroom, they'd eat in the kitchen and as soon as humanly possible she'd have the rotting wooden draining-board replaced by terrazzo; the only alteration urgent.

Beyond the bathroom, the half room she determined should yield up a little gold. Many a shopgirl alone in the world would be glad of such accommodation. Cramped, yes, but spotless and with the rent she'd ask more than reasonable she did not anticipate it vacant long. And close to the indoor W.C. the occupant would naturally have prior claim.

Necessary to keep a hall light burning late, at least till they'd settled in and got their bearings, it was a small price to pay.

Betty was not to know the half-baked lusts of glossy magazines, never buying more than the *Singer Sewing Annual* each year. She filled rather than decorated the house with what was easily available, and no more than necessary. Hers was not a throw-away world, 'instant' had not been coined, there was no philosophy embracing built-in obsolescence. Anything bought was made to last.

Jonquil often wondered how the dimpled copper with the raised letters that spelt out GREEN BRIARS could continue to last under the assault launched on it Monday mornings and tried to frame a way to ask Betty, but couldn't.

'Run down to the corner and get a tin of Brasso,' she was instructed regularly and carrying it home would shake it at her ear and hear it gurgle, finger firm on the flat lid the way her mother shook it.

Cloth in hand, with near-religious fervour Betty applied the Brasso, willing to waste minutes till the polish dried completely before attacking with zeal. Rubbing up from right to left, from the S back to the G, she'd give one final buff and pace backwards to the path to be certain none remained dull. None ever did.

'It's little things that count,' or, 'Take a pride in all you do,' absently she'd address the child should she be within hearing.

Customers never came on Mondays, 'the day for the house' ... and the day for the house meant a great deal of scrubbing,

24

dust-raising, sweeping and mopping while the copper boiled clothes.

The front room fitted out for her purpose, curtained from summer heat and prying neighbours, warmed, but only by a single-bar radiator on cold days, Betty would view it with their eyes when each new customer arrived – by appointment. In such an atmosphere they did not expect cut prices, and by the standards of the day her work was not cheap. Frequently on first visits they'd pipe, 'Oh, what a lovely room, Mrs Spring…' before bending with unsuppressed joy and anticipation to the pattern books, their carefully deposited parcels on a bamboo table donated by Auntie Doris, who'd wanted to do her bit.

Betty specialised in wedding dresses; later her clientele was to speak of them as gowns, recommend them as haute couture. Everyone was prepared to spend more than they could properly afford on the big occasion, and the stitching involved wasn't a great deal more complicated. Naturally for appliqués, bugle-beading, fine tucking or sequins prices increased. And taffeta, satin and silk, which were slippery and frayed if not handled with care, were at the higher end of the scale. Bridesmaids often chose taffeta which was lovely afterwards. Organdie too.

Stiff like hat racks they stood while she patted, pulled and pinned on their second visit and first fitting. Recognising the value of an artificial light, Betty, head to one side, would snap on a small table-lamp at the final fitting in order to tint the brides' flushed dreamy expressions and the folds of the fabrics.

'Lovely,' they would breathe, then quickly, 'what do you honestly think, Mrs Spring?'

Pretty is as pretty does, Betty would think.

'You look beautiful.' Automatically she would make the reply.

Jonquil's eight-year-old world became Green Briars, the harbour of all departures and all returns. Anyone much beyond it seemed to pass over a bridge and cease to exist.

Mr Perkins and Kitty, however, under the roof within a

25

month of the move, lived most of their lives in lands foreign to the child. Mr Perkins a bank clerk, Kitty a junior in Underwear and Corsetry, they were requested by their landlady to lock each of their doors as a precaution. Should anything ever be mislaid she wanted neither accusation nor unpleasant insinuation. Breakfasts were provided, meals at week-ends; hot at Sunday mid-day if given sufficient notice. With the use of the kitchen after 6.15 p.m. weekdays, a shelf each in the pantry, a shelf was shared in the ice-chest during hot weather. Weekly Betty washed and ironed three shirts and six separate collars for Mr Perkins.

When Kitty left and married her young man from Hardware, Lola took the half room. Despite her dirndl skirts, peasant blouses and the dangly earrings she wore even in the depths of winter with a brown overcoat, occasionally she was allowed to take Jonquil to a Saturday afternoon picture show when Betty approved a programme. The gold of her hair challenging the glitter of her earrings after each weekly rinse, no matter how many times Lola dyed what even Betty declared her crowning glory, she couldn't dye the blue of her eyes. There was an indisputable honesty about the blue of her eyes.

To Jonquil she was a beautiful grown-up girl, the prettiest she'd ever seen, and when Lola, extravagantly affectionate, kissed her the scent of gardenias drifted to the little girl's nostrils warm from the older girl's neck and there was such an aching in her throat the child could hardly speak. She adored Lola whose lips moved quickly and lightly like a butterfly's to joke with her and whisper secrets and spread a softened barrier against rules and regulations Betty considered necessary. And Lola never spoke to her in the tone grown people used when speaking to a child.

'I'll see to it, Mrs Spring. Leave it to me. I'll look out for Jonquil. See that she eats her dinner. Yes, she washed her hands, cleaned her nails.'

Lola became the older sister Jonquil never had, the frivolous mother she never had, a tight and protective bond growing between them, to strengthen with the years. Jonquil almost

26

believed Lola could see through the bones in her head to read her mind.

'What I mean is … ' Jonquil would begin.

'I know what you mean,' Lola would interrupt, laughing and pulling her close, hugging her about the waist or shoulders, Jonquil resting her face against Lola, grateful, happy and even if cramped never wanting to pull away.

Lola gave her a guinea-pig in a cage some young man had been persuaded to knock together from a butter box and chicken wire when her ninth birthday was due, despite Betty's disapproval.

'Well … ' Betty voiced doubts but finally came to consent on the strict arrangement that one or other of them cleaned the cage daily and collected unwanted greens from the closest fruit shop.

It was a time for hope.

Chapter Three

Must you lose something to discover it's priceless? she thinks, not clear which particular treasure has been repossessed by a cruel fate.

The night landscape without figures closes in. Tears well in her eyes. She doesn't cry easily; not any more. Tears bulging with secrets, smiles bulging with secrets, she tries to smile. Her feet hurt, unsuitably clad for walking in the high heels they're swollen, mashed. The joints knobbling the big toes ache and refuse to be ignored.

She stops. Cold, she's thankful for that; to walk on a sun-baked pavement would be torment, the heat rank, an affront rather than a pleasure, smelling of powdery cigarettes and the scrapings of toast.

She looks to the flats, the drawers in the human filing cabinets where most of the occupants sleep at this hour warmed by the electric blanket. From their beds she hears the sounds that filter up from the streets, blurred, stealthy; the far-off whining as a car takes a bend, a garage door decorously unrolling, sliding down to fasten and lock, a house cat reverting to the jungle, the wicker basket temporarily vacated, tray of Kitty Litter unused. But she's not in their beds, she's outside with dismal attachments they can't see or hear. One of their pampered cats yowls. Her spine jerks to the primitive sound. Exposure, adventure, revenge, it's feeding now on natural habits, to return with the sun to a bowl of homogenised milk.

She hurries on. She longs to be tuned to pastoral rhythms, the great cycles of the seasons, but how could it be? She doesn't know much of her ancestry, who tilled her background. Her father long ago turned over the sour soil of a small plot, and if before that his father knew space or harvests or bleating sheep, cow muck, or grass that smelt of cream and honey, it has not been her lot. Of course there were holidays ...

Her childhood was lived at close quarters, lit by sudden flashes of chance. Though Betty tried to keep her fenced genteelly behind the curtains of Green Briars, away from the children in the back streets, the lovers in the doorways, it was only with partial success. Lola had broadened her life to bus stops, fish shops, fairgrounds, railway stations as well as the celluloid worlds of Fred Astaire and Ginger Rogers, Andy Hardy and later Debbie Reynolds. Lola had hinted at other pleasures too.

Ribbons of pain tighten her right foot. She stops, foot raised. Under the next street lamp she promises to see to it. Circling an ankle the shoe drops and flamingo-like she stands a moment before hopping to lean by a wall newly built up from stone, the cement not quite dry, tacky. She should care it will mark her skirt, but doesn't. About to lean, remembering the empty shoe stands where dropped, she hops over in order to retrieve it and lowers her raised foot to the ground.

Bending in the pool of light, neck stiff, she can just distinguish two names shakily drawn in the cement recently laid on the pavement too.

'Susan Tonks', she deciphers, and ... 'Greg'.

Greg who? Anonymous as long as this cement lasts, in all likelihood the exercise interrupted by a disapproving adult. 'Susan Tonks' will have a more lasting impression, as if it matters. She sniffs. 'Greg'. Probably bolted; pencil, nail or stick, the defiling instrument, stuffed into a pocket tight already with dirty handkerchief and remains of an apple.

Leaning against the wall, gracelessly she supports her bottom to peer once more at the children's names.

'Susan Tonks'.
'Greg'.
'Jon … '

'Dare ya.'

'Dare me what?' fluted Jonquil who knew very well.

'Dare ya. To write ya name in quick while nobody's lookin'.'

The path which had been uprooted to deal with defective drains had been laid again that morning. It edged the asphalt of the school yard and curved out of sight towards the wash block.

'Keep away from the new work,' had been cautioned at assembly after the hymn; the caution expanded to punishment for anyone defiant enough to ignore the warning.

Jonquil at eleven was not given to open defiance. She always tried to tell the exact truth but had this not been, a self-defeating candour would have given any inaccuracy the lie. Her remembrance of another warning was vague yet compelling. She couldn't recall who gave it … was it her mother or Auntie Doris or her mother's friend, Enid, who helped with the button-holes?

'Tell the truth, Jonquil. God doesn't like little girls who lie.'

Somehow, mysteriously, insinuatingly, there was planted an ominous suggestion. God had her father in his care and if she ever wanted to see him again …

Recently she'd begun a dialogue with God and He, all-seeing, gave most satisfactory answers to lesser questions. His responses particularly helpful as she found herself growing more and more out of accord with her mother's wishes; desperately she tried not to let it show. Often she disliked Betty though she loved her, but could not bring herself to love Auntie Doris, blood relative, her soft moustache thickening with every visit.

Jonquil tried to be good, helpful and uncomplaining about her clothes, sparkling with left-over buttons and Peter Pans of satin and lace where other girls her age were collared in piqué. If secretly they envied her glitter not one was kind enough to let her know.

'Wedding finery,' they'd been known to snipe; the inference her mother too frugal or too tasteless to know better. How wrong they were: none in less than a decade able to do other than dream of passing through Betty's exclusive portals.

A direct challenge to God was also on her mind. Why had HER father died? But she'd pulled back to tell herself who she was, where she lived, concrete facts, not having the temerity to risk swift retribution and perhaps be robbed of her mother. Her busy, bossy, no-nonsense mother. Thoughtful, reconsidering, Jonquil conceded He must know. Hadn't He sent Lola?

After God her passion was for a piano, but guessing it unwise to ask Betty to lay out so huge a sum, didn't. Anyway Lola had promised as soon as she could save the down-payment — whatever that was — they'd have a gramophone. So there was nothing but to be satisfied with the wireless and 'The Witch's Tale' was a Sunday night treat.

Aching on occasion to sulk openly, refuse to make her bed, wash up, she seemed unequal to open warfare. So she appeared equable, tidy and co-operative, pecking at Betty's cheek where she craved to strangle her with love. Hugging Lola, fondling her hair and hands, she was deep with fathoms of affection still unmeasured. Who could heave the lead, sound the depths? She groaned in a kind of despair and found herself back in the school yard.

Alert and watchful the group edged closer, circling her, eyes slitted, mouths open. The adenoidal girl with whom she'd shared her playlunch seemed to have forgotten the jam tart.

'Dare ya.' She found it hard to deal with such treachery. Her eyes dizzied. She ached to explain she didn't want to scratch her name in the wet cement with the nail thrust into her hand. Fingers pointed at the messy grey patch on the ground; one pudgy hand spread palm downwards to it, jerking back within inches of the stuff. The sneak. She had never willingly broken a rule in her life; didn't run along school corridors, didn't eat in the classroom, didn't speak in the library.

She wanted to back away, her huge eyes staring. They pressed closer, prominent among them, head and shoulders above the rest, a boy with a cauliflower ear and perpetual scowl. It was common knowledge that his family was mad so he'd been branded as a warning. A fluttery pair of girls nuzzling forward, gnawing like rabbits on lower lips, over-balanced on tiptoes scattering the crowd as they went down.

Re-forming like cattle, 'Dare ya, dare ya,' sing-songed amongst them, a peculiar sound, the sound sleep-walkers might emit.

'Dare ya, dare ya.'

More ran up to join the group, antagonistic, annihilating. She felt she'd been dropped down a well. Minutes ticked away and if by a clock the time was not long to Jonquil it was endless. Someone yelled, hair pulled.

A strangeness began to creep over her skin and suddenly, wilfully, she wanted to bite and kick, hurt them all. She was against every single person in the world, she wished a flood would drown every person alive or a fire char them to mountains of ashes. She wanted the whole world to die. She wasn't to know it could just as easily have been Heather Frost with the slow eye or Rachel Goldsmith who had permission to spend Scripture in the art room. Astonished at herself, she wanted to spit and hit them, every one, not because they'd singled her out ... Flooded by a desire to wound them, each and every one, her cause was as old and as battered as the moon. She hadn't asked to be born. It wasn't her fault her mother had named her Jonquil and allied it to Spring. Even Mary Piddell didn't get as bad a time and Thelma Crapp, big for her age, had been taught to wrestle by her brother, Theo.

'Jon/quil Spring's a cowardy custard, Jon/quil Spring's a cowardy custard, Jon/quil Spring's a ... ', lovingly the taunt lengthened and stressed the syllables that made up the odious name. Piping above the others, unjointing it with sadistic pleasure a discerning enemy shouted:

'Jon–quil, Jon–quil, who'd wanna be Jon–quil. Jon–quil, Jon–quil ...'

The barb hit target and Jonquil dropped to her knees, the much-lengthened hem of the school dress riding high. New it had been the longest in the class, now the shortest, and she'd determined only yesterday to rip the bodice and force Betty to make another even though she'd be going to high school next year.

Her mouth was dry, her eyes wet. Twinges of pain stung her knees scraping on the rough surface where she was forced to kneel. A sense of injustice gripped the thin little chest. Breathing was difficult.

A disagreeable voice at her side growled.

'Jon–quil duck's bill, Jon–quil duck's bill' in raggedy rhyme, and she turned to an older girl, chin and nose reddened from squeezing pimples. 'Jon–quil duck's bill.'

Jonquil thought she was going to be sick, in a flash saw the concrete with the confetti of her lunch spewed there. Who would clean it up? she wondered and swallowed hard. From behind she felt her elbow jerked, and was close to overbalancing into the stuff with which she had to deal. Like a drowning dog she paddled for shore, began to scrape her name.

J ... O wobbly ... N ... and with perfect timing a bell rang. The hubbub that was the playground stilled for seconds before a confused order resumed. The elbow that had been jerked was grabbed, this time in a pincer grip. Two hands dragged her to her feet and she looked into a pair of pale eyes, distressed.

'Come on,' said the owner of the eyes, Dorothy Burns, whose family Betty conceded grudgingly to be kind, if mad, since they'd added two small cousins whose mother was coughing away her life. 'Come on,' repeated Dorothy Burns with a show of the sympathetic contempt with which the invincible lead the weak, and a friendship which was to last thirty-six years was born. Jonquil, moments earlier never wanting a human being ever to speak to her again, listened.

'Come on.'

Before quitting the playground that afternoon, with a

planned nonchalance Jonquil found hard to sustain, the two girls strolled towards the incriminating letters: J ... wobbly O and N ... Jonquil hesitant, Dorothy confident.

'I'll get rid of it.' Dorothy, fist on her hip, was decisive.

Jonquil had never heard anything so brave in her life; but the letters were beginning to set. She hunted in her mind for a good response.

'Ooooh,' she breathed, feeling in spite of this unsought intervention her goose was cooked, someone would see and testify against her. 'Ooooh,' she said again but with whistling admiration as Dorothy after a quick glance to be sure no prying eyes spied, no listening ears stiffened out like cabbage leaves, ground a heel into the offending letters and obliterated them.

Arms lightly interlaced they left the school grounds. Carefully they crossed the road between flags, and Dorothy just as carefully chose two malt sticks from the sweet counter at the nearest shop. Jonquil reluctant to accept, reluctant to recognise her own good luck, Dorothy with unflinching pale eyes pushed a malt stick into her hand as decisively as she'd pushed a heel into the concrete.

'Jon,' she said, but Jonquil, busy stripping the wrapper back, made no answer. She didn't realise she was being addressed.

'Jon,' Dorothy repeated emphatically, and she heard her name split, chopped by Dorothy's axe, accurately halved. Her mouth trembled, she feared she might cry. Instead a light dawned in Jonquil Spring's beautiful eyes that shone with affection and gratitude towards this new-found friend and sage of twelve.

Jonquil: Jon. Why, with all the emotional disadvantages, had she continued to suffer it? Jon? Could she do it? Could she become the three-lettered 'Jon'? Yes, the answer rang back, yes, yes, yes. She could feel the beating of her heart. When she spoke her voice was a whisper, barely audible.

'Jon.' She tried it. Then again louder, her voice sounding absolutely new to her. 'Jon,' and mentally detached the offending 'quil' for the rest of her life. There would be occasions which would demand it, formal situations, but never again would it pull her down to the depths of hell. Other ropes would do that.

'Jon,' Dorothy was asking, 'did your mother want a boy?'

Bewildered, Jon did not know, did not think so.

'Your dad then?'

Slow again to grasp the meaning, when understood, she had no answer. A boy? But how could that be?

'It's very important to be wanted,' Dorothy stated flatly, her words not in the least open to question, and firmly took Jon's hand as if afraid she might wander off by accident.

Jon trembled walking slowly with a watchful air and blinked at the sun, a yellow agitation, as they turned the corner and drew closer to home. She would like to ask her mother how much she'd been wanted, but even the thought of such an exchange made her nervous, fidgety. There was nothing she could do to show how she felt.

Don't think I care, don't think I care, she tried to tell herself. But she did. It was all a giant jigsaw and every piece had been fitted by other persons, other events.

It's very important to be wanted; Jon made room for this in her thoughts.

'Were ... were you wanted, Dorothy?' Her voice had a strangled sound.

There were few uncertainties in Dorothy Burns's life; those that would impinge with the years would be settled by a firm hand at the tiller, deep waters safely navigated, dangerous reefs negotiated, coastlines kept clear.

'Yes.'

She gathered her words, 'How do you know?'

If Jon could have read her friend's mind it would have revealed an approach to life that was simplicity itself; if you don't know find out. Some might be born to endure, others favoured by a silver spoon of one kind or another, Dorothy was to call a spade a spade and bristle with indignation if answers proved elusive. Reasonably also, Dorothy was prepared to be convinced, but during her formative years a confidence had been planted that troubles could be overcome. In later life when Jon was to feel threatened, frightened, unprotected, Dorothy in the main was to feel stable, able and sure.

'How do you know?' Jon repeated the unnerving question. 'That you were wanted?' Close to lost as she sucked the sweet.

Dorothy ran a long tongue round her mouth. 'My mother told me. When I was small. She told us all.' The words were slow, each sentence like a song.

Was this the usual thing in big families? After all there were four Burnses and now two additional cousins to make six.

'What about your cousins?'

'They're wanted too.'

No one was unwelcome under the Burnses' roof, which tended to tight living with Mr and Mrs Burns's generosity. They bordered on a public kindness; stray animals tolerated too, though the line had been drawn at ferrets. When one of the Burns boys laid claim to an unwanted ferret he came up against his first 'No'. Mice, yes, ferrets, no.

From that day Jon was grateful. Dorothy helped her improve at school and in her own way Jon helped Dorothy, providing her, like her parents, with a lame duck to carry to the pond and coax on to the water. Lola was happy to take them both about with her and Betty, reputation providing more and more bridal parties to dress, did not object. They made a curious trio; Lola flashy, warm, Dorothy practical above all and skinny Jon, her mind empty of grudges and malice, who looked younger than her eleven years, unable to think of a world without either Lola or Dorothy, both of them willing to listen to what she, Jon, had to say, as a person with worthwhile opinions. Betty never listened. Everything seemed near and possible.

Despite the pressure of her orders, Betty with prodigious energy was not prepared to let her daughter slip far away. She insisted still that she think for her, had the maddening habit of answering for her and hadn't the remotest idea she was driving her daughter from her.

'Yes, we're very close,' she would tell anyone who asked of Jon, but they were close only in that Betty continued to consider her child an extension of herself, grudging her a separate identity. She would have been appalled, totally unbelieving, at any suggestion of neglect.

'Neglect her!' There would have been an explosion. 'I work hard for her, hard. Never take a holiday. I do my duty by my own. I have never failed her.'

And if Jon had voiced the question she ached to ask when eleven, what would Betty Spring have replied?

Am I wanted? Jon, suffused by a feeling she couldn't name, had begged silently of her mother, hunched on a stool, feet on the rung, as doggedly she attacked set homework, at the end of the kitchen table, summer, autumn, winter and spring.

'Fetch me the marking wheel, a reel of magnolia silk, the pinking shears, the ... ' Betty, voice definite, organised, found it necessary her daughter run errands. Perhaps she thought it bound them closer, perhaps ... Or perhaps for Betty the keenest pleasure remained in the wanting, no matter how small, not the satisfaction. From her growing daughter she needed some dutiful response, sought it in sharing the trivia which made up the rounds of their days. Subconsciously she expected some return. After all she planned to keep Jonquil on at school, a conclusion reached as she observed certain benefits of education amongst numbers of the perennial brides – their beliefs in all the promises of the middle class burning like landing lights on a midnight quay. Charges doubled, with the increases came young women who crossed the city from better areas, whose grammar Betty had come to appreciate as well as the voices with which they minced and bowed.

'Fred, your late father, would have wanted it.' She bolstered her determination, extending scissors and shaking them to mark the words, ready to impart this again and a lot more should Jonquil herself raise an objection.

'Education's a great thing,' she would often slip like sugar into tea, when mother and daughter sat together, eyes downcast, proper piety sketched on her face ... not her usual demeanour.

'All very well for some,' Lola would contribute if present. 'But you can still have a lot of fun without it.'

'That's not my idea,' with a sniff Betty would retort, who surprisingly liked pretty Lola, hopeless with the little money she earned, never saving for a rainy day, believing tomorrow would never come, but never to wither, brokenly succumb to the passage of time. With an engaging optimism, Lola, like an inviting room extended unlimited hospitality, was bright, healthy and co-operative always.

'Live and let live,' Lola beamed and the glinty hoops in her ears dangled; Lola who next year was to fall victim to a railway porter, leave them for six months to return with a baby close under one arm, illegitimate, the suitcase with all she owned fastened by a strap to the other.

Surprisingly Betty was not to bar the door, though the girl's disgrace was monumental in her eyes. Betty took Lola in as her good deed in a naughty world and in doing so made a shrewd choice. Years later Lola's baby, Tom, with his quick mind and commercial instinct, was to be a trusted member of Betty's empire when it expanded into real estate. Where Tom learned his business acumen was a total mystery; certainly not from his feckless mother, doubtfully from the railway porter who took a train north, destination and whereabouts unknown, after his son's conception.

Earlier Betty was to blame herself for allowing Lola to use the telephone, newly installed. The ill-fated appointment might never have been made otherwise; but if not the railway porter there would have been other candidates, common sense forced in on the older woman.

Lola was the one chink in Betty's reverence for the conventions of her time, which were strict and well-defined. Perhaps by recognising them lacking in Lola she expected to promote them in her daughter, who answered the telephone patiently and carefully. After Lola was allowed to return with the evidence of her disgrace, Jon resented her mother less.

When Betty was selfish she made allowances, when tired and cross, tried to be patient. She was after all her father's daughter. Would she remain so? It seemed a strong likelihood.

However, the older Jon grew the less her ideas and hopes accorded with those of her mother, and if in a situation requiring her to speak of her mother, she talked more of Betty as an idea than a person. She did not want to be convention-bound, material, unmaternal. Manipulative. She began to pray not to be indissolubly linked to these traits and in answer came the hint that she'd have to scheme to break away. Her mind zig-zagged. She had such a craving to live her own life out of her mother's sight, out of her mother's house.

First you're born and then you die ... and in between before I'm an unresponsive old woman in a wheel chair – the image chilled her – I'm going to vibrate like a drum. She hugged herself, searching for the right words to tell herself how she felt. She'd become some ship-jumping sailor turning her back on the sea – her mother's domain – to make good on land. Her affections, engaged as they were with Lola, little Tom and Dorothy, the growing Jon recognised the resultant tie of Lola's sexual forays as well as the limitations of Dorothy's practical nature.

On her seventeenth birthday Dorothy declared intentions of becoming a teacher, to be followed by marriage to either a fellow teacher or a missionary ... 'in order to lead a useful life'. Her choice was a missionary after leaping the first hurdle. Twelve years her senior he was short, benign, willing in God's service but not able for long. Posted to Nigeria, his heart brimming with loving kindness, but his wife more positively equipped by a course in first aid and health care, he succumbed to recurring malaria and had to be invalided out. Ever intent on making her circumstances workable, Dorothy steered him through long course in hospital then a longer course in accountancy. In time he proved more able in the counting of business figures than God's children. It was a happy union.

As her spindly little body grew and matured, Jon fed on a romantic dream.

You belong to the whole glorious mess of human possibility, she would tell herself as Betty told her what to do, what to eat, what to wear, where to go and with whom. It was a grandiloquent phrase she had picked up somewhere and she wasn't sharing it at home. Still adhering to the truth, for what did she have to be untruthful about? she began to develop workable ways of saying one thing and believing another.

Home was no longer Green Briars, though cannily Betty retained that property, in time to be zoned industrial and increase greatly in value. This house was bigger, the address better, even if the neighbours were less friendly. The surrounding dwellings, practical and ugly, were embellished by the latest inventions of a material world. Junk was not yet in revival, antiques were an encumbrance of familial affections, neither desirable nor potentially valuable.

Betty had confounded her elders, peers and Auntie Doris, who had only just stopped peppering her homilies with:

'A woman can't get on in this world alone.'

'Just you watch me,' Betty had snapped back, and that old dragon had swallowed her anxiety to find fault, calmed by the considerable return Betty had made on her nest egg. Having persuaded her to lend the money that would otherwise have been secreted in calico bags in the big wardrobe, if permitted she inspected the books with as piercing an eye as she inspected Jon's neck and nails whenever she inflicted herself on them for a visit.

The whole glorious mess of human possibility, Jon would close her eyes to sleep, or more properly dream.

But nagging, an irregular toothache, was the sense of something beyond reach, if not another realm a disguised corner of her world never disclosed at home or school. Painfully in these years she groped towards an indefinable 'Something' wilfully concealed, she'd grieve, like the tide rolling in to puncture the sand with minute air bubbles but rolling out again smothering them before she was able to peer in and see.

She came to believe if just once it was possible to stare into the blinding core of the sun, veils would be drawn aside and she would have access to something she must find. But ... impossible, the only answer was to retreat back into the known where life's promises came down to a white wedding.

Growing in an unreal world of wedding dresses, paeans to perfect love, flights of doves from the tower, glittering scraps of satin, silks and lace, glittering scraps of second-hand dreams, of love everlasting, love eternal, love glorious and victorious, how else could it be? She wanted above all else to grow, and soon, to be fully female, fully feminine and fully desired.

'What a lovely bride,' she heard them all murmur, the church ushers, the photographers, envious friends and sighing cast-off swains. The bridegroom no more than a shadowy outline like all her official and unofficial heroes, she dreamt of a high-throated opaque gown of virginal white and a flimsily wicked negligee of signal red.

Was her life to unfold this curiously predictable story?

'Perhaps I was foolish,' she was one day to confide to Lola who was supposed to know about men.

Chapter Four

Thoughts stutter in her head.

'Remember, without me you're nothing.'

'God give me strength.'

'Do you imagine my needs are being properly met?'

'If there's a scrap of love left go out and dig.'

'Bad-tempered creatures must expect to be told lies.'

'It was so long ago.'

'Another day has begun.'

She lifts her head, tilts it back. Stars crisp as chips swing high in the sky which is vast, aching with distance and silence, an interminable landscape.

Another day will begin, she tells herself and a smile curves her lips to think of the men and women, so close yet so far from her, who will start that day fresh as salads from their dreamless sleep.

Dreamless sleep, she's positive, must be beneficial; harmonious and as balanced as an arrangement of cloud over the swell of the sea. In the weaponry of human dealings sleep, undisturbed by fragmented images, must give power and strike to the business of wakeful hours.

'What did I dream? Last night?' she queries and with stumbling awkwardness can remember only a jammed door. 'What a cliché,' she titters, to sober to a clearing picture of that door. Iron studded, heavy, battered. And behind the door?

'Secrets I can't uncover.' Words gag in her throat. 'It's no use, no use. Even if I could, I couldn't interpret.'

She trudges around and around in cloying slow motion.

The wind stirs a muffled barking of dogs. Her pace slows. She stops and stretches a hand to brush guilelessly against a bush soon to flower into starry-faced daisies. Sparse specks of white enliven the green darkened by the light, but below ...

'Snowdrops.' She sighs and has an abrupt conviction the clumped snowdrops are consuming all the oxygen from the night. Gingerly she reaches out to convince herself they're real. There's a dryness in her mouth and the fingers of the hand she spreads, not to touch, only to encompass, tingle, prick. A shadow, as smooth as a seal, slips silently by.

'Snowdrops,' Betty's nostrils contracted, inhaling the heady scents of stephanotis or orange blossom. 'If you want no perfume go for orchids, of course. But ... snowdrops!' Her voice had softened to become placatory. 'If you must, of course.'

When Betty said 'of course', she rarely meant a natural logic would follow.

'Well, pet, it's your wedding.' Since Jon had brought Gilbert home she was more pet than dear.

Betty had developed high ambitions for her daughter, socially. And why not? Hard work and determination had brought their rewards and while, curiously, she hadn't expected from Jon the same dedication and stamina she herself gave to their rise in the world, she lived in anticipation of a young professional son-in-law. A good life for Jon to Betty meant a good marriage. Perhaps she should push these ambitions of hers a little further. Or a little faster. If she were to settle something substantial on Jon, wrap this quiet girl in a more glittering package ... Never would she contemplate leaving the fruits of her enterprise to charity, though naturally there'd be a token. The Salvation Army would receive it, and the Friday nights of her childhood assailed her; nose twitching down the years. Polish as boots were cleaned, Brasso for the trumpet, and the overall smells of poverty ... cabbagy soup, close sleeping, fetid drains. Sniffing, another all but forgotten aroma turned in the air; the brilliantine that plastered young Fred Spring's sandy hair like greased straw. What a lifebelt! And in a mood of exhilaration Betty descended on Burton, Ross and Burton, the solicitors who handled her affairs. Hadn't the Chinese gardener who brought vegetables to the door told her often enough: 'Old Chinese proverb. Wealth not cross three generations.' Jon became the owner of Green Briars as well as a duplex, the rents to provide a steady income, capital gain significant, and Betty, expert in matters financial, relaxed, a rabbiter having set her snares.

Jon at twenty was a pretty slip of a girl. No beauty except for the eyes, the sandy hair that Lola taught her to enliven with lemon juice framed the oval face and if her skin tended to sallowness it was fine skin. Lola, manning the boats again, had taught her to blush with a range of cosmetics and the effect could be disconcertingly good. Nose neat, mouth full, soft, there was no hint of meanness. Easily delighted, happy but not easily animated, she tended to hold down any animation like fluttery paper under a weight.

Betty had no objections to Jonquil marrying at twenty.

'Young, well yes,' she said, 'but it's a lottery after all,' and thought of Fred for the first time in a long time. As the years had passed he might never have existed, except on occasion when she looked closely at the result of their brief union. Brief? Seven years' duration, but he was an ordinary man with a simple good nature; a man who wished to be obliging and so was easily forgotten. Betty like a scavenging street beggar had grabbed at what was available for sustenance ... she was made that way. Glad to have Jonquil marrying, somehow tired of motherhood long ago but never bypassing practical matters, Betty hoped she wouldn't be forced to resume it at some stage after the wedding. There were fish she still had to fry.

The decision of what Jon was to do on leaving school, three years ago, had been solved with little difficulty. There was no appropriate place for her in Betty's workforce; a tough and grown-up world for juniors with repetitious jobs over long hours for small wages, a tough and aggressive world for the cutters, designers and sales personnel.

Barely a handful of her class had gone on to university, but Dorothy had won herself a scholarship to a teachers' college, With no striking talents, though art teachers unfailingly praised her painting, Jon's education was not brilliant. Tentatively suggesting art school, if Jon experienced a little grudge against her mother who failed to take the suggestion seriously, it didn't last. She wasn't all that good ...

Aunt Doris questioned ... was the tone sour or insistent? ... 'When was a clever woman ever happy?'

Jon, given to staring at her reflection in the privacy of her own room, on good days would see herself mirrored back, a violin tucked professionally into the chin. In her ears would ring the applause, thunderous, from musically sophisticated audiences in Paris, London or Vienna. On the other occasions clearly reaching out would be a white-jacketed figure, sweat beading brow and upper lip, sandy hair aseptically covered, as calmly she assisted Dr Schweitzer, distant drums beating out to the populace that another white saviour served by his side.

No, there was little difficulty in finding an occupation for Jonquil. Nice girls studied to become kindergarten teachers. With tightly belted waists and polished shoes, decidedly these young ladies did not venture into jungles, nor could they ever be induced to go out with a drinker, let alone a married man. Their timid jungles were enclosed by a prescribed circumspection, and their circumstances. Lunches cut from starch-reduced bread, they would set out daily, gaily, for instruction in painting, puppetry, child psychology and voice production. They notched up a goodly mark if taking with them an elementary knowledge of the piano and a pleasant singing voice.

At this proper place where few conversations probed surfaces deeper than what they were wearing, where they were going, whom they were dating – or hopeful of dating – Jon made another friend, a 'best' friend, above whom neither chill nor sulphurous vapours rose to signal a future warning.

Chubby Laurel Thompson; who had a rounded dolly face, refined voice and rounded vowels. Dressed in as much pink as permitted by a doting mother, her eyes were given to roving in a teasing way, head turning in a conniving way with short little jerks as she spoke. Soon they were to be known as Laurel and Hardy, inseparable.

'What on earth can you have to tell Laurel?' Betty would frown exasperated as Jon, one foot inside the house, would dash to the phone. 'You left her less than an hour ago? What else is there to say? All right, all right. But don't take all day, I'm expecting a call. Five minutes,' and she'd scowl at the clock which straddled the shelf above the telephone table.

'Was he on the bus?' Jon squeaked, breathless as the receiver lifted at the other end. Listening rapt while Laurel detailed with a high, soft giggle, the hairstyle, greeting, expressions, the tie he was sporting that day; he, the son of the Thompson family doctor. Did his father's occupation project a great future? Who could guess, the young man was more concerned with his acne.

'Boy mad,' Betty would relate to Lola, and Lola made a mental note to give Jon some straight talking, knowing her mother couldn't be relied on to advise the girl on contraception ... such as it was.

Jon, happy for Laurel and her wonderful bus rides home, nevertheless was stabbed by envy. Would such delights ever be hers? Each day was like the day before, but some were longer? There seemed this sameness in her life, not quite plodding round and round in circles like some biblical beast grinding grain, but a sameness. And when with Laurel she had come to suspect the wolf whistles they both made a confused half-pretence to ignore were never directed at her. Would there ever be for her a present, let alone a past, brimming with conquests, accumulated at ease?

'And then?' eagerly she asked, to be told he had had no change and Laurel had paid both fares.

'He's promised to pay it back on Saturday and ... ' Laurel recounted this as dramatically as the accident she'd witnessed once where glass shattered from the headlamps was pin-pricked with blood.

Jon's world seemed set to remain for ever female. The landscape of her life shelved flatly, layered between Betty's well-ordered house and the well-ordered college routine. Laurel, from the protective thickets of her middle-class existence, hinted at a promise that just might, possibly, produce a grand scenic slope. Her brother, William, recently graduated dentist, living away from home as he worked in a practice in Newcastle.

'Everyone loves Bill,' Laurel enthused and watched keenly for Jon's reactions. 'He's gorgeous, just gorgeous. Everybody thinks so.'

'Tell.' Jon, eyes wide, was at pains to disguise full interest but Laurel wasn't fooled.

'Tall, dark and handsome; a sort of femme fatale in reverse.'

'What do you mean?'

'Scrumptious,' and Laurel elaborated on the tall, dark and handsome. 'Six feet and half an inch, yes, the half counts. His hair's curly like mine, but ... ' Laurel closed eyes, sighed, 'but as black as a raven's wing. I adore dark hair, fair can be so negative, you must agree.'

Jon plunged hands deep into the pockets of a tartan skirt, the only way to stop them flying involuntarily to her head. From time to time with Laurel she felt urged to split into two parts, the Jon Laurel knew and another Jon, accusing, brutally candid ... less vulnerable.

'His face, well you could say, craggy. Ever since he broke his nose ... but, he was the best in the team, he should have been captain, everybody says so. As I was saying, his face ... it has a strong appeal to women ... '

'Women?'

'I consider anyone over seventeen a woman.'

'Go on,' Jon prompted, submitting hypnotically to her imagination, Laurel providing the bricks on which to build. She saw him, tall, broad, the white coat of his trade stretched taut between shoulder blades as he bent with blinding teeth and Spanish eyes towards a patient, a lovely young woman ... his breath sweet, voice mellifluous as he requested:

'Rinse if you please,' then, 'Open wide' ... the scrubbed hand, trimmed nails expertly manipulating a probe as he bent again to the open-mouthed patient, elbow lightly brushing her breast.

'Close your mouth. You'll catch a fly.' Laurel, diverted from her description, paused. 'And he's got a great sense of humour. It runs in the family people say, and in about five years ... '

'Impetuous.' Jon said it, carried away in the Newcastle surgery where, after deft removal of the cotton-wool padding her cheek, he was on the point of inviting her to ...

Laurel stared at her, wondering if she was being sarcastic, irritated almost to the point of refusing to say more, the room close though the windows were open.

'Don't you want to hear about him?' she pouted.

'Yes, Laurel, yes. Of course I do,' Jon shuffled feet, uneasy, slightly troubled. 'He ... well, he sounds like you said, scrumptious.' She'd never known anyone scrumptious, perhaps never would. 'Go on. What else?' and Laurel forced Jon, her mouth drying like rain on a hot pavement to laugh nervously, say awkwardly: 'Bill ... ?'

'William to you. You haven't met him yet.'

'William,' whispered Jon and felt naked. Strains of Lohengrin filled her ears above the sounds of traffic intruding into the students' room with electric kettle, chairs with flowered cushions and a rock-like sofa on which the girls could lie on bad days.

'Well, he's taken out dozens of girls; he's great fun as I told you,' and Laurel streamed on, obliged to explain that in her prosperous family's view few girls would meet their son's standards, let alone their own.

'I daresay he's only attracted to really beautiful girls?' Jon ached to hear William Thompson sought out character and depth. 'You're deep,' once Laurel had pronounced, and though hadn't liked to plumb the exact meaning, it had clearly been some sort of compliment.

'They're always attracted to him, but ... ' she left it in the air dangling perilously, tantalising like Lola's earrings.

'All the same,' a certain melancholy engulfed Jon and she gritted her teeth.

'Don't be like that.' Laurel was irritated. 'After all he's nearly twenty-four. He can pick and choose. And we're just eighteen.' She was not only irritated by Jon. 'He calls me a snivelling brat who can hardly spell when I try to get to know his friends.'

'All boys treat young sisters like that.' Jon, cast down, felt she must bolster Laurel.

'How would you know. You! You live in a household of women. What could you possibly know about it?'

Stung, Jon spat out: 'Well, it's not a harem. We're not closed off from the world ... '

'What? Go on, Miss Worldly Wise.'

'Well, Lola says ... ' and Laurel's attention was caught.

'Go on, go on,' Laurel was close to begging, and lowering their voices they were thrown into a delicious guesswork and state of speculation on the subject universally enthralling to girls of their age.

'I don't think I'd like it really.' Laurel's voice was pleasured. 'Anyway, not before I'm married. Would you?'

'Lola says ... '

'Yes?'

'Lola says, don't make up your mind till you've tried.'

Laurel, disconcerted, gulped. 'But ... '

'Lola says, it's ridiculous to think only men are randy, and that lots of women can barely control themselves. Overwhelming passion, Lola says, is not just in the mind, and women ... '

'But we're only eighteen.'

The temptation was too strong. 'I consider anyone over seventeen a woman,' lips drawn tight for a moment before she exploded.

'That's all very well.' Laurel tried to recover a little dignity, but failed. The subject was too intriguing.

'It's not only men who seduce women, Lola says … '

'How do they do it?' Laurel must know and began to conjecture. 'They probably wear tight jumpers with only a bra underneath and … '

'Lola says, they don't wear anything underneath. And they never wear tight belts because that makes it easier to get at them, and in summer the buttons on their blouses are loose … '

'To pop off?'

'I suppose so,' said Jon who didn't know. All her buttons were sewn on to stay, still there when the clothes were ready to be discarded.

'And their eyes flash a message,' Laurel squeaked, 'which says … take me I am yours. Jon, I read a book … funny, I found it in the bottom of Mummy's wardrobe between the boxes where she keeps her gold shoes … and it was about this girl who went sailing with her cousin who was much older than her, and a storm blew up and they had to make for land and the nearest bay was this little cove, which couldn't be reached except from the sea. Well, when they finally had the boat secure, they were wet through to the skin so he said, this cousin of hers who was about ten years older at least, they must find a cave and light a fire. Well, all that took time and then … then, he said she must take off all her clothes otherwise she'd catch pneumonia. Well, she did, because she thought he should know, being so much older I suppose, and then … then, well, he took off all his clothes … and … well, they did all the things married people do, and … well it told every detail.'

'Did she get pregnant?' Jon asked, calculating that William Thompson was six years her senior.

'I suppose she must have … eventually. Because they kept doing it and doing it every Saturday and her family was so pleased when she took to sailing because she'd been a bookworm and they thought it much better for her to spend Saturdays out of doors getting fresh air!'

With the next mail came a brief note to the Thompson family. William would be home for a holiday and wanted to acquaint them with a friend with whom, eventually, he might set up in partnership. Too many dentists worked a solitary practice; the young men planned two surgeries side by side, which should give each the opportunity to reduce golf handicaps. Gilbert Jamieson's birthday was within a week of his own.

The aura of the approaching guest, of fast-approaching excitements and possible good times, hovered expectantly over the girls.

'Gilbert Jamieson, Gilbert Jamieson,' Laurel intoned day and night, her mind busy with hasty plans. 'I've fallen in love with the name,' and began to engage herself in what she confided to Jon was the essence of life. As far as Jon could see this consisted mainly of trying new hairstyles and fruitless attempts to peel off some of her surplus weight. Laurel, fond of food, could barely restrain herself between meals and hadn't the willpower to stick to any of the many crash diets unearthed from the women's magazines where her svelte dreams lay.

Perhaps, Jon thought charitably, she was ashamed to go hungry in order to be beautiful, but whatever the reason Laurel was a querulous companion.

Gilbert Jamieson. At twenty-four he knew too much, he'd seen too little. A scholarship boy, he never wanted to look as far back as the corner fruit shop—with its sidelines of eggs, milk, soft drinks and confectionery—where he'd had to weigh up potatoes after school and delivery orders from the big basket attached to his bike.

Knowing what he'd considered trouble in his time, trouble in the form of empty pockets, he had every intention not only of filling them but keeping them brimful. If he was a man with a dream inside him it was wired up to a calculator. His way of putting it: 'I like to clarify the issues.'

Tall, well-built with neat waist and lean hips, his legs loosely fastened to his body as he walked in a rambling way, he was almost but not quite handsome with heavily lidded grey eyes and mahogany hair. It was the nose that left him attractive rather than handsome: blunted, chopped short as if he'd been born just prematurely, before the last button was fully formed. But he'd overcome it quite well, elongating it with a neat toothbrush moustache, the vogue of the day. Where Jon had learned to abbreviate her most telling defect, Gilbert had learned to lengthen his.

'Jon,' Laurel bubbled at the first possible opportunity, two nights and a day after the young men's arrival, 'yummy scrumptious. Absolutely. And with those come-to-bed eyes like the millionaire polo player in that book with the heroine, Deirdre, who was slim as a reed and thrillingly pure.'

'What about his teeth?' If a dentist didn't have good teeth, who would?

Dismissively Laurel ignored the question. His teeth weren't bad in shape, if yellowy, but blinded by love all colours blended to her rainbow. 'The timbre of his voice ... '

'The what?'

'Timbre.' There was a sigh. 'The tonal quality,' said Laurel who'd looked it up in *Webster's* after coming across it in another of her mother's hidden books, and pleased to display it before it floated away.

'Did he notice you?' Jon wanted to know, and Laurel to her astonishment took this as an unprovoked attack, her reply cool; choosing to forget that her brother's friends rarely treated her as more than a nuisance, at best a playful pet with whom they cared to spend no more than limited time.

'I find that a most uncalled-for remark,' said Laurel, not quite high in a dudgeon but climbing towards it if Jon wasn't immediately apologetic.

'But ... I ... I ... ' her tongue heavy in her mouth, dumb.

'I know what you meant.' Laurel's vowels rounded full circle. 'And you're wrong. Gilbert certainly HAS noticed me. In fact ... ' but she caught short the confidences she was longing to pour out, to mince ... 'and what have you to report of interest?' stress deliberate on 'interest'.

'Don't be like that, Laurel. Tell. Do.'

So she was told of the trivial courtesies Gilbert Jamieson had paid Laurel, all her family in fact, for recognising the richness of their environment ... house spacious, two guest rooms and billiard room, a gardener whose duties also ran to rolling and marking the court, and extra meals at short notice no problem ... there must be no risk that the Thompsons' acquaintance should not develop to the same friendliness he shared with their beloved son.

Gilbert, like Jon, was an only child, and just as well as the fruiterer's shop had been operated mainly on credit during the depression. Afterwards the customers had continued to rely on clearing the slate as infrequently as possible, stalling; Mr Jamieson being soft in the head, nagged his wife, Rose ... Gilbert's mother ... incessantly. From this numbing tirade there grew in Gilbert a fundamental disrespect for women. Rose, the first woman he knew intimately, her influence greater than either of them could suspect. Gilbert did not see marriage as a desirable state unless he married well.

'Absolutely yummy scrumptious.' Laurel couldn't improve on that, and Jon wondered when she was to be privileged to meet this god. Was she to be included in unknown pleasures?

Laurel streamed on. 'At dinner last night he held out Mother's chair, and what do you think? Can you guess? No. He ran round to the other side of the table, no, that's not right. He didn't run ... but slid gracefully to the other side, like ... like a well-oiled ... I was going to say Rolls, but that's not exactly what I mean, well ... you know ... gracefully. And, Jon, that terrible joke Daddy tells about the Irishman who orders six whiskies, six beer chasers ... and is asked by the barman if he needs a tray. You know. No? "No," says the Irishman, "I've got my hands full. How could I carry it?" Yes, that's the joke, and Gilbert laughed. Not just to be polite, but as if he really appreciated it. What do you think of that for superb manners?' Laurel drew breath little knowing how soon she'd be titillated by his jokes, privately told her, which would stop just short of indecent.

Heart palpitating against the pink rayon dress with darker pink sash, she decided to share the dreamy isolation of the two nights and one day since Gilbert Jamieson had been their guest and first extended a hand to hers on introduction. Stunned by such courtesy, exceptional in their circle, she had shot out her own to feel cool fingers clasp hers, hers, she was mortified to find, sticky.

Jon waited silent, certain there was more, flattered and frightened by disclosures she sensed imminent.

'Jon ... '

'Yes.'

'I have fallen in love,' her voice bold and strong.

'Laurel!' Jon, who with a little more worldliness would have guessed, was staggered by this revelation.

'I have fallen in love,' Laurel repeated, glowing, expanding in Jon's disbelief.

'But you don't know him.'

'Don't know him! You're the one who doesn't know him.' Laurel's indignation was short-lived. 'I feel as if I've known him all my life.' She looked at the other girl sharply, then skilfully misted her eyes, the appeal not lost on Jon. 'From the moment I was born, from the moment I took my first step, from the moment I ... you know. Oh, well I don't suppose you could possibly understand.'

Understand Laurel? It would have been attempting to dissect a soap bubble. Jon didn't understand.

Tucked away out of sight of the house, a bank of rhododendrons between them and the tennis court, the open air blotted up their words; Laurel's words, for Jon's appropriately were few. Smiling, though her mouth felt wooden, they were fewer still when later introduced to Bill Thompson and Gilbert Jamieson, Gilbert firmly ensconced already as friend of the entire Thompson family ... with the exception of the daughter of the house. She didn't offer friendship, but love as a full-time occupation. She thought of nothing else, ranging wildly from the erotic to the modest then back to the erotic again.

'You're so bourgeois.' Laurel's pupils dilated, amazing even herself with the lengths to which she was prepared to go. 'I don't suppose I can expect you to understand.'

Jon didn't understand.

Two years later when Gilbert Jamieson married Jonquil Spring, Laurel Thompson didn't understand. How could she be aware careful investigation by Gilbert Jamieson – defensive about his own income, deliberately vague about his assets – had revealed the Thompson wealth unsound; a show of opulence, no gilt-edged bonds to back it up, little money in the bank. And no settlement for Laurel. The basic issues clarified.

Gluttonously Laurel's eyes devoured the bridegroom as he stood immaculate at the altar, the fashionable church filled, guests fashionably attired. Thin and elegant, dressed as a pair with Dorothy Burns in pink *peau de soie*, a darker pink sash caught at the waist, Cecile Brunner roses strangling in her grasp, she walked with the artificial jerk bequeathed to her by a modelling school. She didn't understand.

Jon's eyes, large and unblinking in a powder pale face, shone as she and Gilbert retraced their progression down the aisle, united, Gilbert patting at her ringed fingers looped about his right arm with the nonchalance with which an assured man pats at the cheque book flat in his breast pocket.

Betty, hypocrisy not one of her sins, did not cry.

Chapter Five

'The long day wanes; the slow moon climbs;
the deep moans round in many voices,'

she intones. Tennyson? She thinks so. The air is cold, the temperature dropping and glacially, distantly, the moon is a slice of ice, chilling, comfortless.

'Don't look at it,' she tells herself. She wants to be warmed and with no other alternative, listing forward on the balls of her feet, strides on. Approaching a parked car she sees it occupied. Two figures lump into one in a tight embrace and the car radio sings for her as she draws closer. Decidedly they're not listening.

'By the light of the silvery moon,
To my honey I'll croon love's tune ... '

This song is old, old enough to have been sung when her parents courted. She stifles a smile; was her mother, Betty, ever caught up in an awkward young love? Unlikely.

'Honey moon keep a-shining in June,
Your silvery beams will keep love's dreams
By the light of the moooooon.'

Remembering little of her father she tries to conjure his face, but there's none ... nothing but a blurred shell of cherishing. What would they have meant to each other if he'd lived? She likes to think theirs would have been an ordinary miracle, an enduring affection. Who can tell?

Honey moon. Honeymoon. What can it signify in two separate words? Honeymoon presents no literal difficulty; a holiday spent together by a newly married couple. But Honey plus Moon? Sweet waxings and wanings dependent on time of month? Or simply the waning of affection?

She was anxious for the first time for their life together when she honeymooned with Gilbert at a hotel, newly constructed on a cliff as old as time, a buckled piecrust of strata below which the sea cobbled along the length of a beach to feather-stitch the farthest reaches with froth and foam. Gilbert as frisky as a buck rabbit, she was bruised by the heat and torn by her husband.

She hears his voice as if it were yesterday, powerful as it boomed from the bathroom where he faced himself and shaved.

'I've never seen marriage as a desirable state, darling, unless one marries well.' He let a rich chuckle loose. 'Agreed?' Had he winked at the half-shaven Gilbert he faced, battening down the lower lip to trim the precise bristles below the nose as she came into view, tears threatening? 'Sentimental little mouse,' he smiled or snarled, she couldn't judge as he stroked a clean-shaven chin. When her hand crept into his he tightened it a little, reassuring her, a little.

'Yes,' she said, and to no one in particular.

The car with the kissing couple is well behind her now, and she's fast approaching one of the harbour reaches. A long dagger of water stabs into the land, glistening like wet tar in the night light. From here it extends to the sea which extends to the world.

A ship's siren sounds, moaning like a haunted sea beast. There's small comfort in this sound which smacks of the uncertainties and powers of the sea. Tugs service the liner signalling with fussier, higher, more abrupt hoots.

The siren sounds again; there seems no end to it.

The cabin was on 'B' deck and the head steward, when she

entered the dining saloon, led her to be seated at the purser's table. Intent on improving his professional life, Gilbert had decided after due consultation with Bill Thompson that each of hem would benefit by two years' work in London.

'I'll mind the store,' Bill had offered, 'you can be first,' generously his partner thought, knowing that Bill, engaged in a civilised once-weekly afternoon affair with a friend's wife, could be at risk.

Gilbert with little reverence for the institution of marriage planned to continue his own ... on his terms. Though she was intimidated by social life, in the early days he had liked to dress Jon up, propel her to balls and cocktail parties, where he'd watch to see she wasn't stranded before channelling himself towards the more vivid of the females present to indulge in public flirtation. These activities didn't go underground until later. When he arrived at the stage where he felt his wife couldn't supply the life he was vaguely worried about missing, he supplemented the diet with other women; these, as years went by and he grew older, growing younger and more nubile.

With a strong sense of survival, where Jon had at this stage of their lives little idea of self-help, few deepening doubts, he believed her to be, and always to remain, docile, pretty, hero-worshipping but first and foremost docile.

Surprised at the resistance she mustered when breaking his news that it would be advantageous if he sailed first for London, established a flat before she followed in three months' time, he'd badly miscalculated the reaction.

'Three months!' Jon was horrified.

'Yes, three months, darling.'

'That's not necessary, Gil.'

'Please. Let me be the judge of that,' he stiffened, piqued at this opposition to a carefully laid plan, completely settled in his own mind. First he'd enjoy the voyage; having heard women went mad at sea throwing morals overboard as the anchor weighed, he wanted first-hand confirmation. The Red Sea ... whew ... a hand dabbed metaphorically at his brow.

Several weeks in London alone to explore delights that couldn't wait till Jon arrived ... Soho, Maida Vale, Shepherd Market ... he'd certainly change the guard by the time she docked!

Jon's expression was mutinous, her voice more positive than he could remember: 'I can't see any reason at all for such an arrangement. I'm definitely against it.' Threatened, she stamped a foot to emphasise qualms buzzing unrelatedly in her head. Raising her voice she shouted at him for the first time. 'Give me one good reason, just one good reason why you should go off alone and leave me to follow?'

'There is absolutely no need to raise your voice ... '

'And absolutely no need for you to make such a decision.'

Gilbert thought quickly. 'Darling ... '

'Don't "darling" me.'

'Don't be a silly little goose,' this was the best tactic he calculated, at the same time calculating he'd have his way whatever the cost. 'Three months,' he crooned, 'twelve tiny weeks. And all I want is to have everything shipshape for you.' Shipshape? Ship ... the ship's rails were lined by single women, to a man smiling invitingly, beckoning voluptuously.

'I'm sorry, Gil,' her eyes downcast, she had an unexplainable feeling there'd been a mistake, 'but ... '

The danger point averted, the sigh he exhaled mustn't betray him.

'But I ... I really can't see any reason for us not to travel together.' She felt panicky. Once she'd missed the bus on a school excursion and the long-ago alarm flooded back.

'Darling. Of course you can't. But trust me.'

'I'll be wretched travelling alone.' Again she saw that bus disappearing in the traffic, arms waving streamer-like. 'I've never ... '

Gilbert planted a kiss on her forehead. 'Can't stay a baby for ever,' and renewed his plans, insistent she'd be fine, disconcerting her further.

Lost, forlorn, hollow, she took herself in hand in an attempt not to show it. As Gilbert, set on making amends, divulged their schedules she said nothing, his mood facetious now. She seemed to have used up all her attention.

'It's even possible,' never believing it for a moment, 'you won't spare me a thought. Imagine all those dashing ship's officers making a play for you.'

'Gilbert ... '

He didn't want to hear. 'By a snap of good luck I've managed to get myself a single cabin. "A" deck,' he flashed her a smile but his words carried to her in lumps. 'Plan ahead is what I say. Then you're to share a porthole cabin ... '

'Share?'

'Now listen, Jon, the *Odeena* is a fine single-class ship.' On her face was a determination new to him. He thought quickly. 'Young and lovely wife joining young and handsome husband', he played out the part, 'falls for the novelette's trump card. Shipboard romance! Hearts pound with every flat-chested-borrowing from all local libraries. He, dashing, debonair, she sweet and shy until ... ' he rolled the non-existent wings of his moustache.

'I'd like to travel first class.'

Slack-jawed, surprised, helplessly he spread his hands. 'Be reasonable, Jon. Why not spend the money in London? There'll be so much you'll want ... umm ... aah ... Warm clothes ... '

Any chance of her relenting evaporated. 'First class. In a single cabin.'

'What!' he exploded, prancing like a horse at the starting barrier. 'First class! A cabin to yourself!' Sarcastically his tongue rolled about his mouth. 'Quite sure m'lady doesn't want a day cabin too?' Shaken, Gilbert was deflected only for a moment. 'That would be a ridiculous waste of money.'

Was it her voice? 'It is my money.'

In attempt to recover shredding composure he lifted well-tailored shoulders and smiled expansively, inwardly continuing to rage for the rest of the week, sourly nursing a sense of betrayal.

The purser rose from his chair as she advanced, his girth large, tightly bound by the cummerbund of the evening uniform, complexion florid, poise mechanical.

'Ah, Mrs Jamieson, how do you do?' and she was placed on his left. 'Allow me to introduce your fellow travellers. Then I think a toast to a good voyage would be in order.'

Two bottles stood held in silver. Deferentially the purser's dining steward filled the glasses which were lifted and sipped by: a Mr and Mrs Royston Goodlet, owners of a Brisbane department store, a Mr and Mrs Lance Beresford, honeymooners, the bride years older than Jon, a Mr Gerald Pascoe, construction engineer, a Miss Ethel Moulton, elderly spinster with grazing connections, and a Mr Miles Dey, on her left, art curator and expert in the restoration of oils.

She nodded full circle with the introductions.

'Mrs Jamieson.'

'Mr Dey,' her wan smile was drawn a little more warmly. She was drawn to short names. If ever she had children ...

Glasses replenished, more wine appeared on the table.

Dear God, thought Jon, will I be able to cope with all this? How would she when her turn – for during the weeks of the voyage it would inevitably be her turn – order the wine?

'First time "Home"?' Miss Moulton flashed between large teeth.

'Yes,' and realising more was expected of her added, 'I'm joining my husband in London.'

'Which part of London?' Mr Goodlet meant well.

Floundering, Jon could think only of Gilbert's working address, and though must have been breathing perfectly well felt a constriction thick in her throat.

'Wimpole Street.'

Miss Moulton boomed in. 'Selfridge's or the Regent's Park end?' Perhaps she hadn't been incorrectly seated after all.

James Wheelwright, the purser, who at the beginning of each voyage tended to think he was getting nowhere, nowhere, except older, looked with pleasure to the menu. Meat and drink and a tidy ship were more real to him than his wife in

61

Hampshire, their two children at expensive schools. He'd married late, domesticity made him feel limp, and wished Miss Moulton's relatives had not enjoyed his table so much last trip.

Idling across hundreds of miles of sea, the ship was an entire world, her passengers drinking, playing, recharging languorously in the sun, streaming on through their own shallows and depths, no reflection to be caught in the churning wake.

All ease and indolence, the great white liner cushioned them like a feather bed, quick to regain shape when in their prescribed time these men and women would totter down the final gangplank.

Hot blue skies shared the world with inky nights, the stars hysterical in number. At first affronted by freedom, the echoes of her normal life began gradually to fan away. She ceased to rattle in her kitchen, Gilbert no longer in her bed. Jon began to move easily with the roll of the ship. She screwed eyes to watch dolphins, flying fish, cushions of rocks on the horizon which were islands and the few birds which appeared; the sea an indigo blue, a sullen grey or as green as moss ... rackety or calm as it surged uneasily, unendingly. Ports had a potency and charm she'd never known, apricot at dawn, lavender, blue and pink if approached at dusk, a heap of diamonds by night.

Evening was the most opulent time in her lazy playground; leisurely she'd take a bath, dress, then climb to the boat deck, the games courts deserted, quoits, balls and racquets stowed away at this hour. There she'd follow the melting butter of the sun running with the streams of flames till soused, incredulous at the glassy brilliance of the sea before the moon began to rise.

Though still only twenty-two, Jon's vision of the world had been changed vastly from the mockery and romanticised veneer of her eighteen-year-old dreams, her longing for love burned up in reality. Yet she continued to oversimplify issues, absurdly naive in any encounter which constantly put her at emotional disadvantage with Gilbert.

'A penny for your thoughts,' offered a voice, precise, cultured, English.

'Not worth it,' she smiled at Miles Dey, table companion, art curator, expert in oils restoration, cultivated, gentlemanly, the man on her left at three meals a day – thirty to date – short, lithe, brilliant-eyed, and she sensed belonging to a world to which she could not aspire. A frown puckered between her eyes and she realised she'd been more relaxed with this man at breakfast than with Gilbert, her own husband. Gilbert never at his best in the mornings, tending to answer questions with a grunt; culpably she felt a need to justify his behaviour. There was little justification.

'No bargaining,' he laughed, 'save that for Aden next week.'

'Have you been there?' Yes he had, his tone low and conversational.

'Join me for a drink?' he asked, she hesitated, the sky growing purple, juicy as a grape.

Jon knew she wasn't a young woman whom people scrambled to entertain, but sensed the invitation genuine. She should have felt confused, but didn't, there was a certain clarity ... He was appropriate to her life uncharted at this time in unfamiliar waters. He didn't press the invitation but stood beside her, effortlessly leaning on the rail, looking fixedly into the night. Behind them, thin and stranded and temporary, the sounds of a party in one of the bars webbed by coloured lights, before them the sea which lived on forever burdened by its legends: there was a terrible void. When Miles Dey turned to her she was shaken by a sense of freewheeling to an unknown planet.

'Let's have that drink,' and easily took her hand. 'I've wanted to ask you often, but ... you seemed locked into some private world.'

He'd been studying her? He must have guessed she was shy. At his touch there was a triggering self-possession she'd never known before, his closeness she found reassuring. Stunned to be the focus of his attention, later she questioned herself hard and long. Was it a trick or the heavily enchanted light? Some supercharged flash of recognition? When you throw a stone do the ripples ever cease?

Convinced that anything she chose to tell him about herself would interest him keenly, she was no longer interchangeable with any other woman. Awed, she felt nearly beautiful.

'What will it be?' He ordered drinks above the idle wash of voices then leaned forward and their voices meshed with the chink of glasses and ice, smoke spiralling from cigars in the mouths of dinner-jacketed men, perfume from their gowned companions. Encircled in affluence, they were enfolded in the liner's luxurious life. Intrusively a siren sounded.

'That sound,' he grinned, 'it's like ... like some great haunted sea beast.'

Jon alarmed, glass in mid-air asked: 'What is it? What can it be?'

Lightly he covered her hand, bringing it with the glass to rest on the table, grinning still, but kindly. 'Just lights on the horizon, another ship ... '

'Ships that pass in the night?'

'Yes.'

'You're so very young,' he said the following day, then, 'Tell me about your husband,' and listened carefully, though at first she didn't know how to answer. His forehead touching hers, he wanted to weep for all trapped creatures. Loveless marriages end only in punishments, never rewards, he was sure.

Tell me about your wife, Jon ached to ask, but restrained herself. What would it matter anyway? Why waste time in speculation?

'I have a wife,' said Miles who might have read her thoughts, and looked at her closely.

'How long has this been going on?' Lightly she tried to catch the right, the expected mood, crushed by a jealous weight.

Folding her hands in his, he was grateful. 'Ten years.'

'Ten good years?'

Slow to answer he considered. 'Yes. Yes it could be described that way. Probably been kept that way by an institution we call the Saturday row.'

'Children?'

'Two boys.'

'Are they like you?'

'People say they resemble me.'

'Don't tell anything more about them. That's enough.'

'Yes.'

Love to Jon was a thin highway of glass on life, never before trodden. Heaven teetered on the borders of hell.

They parted each dawn, with a need to be together again as soon as possible in order to have life confirmed.

Miles Paul Dey, Jon kissed each single syllable of his name in her mind. How can he feel this way about me, mousy me? repeatedly she asked herself, but knew by instinctive guile that he did and she did and that whatever happened in her future she would have shared a decorated world, alive with colour and joy. There was no single woman in the entire world, she knew, happier than she was. Not one.

No pair of lovers, no pair of fingerprints, was ever built to an identical pattern. Who could know that what they felt for each other would ever be experienced again? Tenderness, passion, respect, but principally joy, a lilting, zinging joy which kept the rest of the world sightseers, spectators apart.

'You're a witch woman, you've laid a spell on me,' Miles would tease, eyes filmed by softness, both their needs imperative.

Tailor-made, she smiled, tailor-made to contain you.

She should safeguard her marriage, retreat, she told herself and didn't believe it. She felt no devotion towards Gilbert, none, and only lamented the time she and Miles would be apart. It's so wasteful, she believed and laughed to remember that Betty had brought her up to think of waste as sin.

'Sin,' she confided to Miles, 'if this is sin, where's the value in life?'

Miles made everything out of nothing beautiful.

'I didn't know I could ever feel this way,' she said, the ordinariness of the words inadequate, stupid.

'They're part of every language, always have been, always will. Whatever else we invent we can't find new words for love.' She let his words linger and spin inside her ears, on and on and on.

His voice was gravelly, 'I do love you.'

She uncurled like a cat to see him better, dazzled, bewildered, jubilant, as if at last she'd been privileged and looked directly into the sun.

'There's not just one woman for one man, one man for one woman. You know that. Perhaps during each of our lifetimes there could be five, ten, whom we could equally love. You realise that?' and lifted her chin.

'Mmm,' she nodded absently, eyes searching his face, one hand rubbing softly at his cheek.

'You know, historically,' his lips dabbed at hers, 'love's a modern invention. An obsession with us westerners.'

'Mmm,' she sighed.

'There have been whole civilisations that haven't catered for it at all. Millions of people spend adequate and affectionate and ... and adjusted lives without it!' Her smile was loose, tender, as he went on. 'In Asia, in Africa ... '

'You mean arranged marriages?'

They talked with woven voices.

'Mmm. Traditions are too relevant to more than half the world to be left to sentiment and chance.'

'Sentiment and chance,' she echoed. 'I like it.'

'You're not listening.'

'Yes, I am. Truly.'

'Well, if love creeps in after the marriage broker and the parents have bargained and negotiated, it's a marvellous bonus but ... '

Jon trembled. She'd never made a more definite statement in her life. 'I love you.'

'Hush,' he murmured.

A mass of fidgeting little craft, boats precariously loaded, buzzed at the liner's hull when she came to anchor in Aden, one side facing towards the town, the other to the cluster of huge oil tanks shimmering silver in the sun.

Moored fore and aft to buoys, the shore hazy, dun-coloured like an old lion, flashes of golden beaches at its feet; rocks rose piled up in a dusty heap, arid and sharp to jagged peaks.

Steam-driven tugboats panting asthmatically ferried to the landing stage, bumping heavily against the quay to tie up in a tangle of shouted instructions from a waiting crowd.

The heat was savage, drenching them with brutish force.

'It's a hell hole,' Miles smiled at her, 'with a choice of one road. Right to Steamer Point and the Governor's residence. And there's the N.A.A.F.I. Club fully equipped down to sharkproof bathing beach. We'll ... '

'Is that where we'll go?' She realised how rarely they spoke in terms of the singular: it was 'we', and soon she'd have to do without him. The thought of it gave her a crashing sensation, she felt she was plummeting fast in a lift.

'No. We're not going there.'

'Then where?'

'Willing to put yourself entirely in my hands?'

Vigorously she nodded.

The heat was torrid. Through a fringe of beggar boys with wrinkled little upturned palms and pi dogs slinking like loosely boned shadows, when they reached the shelter offered from the sun by a handful of flaky buildings and a scattering of shops the leaden ugliness had combined with dust and a rotting smell. Faces dark as walnuts peered from under catheas, the white of the headdress and headropes in sharp contrast, the women as squat as ducks, black galabias concealing family wealth in silver and gold about arms and throats.

Miles, one hand tightly catching hers, imperiously lifted the other to hail an ancient Buick. Haggling with the driver, the fare settled they climbed in and gears grating turned to the right, hot dust grinding like pepper under the wheels.

'We're going to Crater Town,' Miles informed her, 'Aden proper. It's roughly five miles, stands in the crater of an

67

extinct volcano. And ... ' he looked lovingly into her eyes, 'if you're wondering, the mean annual temperature is 83° Fahrenheit.'

'In the shade?' She lifted the hair off her neck.

'In the shade.'

I'd roast in hell with you for ever, Jon thought, and be happy.

Ahead a filmy haze half hid a string of camels, the splayed feet hitting pools of dust like padded saucepan lids. The road, steep and winding chiselled out of the lava, tunnelled through living lava to reach a dirty huddle of houses which led to a few larger administrative and commercial buildings. From the police station hung a Union Jack.

Dwellings, a cross between tent and humpy, were forced closer into narrow alleys, listless beggars in doorways animating to whines and a nasal entreaty as the car slowed, stopped and they stepped out, one miserable wretch unwrapping the raw stump of an arm in silent supplication.

'Miles,' Jon clung to him, sickened.

His arm tightened about her. 'It's all right, all right.'

'Is it ... is it safe?'

'Of course, providing we keep to the open street. Anyway,' he pointed, 'look at that smart fellow over there. One of the local police and they all have a smattering of English.'

Lean faces, features aquiline, obscure dark eyes stared openly as they were channelled into a shrilling market, round-faced Indians from Goa and Bombay the shopkeepers, names ... Ramdas, Padel, Desai, Ashok ... declaring their origins. Tired fruit and vegetables knuckled for space beside tins, rice, loops of red mutton and goat meat, rolls of cloth and cooking pots.

Tethered goats and bleating kids, tin-smiths mending kettles, silver- and goldsmiths with displays of bangles, bracelets and rings filled the streets, overflowing fat men and lean bags of some sort of bean obstructing their way. Children in rags, flies at the honey of their eyes, pranced behind them, clear voices pitched high. A fox-trotting donkey, released from a halter, neatly dodged them, the owner's curses guttural, an all-pervasive smell hung thickened like cream and the heat blistered relentlessly bent on sucking them as dry as the further peaks all around.

'We'll have to find something to drink.' Miles led her into the darkened depths of a stall where a tailor sat cross-legged, head down, stitching lethargically.

'Hungry?'

Jon shook her head. 'Just a drink ... '

'Just as well. Even I, who adore you, would be taxed to provide you with a safe Epicurean delight. There's probably tea or coffee revolting with goat's milk, but we'd be mad to drink it.'

Jon sank on to a low stool.

'Ah. God bless America. Will Coca-Cola do?'

'Lovely.'

The shop seemed to fill with coughs as more and more figures followed them in, lining the walls to gape unblinkingly, one a young man with wheedling speech, the rest silent, grave.

'Miles?' Some primitive instinct urged her to move.

'Drink it, Jon, then we'll look at the mosque.'

Later, choosing with care the goldsmith, he chose with greater care a bracelet for her.

'Love's built on truth not dream,' he said, 'and ... '

'Yes?'

'And ... if later you come to think what we feel for each other is dream, well ... this is a small, real thing to remind you it's real.'

Is real? Was real? Feeling her heart heave, thinking how fear lurked just below the surface of joy, she clung to him with a bewildering disregard for the overcurious eyes that followed uncomprehendingly, removed from such a display of emotion by the walls of centuries.

Despite the heat they were among the last back on board, the water at the foot of the gangway broiling; planks of boats with sheets of sails doing a brisk trade in shoddy souvenirs and brass from Birmingham, garish carpets and Taj Mahals from India.

69

'Look at them,' Miles nodded towards the gossips in their deck chairs, Mrs Goodlet pearl-chokered and Miss Moulton desultorily waving a fan, tongues clacking though the heat stilled the rest of their bodies. 'Look at him,' Miles's eyes swivelled towards Lance Goodlet, asleep, mouth slack, panama at a racy angle. 'He's been filleted; there's not a bone left in his body.'

Jon grinned, 'No soup for me tonight … '

I'm beginning to be frightened, confused, she wanted to tell him as day by day Tilbury loomed closer, and desperately she made the attempt to resolve in her own mind whether any family was more important than its individual members. Instinctively, Miles seemed able to penetrate these thoughts she knew should be hidden. It's so unfair, she screamed silently, bewildered by the injustice, so unfair. Why can't he be mine? Why shouldn't he be? Mine, mine, mine.

'We've been lucky,' he told her, and each star stabbed the sky with a stiletto glint, unsaid the recognition that anything worth having had its price. He prayed their encounter wouldn't tear her energies, drain her will.

'Yes.'

'What will you do while you're living in London? It's indigestible, so much to see and do. What will you do?'

'You won't laugh?'

'Do you think I would?'

'No.' She hung her head. 'I'm going to try to get myself some education. If I'd been correctly educated … knowing you … ' she hesitated.

He broke in. 'If you'd been what you call "correctly educated" you might have been irreparably damaged.'

She tried to smile. 'Miles … knowing you … if it had been possible for us to live together, you would have grown bored with me. I know so little.' The vacuums in her knowledge became more startling every day.

'Jon … '

'It's true,' her voice dropped, 'but we'll never know … '

'No.'

She looked away before she spoke.

'We can't see each other after we land ... ?' Something seemed to squeeze her heart so hard she was wrenched by what she felt must be a crack. Intended a statement, it was a question she wanted to protest and argue.

'You know we can't.'

'Of course,' she agreed and believed she would wake up every night in her life and recall him so vividly he might almost be there beside her. 'It'll be Gilbert,' she screamed and when calm again tried to explain.

'Jon,' he touched her lips with light fingers. 'What I'm going to say, well ... it's grossly impertinent, but ... '

'Yes?'

'Think about having a baby.'

'Yours?' Her eyes were incredulous. 'Yes, yes, yes.'

'No. Be sensible. No, I couldn't be as irresponsible as that. Neither must you. We couldn't, you know that.'

The dream vision of a child, hers and Miles's, could last only a moment; love smudged by hate. She bit the knuckles of her fist.

'Gilbert's?' She was repulsed by the idea.

'It would be your child too.'

'Oh Miles ... '

'Jon, listen; we're all somehow caught but life's not only affirmed in the intense moments, but in the continuance.' Wanting a baby must have been one of the longings that had tempted her into that marriage. He drew her closer. A pervasive sense of loss, a mixture of grief, guilt and nostalgia for something that immediately was gone, struck hard. Breathing fast, her breath gradually slowed to his, her tears damp on his neck.

Like all true partings it was difficult.

The ship docked at Tilbury, uninviting, and the train through Essex to St Pancras was interminable, dragging through the treacle of the flat countryside. She spotted Gilbert in the turmoil of the station before he her, and felt older than at any other time in her life. Tall, his leanness overlaid with a little fat, curious she'd never before recognised him as vulgar.

Puzzled, Gilbert found her tense, yet strangely beautiful, her eyes burning, over-bright.

'Jon, my little wife,' he warbled in the voice used during their courtship, and the heavily lidded, droopy eyes looked at her, licked her, she thought, like a spaniel licking a bone. The kiss he'd intended planting full on her mouth brushed her cheek. His voice sounded scratchy, rough. Crude? 'Well, here we are together again. In the big, wicked city of London,' he stared at her as if they shared a secret scheme. 'You'll love it here.'

The flat in Camden Town was off Albany Street, a short walk from Regent's Park and the Zoological Gardens.

'Lucky to get this, darling,' even Gilbert's most insignificant acts had to be heightened by some adroit skill; but she agreed on seeing it they were lucky.

Basement, ground, first and second floors of a sizeable terrace house remodelled to flats, theirs was right at the top, an iron balcony overlooking a mews and a neighbouring pocket garden where a pair of Siamese cats were loved like children.

'A good furnished flat is hard to come by, Jon,' and appreciating his pleasure he sank into one of the armchairs on either side of the fireplace. 'Look about, my girl,' he instructed, to leap up and lead the tour through the three rooms plus bath and kitchen. 'Note the heating, Jon ... fireplace and an oil burner. No shilling-in-the-meter for us, eh? We'll be snug as two bugs in a rug. Or, let me put it in the English style,' his voice imitative, 'as snug as two badgers in a burrow. Ho, ho, ho.'

Gilbert's hands, Jon's eyes on them, looked parboiled. Was his chin beginning to jowl or was it the angle at which he held his head? I mustn't cry whatever I do, she was thinking, filled with dismay.

'What is it, my sweet?' He loosened his tie. Yes, he was pleased to see her.

'I'm ... '

'Excited to be here?'

Nodding, she gulped, quivering with the necessary smile.

'Well ... London ... it's so exciting. I can't wait to see more, get out and explore.' How lame it sounded.

'Come to Gilbert.' He spread-eagled arms and she was flooded by nausea, knee-caps jellied. 'It's been a long time.'

How long ago, aeons in time, since she'd thought he'd offered her love. Turning her back she covered her face. 'Give me time, Gil,' she stood very still, eyes closed. 'It's all so different after the ship.' She looked about the room as if unsure how she'd arrived.

Gilbert could afford to be generous, exhausted himself from the previous night. 'Silly little goose. You know me. We both have our rights.'

What does he mean? she shuddered, alarmed. How and where do you strike a balance between largely incompatible sets of rights? The world, on parting from Miles, seemed drained of sense.

The sheer weight and size and muddle of London was a confusion, but the spell of enchantment spun and sung of it for centuries wooed her too. Any time, day or night, in any one of a hundred locations the world was on display, the good and bad of clamorous city living. Millions of bodies, millions of minds scurrying secretly in and out of tubes, buildings, strolling openly along the Serpentine or the Embankment. The great spread that was London with acres of rooftops and chimneys, the alleys and courtyards, elegant Regency terraces, squat Victorian villas, unbeautiful blocks of flats and the vast counting house of the City was in fact there for her to explore.

Walking and wandering, Gilbert engrossed by English teeth in Wimpole Street, never before had she seen such flowers as banked in gardens and squares or blooming in the buckets of stalls. She delighted over the pigeons strutting in Trafalgar Square to volley without warning into the skies as though shot from a cannon; she visited all 'the sights'. In this congestion of living she marvelled at voices supposedly speaking a common language, English, mixing with more secretive foreign accents, evasive and difficult to understand, as impressed like all newcomers, she watched the guard change at the end of the Mall. There was a physical toughness about London; so many Londoners, cheery, gracious, uncomplaining in the cramped and ageless old arms.

Intoxicated by idleness she gloried in museums, concert halls, the theatres ... 'a regular little culture-vulture,' Gilbert described her to friends made in clubs and pubs ... and wandered guidebooks in hand, through the galleries of the National, the Victoria and Albert, the Wallace Collection, the Royal Academy, the Courtauld, all but the Tate. One day perhaps she might bring herself to go there.

'I'd like to take art lessons,' finally she told Gilbert.

'Ah. A blooming little Leonardo. Is that to be it?'

'Don't be absurd. I'm thinking of joining a studio near Russell Square.'

'Joining the Bloomsbury set,' Gilbert slapped a Prince of Wales knee and convulsed over coffee, sobering at Jon's face. 'Don't take it all so seriously.'

'But I do,' indignant she had to take him seriously, a need gnawing to be separate from him.

'Darling, come first light Saturday I'll go out and buy you tubes of oils, a palette and a smock. How's that?'

She looked at all the corners of the room, and spoke very clearly to shut out his voice. 'I'm going to work in water-colours.'

'Oh. I see.' Yes, he did see water-colours a better hobby medium. Lady water-colourists; easy to envision, seated primly, knees together, dabbing a delicate pink here, an inspid washy green. 'Any other plans?'

Jon couldn't be sure he wasn't laughing at her, had the feeling he was no longer fully interested though he continued to look at her. She framed the answer carefully. 'I'm also going to study French. And history.' No need to tell him it was art history. Nor did she mention the reading lists in the assault she planned to make on her general ignorance. She might also tackle the Russian novelists.

'Blow me down,' Gilbert slapped his knee again. 'You are going the full hog.' Did he drag the words out in a mocking way? Just a touch vinegary? 'Equipping yourself to earn a living next, yes, that'll be next.'

How's it going? What have you been doing? She knows he will come to ask, stagnant phrases, never questions. She sighed deeply. Would she continue always to 'feel' with the crushing pain of an adolescent when wounds should have healed over?

'Yes, that'll be next,' he repeated as he looked at his watch. 'Well, this bread-winner must be off,' and pecked her cheek absently.

The door closed behind him, she waved at the window then sank down to the floor and began to cry.

Jon didn't know exactly why she cried, and if it wasn't her situation what? Why should she be singled out for happiness or betrayal? Yet she did believe that everything would turn out to be all right. She was still young and more resilient than she could guess.

Chapter Six

Her teeth chatter. The day began a commonplace enough day.
But ... Shapes in the distance are ragged. She's in a large and
heavily populated city, but it's wild and silent, alien: interchangeable with a sparsely wooded mountain terrain, trees
tufted with the nests of ravens, gaunt, forbidding. Should
wolves come slinking down from their hidden ways to devour
her, snarling and bristling in the thin light, could they be held
at bay? She imagines the hot, stained fangs in her bones, her
skeleton picked clean like a wicker cradle. Horrible.

Hunching shoulders into her neck, tugging the sweater
down over her hips, she attempts to still her chattering teeth.
How fanciful can you be? We all go through life knocking,
touching, missing, hitting, thumping and throwing stones at
wolves.

'Wolves,' she says aloud and blinks the hills and heavily
shadowed valleys into proper perspective, to follow this
ordinary street and the slight incline. A swinging light reflects
the ordinariness of the roadway, footway, and beyond in a
band of sounds a dog barks. She keeps on walking: left, right,
left, right, left, right.

'What's right?' she asks and becomes two bodies, each with
a tongue.

'Very little's right.'

'What nonsense you talk.'

'What answers then?'

'There are no answers.'

'I won't accept that.'

She should feel hurt and unanswered.

Clustering like crabs, their little shells a delicate pink, on a bare tree ahead blossom breaks out from winter-grey limbs. A few weeks and it will be thick with flowers, blowzy and overblown. The scent will be overpowering, intoxicating, smothering, trumpeting like an elephant that life is regenerative.

'Soon it will be spring.' She hugs her waist and elated now chants ... 'Spring when a young man's fancy turns etc.,' to see lambs cavorting and foals with spindles of knotted knees endearingly close to Mum. It's a recurring cliché which insidiously gives even the most cynical humans renewed hope that all will come right with the world.

Spring? Caused by modifying effects of the earth's position in relation to the sun; the distribution of land, water, winds ...

No. Spring's a production, an excessive production. She smiles into the night; the black dividing night. Here winter marches more sedately into spring. But it can burst upon a wintery world. Startlingly.

Ruth, her daughter, was born in an English spring.

At first Gilbert declared her a victim of hysterical symptoms; he didn't care for the thought of parenthood, wasn't ready to be deposed, and not guessing he wanted to remain the child of their household, sulked. It even crossed his mind to leave. Not that it should tie him down, restrict him any more than marriage, but gradually accustoming himself to the idea of a son, basked in certain knowledge of proven virility. Not that he'd doubted, but the marriage was three years old and birth control hit and miss.

Jon, pregnancy confirmed, had burst into tears.

'What is it, what is it?' Gilbert trying to be kind, solicitous but above all practical was on the point of suggesting if she didn't really want, he knew of a doctor who ...

77

'I couldn't be happier,' Jon sobbed into his shoulder, vowing never to let her husband know that the baby, indisputably his, she claimed for her own. Damp with emotion her condition thrilled and terrified her, bringing her fully to the realisation that her body inexorably would do as it should; fill, flower, bulge and burst.

I wonder if I'll die? she asked herself and in a rare moment of rapport Gilbert made the statement:

'Childbirth is extremely safe these days.'

How would he know about extracting a baby, he only extracted teeth?

'I'm not a bit worried,' Jon looked at him through misty eyes, and wasn't.

As she began to swell with the child she moved with a new power, an entitlement.

Rumours bounced up and down the pre-natal clinic like balls; the expectant mothers seated, gossipy, their lumpen bodies in turn to be pumped and inspected, wedding rings well displayed on laps or what was left of them as they waited for their babies to unlock and be born. Jon welcomed the chance to take a place in the queue, and sit after the tube to Hampstead, clanging up to street level in the elevator and climbing the long hill to Queen Mary's Maternity Clinic. Visits over, when it wasn't wet or too cold, pale sunshine welcome, she'd stroll across to the Whitestone Pond. There small children watched over by cautious parent or nanny set boats on the water with a jaunty solemnity she found so endearing, others whispering wooingly, hopeful of the chance to hold a string.

Peering into prams, the babies bundled neutral little figures, acknowledged by her condition to have the right, the world seemed no longer separate from herself: she felt included. She tried not to speculate on the colour of her child's eyes, the shape of its nose or head, but repeated the universal plea only for it to be strong, knowing she gave her unborn child wishes it couldn't hope to extend into life.

When the contractions began she couldn't believe it. Face

barely changing she told Gilbert, dinner over, who sat engrossed in a different mystery.

'Gil.'

'Mmm?' His eyes didn't leave the pages.

'Gil,' she repeated, her voice begun normally rising to an unnatural pitch. 'Gilbert!'

Gilbert informed became efficiency itself. 'We must time them. Precisely,' and went purposefully to fetch the Wessex alarm from the bedside table. Jon wondered why a watch wouldn't do.

An hour passed, two, three, and she began to believe no other woman in the world had had a baby. Breathing according to Dr Grantly Dick-Read and the instructress at her regular classes in relaxation, the whole thing took on shades of an almighty confidence trick.

'I'll make a pot of tea.' Chameleon Gilbert, she thought, had become very British. Jon rarely drank tea.

'Coffee ... ' her voice plaintive.

'Tea,' the answer firm, 'is better for you.'

How do you know what's better for me? She wanted to scream but grabbed by a tightening band, bit back with the strong feeling she was mismanaging the whole thing. Having read widely on childbirth, every word fled into a recess so inaccessible she couldn't follow. Her mind and body, with dismal cunning, were estranged. Something flailed at her backbone and she cried out.

Gilbert tripping over the mat in the kitchen astonished at the viciousness of the sound, recovered balance and froze theatrically, teapot in one hand, lid in the other. Steam hissed from the kettle. He'd spilled sugar on the floor, each step gritty as he moved in haste. The groans from this stranger in the next room, he supposed, were something to do with him, but ... Would he care for the child? He would certainly care that this son of his, so nearly an actuality, should reflect credit on him, but ... Of course he cared, and breaking the ice-like posture filled the pot.

Jon having removed herself to the bedroom in a stiff-legged

79

and curiously delicate way, felt that if she attempted to talk she would be using the wrong words. As much as she longed for this baby she wished it possible to free herself from the world at least for a day, this day. Having interrogated herself often in the dark prison of the night in attempt to extract the reason, uncover why she'd married Gilbert, she only wished she'd never married at all. There was no one in the world to trust ...

'Here's a nice cup of tea.' Gilbert soothing, she imagined he was jeering at her. He wasn't, the suspicion unfounded.

I'm not a music-hall joke, she tried to say but her voice fuzzed at the angry pecking that had started up again in the centre of her body, the beak cutting through the thicknesses like a knife through butter. How could she be so cruelly exposed? Then a respite; the bedroom suddenly shrunken and quiet. She longed to be entirely composed.

'You must be a good, brave girl.' Gilbert with the look of someone who had waded out too far took her hand and she was grateful. But not for long.

'The hospital. Phone ... and get me to the hospital,' she heard a voice hoarse and insistent, astonished at the pitch of the words.

'No need to shout,' Gilbert shouted back at her, feeling a touch squeamish, believing she was on the verge of passing out. He wanted to be sure she could hear. 'I'll get an ambulance.'

Ruth's travels had begun.

It was a slow and difficult labour. A battered little baby finally a forceps delivery, it was to take time before the bruises on the tiny swollen face and body were to smooth away.

Gilbert, very ready to be told what to do after delivering Jon thankfully into the clinical arms the hospital extended, was easily persuaded to go back to the flat to keep a more comfortable vigil than the draughty corridors provided. With indications it could be a prolonged labour his reluctance to leave was barely token.

'Phone every hour,' the sister on duty smiled humouringly, 'yes, yes, we'll phone you should it be necessary. Off with you.' She had a hand to lend in larger issues, husbands she found bothersome, many of the mothers too. 'Don't make a fuss, dear,' she was to say later to Jon, tight-lipped and a spinster.

Gilbert dazed, having played his part, staggered into a pub for a drink. Key in the street door lock, the telephone shrilled and taking the steps at a run, it jangled on as he fumbled with the key to the flat. Fingers clammy, reaching for the receiver it stopped dead, the shrill silenced.

Helplessly Gilbert sucked his fingers. About to bite his nails he remembered his profession. The phone started again, and pouncing to make a grab breathed rhythmically and counted to five. Dignity, dignity, he cautioned and rolled the number over the line.

There was a momentary pause.

'Gillie?'

'Gilbert Jamieson speaking.'

'I know, I know, hello, hello.'

Mystified Gilbert repeated his name.

'Gillie, darling, it's Laurel.'

'Laurel?'

'Laurel, yes, Laurel. Laurel Thompson, Laurel Gerard, Laurel Thompson.'

Laurel, who determined to marry quickly as she had watched and lost Gilbert as he and Jon joined, had found the necessary ingredient to make her one of a pair amongst the guests that night at their wedding. Single-minded as a silkworm devouring mulberry leaves she hadn't time for the niceties. Furious and slightly unhinged on losing Gilbert, she slept as quickly as she could arrange with both sons of one family to tell the elder she had conceived by him. His was the more trusting pair of eyes. Having resorted to sexual blackmail she promptly miscarried, to find the whole thing wasn't worth it. Briefly she'd tried to reproduce a glossy monthly idea of marriage, but was divorced two years later, divorce then not the common follow-up to marriage. She'd even managed to persuade him to accept the role of guilty party.

'Laurel! What a surprise!' Gilbert spluttered shaken. He

found himself looking round wildly, remembering with sudden clarity the opulence of the Thompson household. Externals only, but ... Five years since first introduced to it, Bill Thompson his partner, a close family friend, yet grim-faced, anxious, he saw the corner shop with its marble scales, musty storeroom, smelt the sacks of potatoes, decaying fruit. The unease passed and he relaxed into the phone; aware that Laurel, once so garrulous, was silent on the line.

'Are you still there? Laurel?'

Not answering immediately, savouring the moment, Laurel smiled sweetly into the confined air of the telephone booth where so many stale conversations lingered. She'd developed a sweet smile; many people including Gerard had almost thought she meant it.

'Laurel?'

'Gillie, darling,' she repeated with a honeyed laugh, her shield against a rotten world. Which might improve, who could tell? They were well met, she and Gilbert Jamieson.

'When did you arrive? Where are you staying?'

'Midday. The Dorchester.'

'Doing yourself proud.' Gilbert, won by her assurance, felt delighted to be in contact. Jon's confidence, grown enormously since her arrival in London, had none of the boldness immediately detectable in Laurel's tone. 'How long are you staying?'

'So many questions, Gillie. Only till the end of the week.' Fingering a large diamond salvaged from another wreck Laurel paused, to have been flooded by pleasure had she sensed his immediate disappointment. 'I've only diverted on my way to Paris, the Spring Collections you know.'

'Spring Collections?'

'A girl must pay her way.' She'd landed a cushy job on a magazine. Fashion was her field.

'Oh, if that's the case we must see as much of you as we can. What about tomorrow?'

Coquettishly Laurel purred. 'I did have plans, but maybe, perhaps, they could be rearranged.'

'Good, good. And how's old Bill? The family? What's happening in that neck of the wood?'

Laurel told, Gilbert listened, questioned, their conversation thick with familiar names, Laurel finally to ask after Jon.

'And Jon? She's well?'

'Oh my God! Laurel, darling, give me your number. I'll ring you back in five minutes, ten at most.' His head felt big and loose. If it wasn't necessary for him to go back to the hospital before morning, perhaps a drink?

Would his wife want him by her side? Certainly not. Jon at that moment felt such a spite and anger against the world for leading her to believe that if you learned to breathe properly a baby fell like fruit from a tree.

Ruth, whom she would not see for another two days, would look like a battered plum newly born, a wizened little crone, but within a month enchantingly pink and white, head ringed with downy obsidian curls, the tiny face a mis-shapen pear to come rounded and right within weeks.

However, birth still imminent, her mother had no resistance to the terrible thoughts that assailed her. They did not include thoughts of Gilbert. Why couldn't this baby be decanted from the engulfing shape of her own body to a neat, named and dated cot? How long must she pour out and expend frantic energies in this single-minded pursuit? Jon, all sense of dignity lost, no longer had a meaning for dignity, as legs strung between poles she was cajoled, directed and stood over, expecting never to be covered decently again. Nothing made much difference, until called back from a dark pit which threatened to erode and tumble in on shock waves, distantly from a far-off echoing forest a voice called: 'You have a daughter. A little girl. Can you hear me?'

What she heard was the scrape of a bow drawn over a single string ... a sliver of a wail as Ruth made her first claim on air space to cry, the sound pitched high like an eastern lament.

'You have a daughter. A little girl, Mrs Jamieson.'

'I know,' she attempted an answer and knew absolutely that nothing would be the same again.

When the baby, her daughter, with miniature fingers knuckling into the purple folds of flesh that made a chin, was laid in her arms, the strength of her feelings outran any control. She wept convulsively.

Jon couldn't study her enough; this child of hers now separate from her own body with her own complicated organs, four limbs, the blurred features that had as yet little form of her face, the ears and perplexed little brow, tiny blue threads of viens, the slack sac of her skin which would fill out to develop along with her wits, her whims, her wants and her good or bad fortune.

'I promise you it will be good,' she murmured, enslaved. 'I'll care for you. I love you so.'

'Hush,' she heard Miles Dey say with infinite tenderness, and this time knew there was no need to think of the time to come when they must part. She was her daughter's keeper and while recognising it a temporary post, did not complain. She's my second chance, Jon told herself, for Ruth must conquer new worlds.

Gilbert, initial disappointment at her sex only to last till her face righted, was trapped by the vanity of fatherhood.

'You see she's like me, don't you, Jon? Just a little. If nothing else, her hair. It's dark and ... don't you think the shape of her mouth ... '

Jon smiled indulgently; she didn't mind, knowing Ruth wouldn't be clay for Gilbert's moulding, or for that matter entirely her own. This baby was a unique person and she'd fight to see she wasn't programmed to freak or failure.

'I want her to go to the best schools,' Gilbert blustered on. 'I had to make my own opportunities, but she's not going to have to climb up unaided ... '

'You don't want to push her up the beanstalk. There could be an ogre in the castle at the top.'

Gilbert looked at her hard. He made as little reference as he could to his own background, but had been forced to reveal something of it to his wife, though never without a knotting resentment in his chest. Pulling at the bristles of his moustache he pulled his face into a smile. Of course it was his place to humour her; she'd had a tough time of it, so they said.

'Darling, we both want the best for her.'

'What's best? Too many ambitions? Too many expectations?' She heard her voice unwinding with her own questions, played out like a slow rope. 'They must be hers, not yours.'

'But ... '

'I've been thinking about it. Seriously. Of course I don't want her poor, materially poor. But I don't want her impoverished in other ways.'

'Darling,' Gilbert patted her hand, slender on the sleeve of the sheet, his face a puzzle. 'I understand,' but frankly found her thinking muddled. A daughter he regarded as a plaything and a responsibility. Which order? He would have declared responsibility. If he'd looked into the crystal ball of his mind and the vapours had swept away he would have seen a man who would fuss over the child, push her out of sight should she become a nuisance, spoil her when she pleased him and when it pleased him to spoil her. He would want her pretty and well-mannered to show off, he would want her to achieve, but, primarily he would want her to submit to his authority. After all he knew best. As for her name; he'd try one last and final time.

'Jon. Ruth's ... '

'Yes.' Had she guessed and stiffened for battle?

'Ruth's a sound name, but have you reconsidered my suggestion? Sandra.' Laurel who'd had to leave for Paris before Jon was permitted visitors other than direct family, had thought Sandra a 'perfectly darling name'.

'Sandra or Saundra?' How to say it? Jon was bemused.

'Either, wouldn't matter.' He gestured with a flattened palm.

Jon took his hand, her gaze direct. 'Gil, indulge me, please. I'd never give a child more than a single-syllabled name. Never allow it.' Knowing her mind made up she was almost enjoying herself.

He didn't like to forgo a cause too easily, to submit pained rather than pleased him. Even in little things ... 'What about

Suzanne,' Laurel had insisted on discussing the name of the baby at some length; it was after all Gilbert's and she felt something of a proprietorial interest.

The flowers from her, a huge beribboned boxful, sent out their sickly perfume.

'Suzanne,' Gilbert repeated; he had a headache but supposed Jon would have nothing as simple as an aspirin available.

'If you'd prefer Rose to Ruth,' Jon smiled sweetly.

'Oh, no,' the answer sharp. It was his mother's name. Rose! Rose ... his puritanical, unchristian mother with her Christian texts constant on her tongue like butter. His mother who had liked to pull him close as a boy, bury his nose in her neat cotton prints and geometrical rayons, which smelt to him of carbolic. Rose, who crunched her words like tart apples. Gilbert spread hands acceptingly. 'A name's a name.' Why not be generous? 'If it's Ruth you want then Ruth it will be.'

Ruth, it was a name echoing out of antiquity. The biblical simplicity had appealed to Jon from the moment she knew she'd conceived. Things, she felt, accumulated around a name. With myriad complexities to face in living she had resolved her child would bear no handicap she could consciously control. Perhaps it would make no difference, it was something that couldn't be proved, but with even the suspicion ...

'Had she been a boy ... ' Gilbert saw no real reason to keep defying her female judgment.

'Had she been a boy he would have been christened Paul.'

In a September spring at the other end of the world, two years later Paul was born.

Chapter Seven

A gusty puff of wind blows out of the still night with the suddenness of a whitening beam from a distant lighthouse. It picks into the night, she feels an extra keenness of cold and the moon is shuttered off by a racing cloud. One moment she's walking in a sparkle of moonlight, the next ...

'Where's the visible world gone?' she begs.

The wind, started unexpectedly like an electric motor, drops. The darkness wells out, throbs. She props as if she might stumble on hidden rocks. There are none. No point in standing where she is; she starts to move forward. The wind flurries up again and putting a protective hand to her cheek as if to save it from bruising, spreads fingers over it like a defensive wall. If she was wearing a collar she would turn it high over neck and ears.

A shaggy pile of newspapers stationed by a gate for disposal is held down by a brick. But a few sheets have blown free. One hooks the toe of her shoe as she moves on, but kicked high in the air, catches again. She makes little goat-like leaps and tries nimbly to disentangle her feet.

'Paper, paper, read all about it.' What headlines shout from this printed page? 'Footlines,' she says, idiotically. 'Old woman attacked and robbed of meagre savings. Young woman convicted of brutal assault.'

The wind falls away again. Stars hazy against the edge of the cloud are freed and shine once more metallic, bright. She stretches her neck to them and, as though some great obstacle has rolled away, the moon hangs in the sky, luminous enough to dislocate the senses.

Scrunching over the newspaper, another sheet spreads wide against an iron fence; spread invitingly, begging to be read. She picks it up. The light is clear enough to reveal a page. 'Amusements'. A guide to entertainment ... current concerts, films, theatres ...

'Revivals, revivals. So what's new?' She runs a slow finger down boxed columns.

Much Ado ...

My Fair ...

Oedipus ...

'Her Majesty's presents' ... this print is larger, darker with the presentiment of gloom in Nordic households peopled by wine-dark emotions, tribal, devious. Ibsen? Strindberg? where the raiders pick off the passive resisters, few to survive unscarred.

Her Majesty's Theatre. She sees two dress circle tickets, lolly pink, and two of the audience dressed in their best duplicity. Nineteen years ago.

Paul's birth was tidier, quicker.

Gilbert at thirty, given to overeating and potentially overdrinking ... 'Man was made to enjoy the fruits of the vine' almost as regularly on his lips as glasses raised to them, but strictly out of surgery hours: his breath from 8.30 to 5 p.m. untainted by anything stronger than peppermint. He had thickened about the girth, flesh shining with fat, and summer approaching was determined to slice back to former sleekness. The neat waist and lean hips of his youth rounded; this did not please him entirely when ordering new clothes, for he'd developed something of the small-time dandy. Nor was he entirely pleased as he slipped from these well-structured garments on extra-marital excursions, though gave it more thought at his tailor's than during amorous encounters. Cars along with clothes had become an outlet for early unmet needs and he liked them foreign, expensive and never the family size. He was not amused, decidedly not, when jokingly after her second confinement, Jon, concerned with tightening her own stomach muscles, suggested he might need corseting.

Emptying the contents of his pockets, a nightly routine, on to a William IV desk ... one of many good pieces Gilbert had realised prestigious as well as sound sense to buy ... he wondered at the unsuitability of many of Jon's remarks. She wasn't an unsuitable wife, no, not that, and if interrogated would doubtless profess his love for her. But how surprised he would have been, rather than hurt, to guess at the depth of feeling she was capable of.

This Jon poured into her babies. Her babies! They had liberated her from a gnawing loneliness despite the fact that her life was liberally peopled, there was plenty of company ... Lola, Betty, Dorothy, Laurel as well as an ever-widening circle who fed them, they fed in turn, on the dinner party circuit.

She had developed a sort of curious loyalty towards Gilbert in the ordinary tug and pull of family differences, shutting ears and eyes to find she could live quite happily. Lola had helped in this when she'd recognised in Gilbert a restrictive, an imprisoning attitude towards the emotions.

'He's sleep-walking with his eyes open,' Lola told her with the smile Jon found unfailingly dear. 'I've done a lot of sleep-walking myself because to get through sometimes you have to believe one day you'll wake up. I don't believe in turning my face to every blast that blows. Gilbert doesn't operate that way,' she saw Jon's confusion. 'He does it by believing everything that doesn't touch him, well, it doesn't count ... it's ... '

'Irrelevant?'

Lola hugged her. 'You're a one. The right word at the right time. How'd you do it?'

'I just read a lot.' It had taken a long time. Jon busied herself turning away from Lola's blue eyes. There had been only one thing she'd been unwilling to share with Lola, and the older woman who'd moved in the background of her life like a bubbling fountain probably guessed but suppressed curiosity, never questioning. There had been no fuss, no appeals, no reproaches, no persuasion; any advice warm as new-baked bread.

'Gil's not good enough for you, Jon. Never has been. It doesn't matter a fig he doesn't take your painting seriously, I can't myself you know, but he could try to understand a few more things ... '

Was Jon answering Lola or simply pouring balm on deeper waters? 'When men don't understand their wives they call it the battle of the sexes.' Sometimes she wished she'd never loved a man; it left you too lonely, it spoilt too much.

Lola had never taken to Gilbert, though she'd made the effort for Jon's sake when at eighteen she'd been first infatuated. Yes, he'd had a certain jaunty style, and while suspecting his blinkered sight of life, she had seen very clearly the overwhelming bourgeois ambitions, which Lola in her heart knew to be trivial. Lola, caught up herself without the securities desirable to a young woman, let alone a young mother, had had few ambitions materially. She'd spent her childhood in bleak discomfort ... as had Betty but how different they were, chalk and cheese ... Betty purposeful, Lola indifferent, but generously life had pulled a trick out of its hat for Lola. Betty, unasked, had provided for her and her baby almost to make Lola the wayward young sister, Lola in turn to pass on to Jon, through no links of blood, some of the qualities her own mother, Betty, lacked. Lola's sufficiency spread prodigally, Lola herself unaware it spread over any demarcating line of need and greed.

Now with hindsight Lola saw that any girl encircled by the suggestive wedding glints of satiny scraps and lace-trimmed finery, might believe that marriage could be nothing but smooth and lacily fenced from the hugger-mugger of living ... a tennis game where unspoken one partner, then the other, took turn about to win. It must have been a cruel awakening. Never in her entire life had Lola planned, and the thought crossed her mind what a lucky thing she'd had no mother like Betty. Very fond of Betty, they understood each other well, but what disasters could have fallen her way had she been the child of such a mother. It was understandable that Jon had had such a craving to live her own life out of her mother's house and orbit. Gilbert had provided an answer of sorts.

'Everything must have some plan,' she sighed in a moment of vision.

Jon agreed.

If Lola had never cared excessively for Gilbert, his response was mutual. He never liked to associate with unfortunate people, never had by choice. Until scornfully Betty drew the sights from his eyes he had treated Lola like a servant, at best a poor relation with more than a hint of patronage. Was he envious of Lola who inspired such depths of love? Little Tom, her son, he considered no more than a nasty accident. But as Tom grew from an enchanting small boy to an attractive youth to a mercurial young man, Gilbert's paralysing depression evaporated as the entwined family connection became no longer a degradation but an advantage. So it was necessary for him to adopt an uncle-like joviality. When Betty plucked Tom out of the business to acquire degrees in Commerce and Economics, Gilbert could barely hold his tongue. He longed to discourse on opportunity overcoming heredity, but with Tom inheriting his mother's affectionate disposition his views were best kept private. Jon would not be drawn into argument on this subject; she'd always loved Tom, could never understand why Gilbert was so particularly enraged with anything concerning Lola.

'Seen anything of Lola this week?' Gilbert picked the contents from his trouser pockets as carefully as he'd pick shards from an archaeological site.

'Why do you ask?'

Gilbert, finger hooking into his key ring, shook it absently. 'Thinking of corsets and excess size,' he was restored to better humour by what he thought was a small victory, turning the joke from his own weight.

Jon looked at him smiling. 'Whatever you may think, Lola will grow to be a real twilight beauty.' Tough in an enduring way, yet wistful with her smooth open face and her eyes, Jon never doubted it.

'How's that?'

'With her nature and a voluptuous body, how could she miss?'

'Voluptuous! Wads of fat I'd call it. Oh, well, if you like that sort of thing,' casually Gilbert laid keys, change, pocket diary, wallet, an envelope and two oblong, lolly pink tickets neatly in a row. Idly Jon's eyes wandered over the array and lit on the gaudy pink. Theatre tickets? He planned a surprise. They'd been out little since Paul was born ...

'Which? What?' she bit back the questions. As he'd planned a surprise she could wait to be told, and turned to cream her face, eyes on him in the mirror.

Suddenly Gilbert made the discovery; glanced suspiciously towards her, bare shoulders tensing. Jon ignored him. Really, it was quite sweet of him to go to the trouble of concealment. She found she was intrigued; he was acting out of character. Fancifully she tried to see Gilbert immersed in international conspiracy. No, impossible to imagine him darkly, daringly international in crumpled raincoat, cigarette burning as he ordered Turkish coffee. Flaking doorways, steamed up windows and hideaway attics, Gilbert sly, unrecognisable with clean-shaven lip.

'Gil,' she saw him surreptitiously slide the tickets into the privacy of his wallet.

'What?' Sharp, knife-edged. Did she imagine it? 'What is it, darling?' He recovered smooth tones, no longer pointed like a picket fence.

'Dorothy's asked if I'd take the children to their cottage at the beach for a week next month.'

'Splendid,' expansive, his hands packed down his sleeked hair. 'Do us all a lot of good,' he coughed convulsively averting his eyes. 'Do you all a lot of good, I mean.' His hands patted down to his stomach and lifting his rib cage breathed deeply. Was he courting a heart disease by carrying extra weight? He'd better watch it, resolved to keep his blood pressure down: he intended to live to a ripe old age. 'Perhaps I should get more exercise. You're right. I plan to live to a hundred. Think I'll work out in the gym at the club a couple of nights a week.' His voice grew louder. With enthusiasm? It was his loud public voice. Had it ever been raised on any issue of political or personal freedom, Jon would have been happy to listen. But he was recounting yet another episode of Bill Thompson's latest skirmish with the wife of a mutual friend. She nodded mechanically.

'And by the way. Are you listening, Jon? Bill reminded me of the reunion next week. All the fellas. Next Wednesday. Wednesday the 18th. Make a note. In your diary. The 18th. Don't want to double up on anything, do we? Do we?'

'Oh. No. I'll remember.'

Later, getting up to Paul, Gilbert heavily asleep, she remembered the 18th. But what about the 18th? The date for the theatre? No, that hadn't been mentioned yet. Night was just breaking into day and brushing aside the curtains, the windows massed a dawn blue. A fresh, green smell as sweet as pinewoods hung in the air. The 18th? The 18th. It niggled. What had Gil said, she couldn't remember. Ruth called in her sleep and was quiet again. I won't think to ask him at breakfast.

Bare feet padding over to the desk she picked up the wallet, and having had no occasion to do so before fumbled to get it open. Yawning, Jon drew out the tickets.

Her Majesty's Theatre. Even. performance Wed. 18th, Dress Circle, D22, D23.

She stared at the tickets which lay on her hand like a socially embarrassing disease. Wed. 18th, but Gil said … She stiffened. Logic baulked, turned in on itself.

Sometimes I think it takes you longer to realise a fact than anybody who ever lived. She tapped her forehead, and turning towards the bed made out the dumpy shape curled on one side … her husband. She wasn't sure when she'd guessed Gilbert paddled in the illicit, but faced with the evidence that this must be more than bedroom entertainment was confounded. Recently she'd found herself softening towards Gilbert; his thickening waist, the lines fanning out from the heavily lidded eyes to give him a comical expression, bringing the realisation that the years they'd been together were lengthening and a matter of indifference to anyone but themselves. The fears, the anxieties of trying to accommodate to existence with him had begun to recede.

Still not thirty, on occasion she'd felt life had been going on a long, long time and sometimes had wished to die, but running out of pretences had told herself she was tedious, dull. The small voice of her suburban despairs could be swamped by news every day ... famines, fires, floods, battlefields. She must define her life and make it work.

But, the great unspecified 'it' was not going to work out the way she'd hoped. Marriage accustomed you to many things you took for granted, but magnified all the things you found bad. Expectations she saw like fairy-tale pictures: turreted castles, trees and flowers for ever in bloom, bluebirds, princes on high-stepping steeds, princesses with golden locks, gauzy gowns and loving parents, fairy godmothers with magic wands to ensure that everyone lived happily ever after ... beautiful bubbles removed from reality. As if the world had ever been fair and properly regulated!

Returning the tickets to the wallet in half-acceptance, she jerked open a drawer of the desk and fumbled inside. 'What do I want?' she whispered alarmed. A neat little Luger, a pearl-handled dagger? Neither, but her hands were clammy by the time she crossed the few feet and climbed between the sheets to lie stiffly, trying to keep her body from relaxing and possibly touching his. She was indignant. How dare he be so underhand? Indignation swelled; she worked up a short-lived fury. She stared up at the ceiling, the corners dark, the light soon to dispel it to an early grey and cancel away another night. Regretting that she'd weakened to some form of acceptance, she alternated between humiliation and disgust. Then she began to cry, but not much. The absurdity hit her;

she wasn't so affected by his infidelities but her own situation, its inescapability.

'I'll leave him, I'll leave him,' fisted hands tightened to strike him as he slept, but with small children it couldn't be easy. Supposing he tried to claim custody ... supposing he tried to smuggle them out of the country ... supposing ...

At breakfast she said nothing. Fears of the early hours had receded, she was conscious only of a weary rage.

'My eggs. Aren't my eggs done?' he asked and she turned on him, agitated, eyes she supposed darkly percolating like the coffee on the stove.

'If the service isn't to your liking, hire another cook.'

Gilbert blinked, stared at her, shaken. 'Jon darling ... ' to her ears his voice oily, 'had a bad night of it, have you?'

'I've had worse.' She pushed her hair back and watched him avoid her eyes.

'Go back to bed. Mrs Leonard'll be here soon.' He sucked at his teeth; he did it methodically after every meal routing out particles of food. 'Let her look to the kids, I pay her enough, and', Gilbert believing this unknown domestic crisis solved, 'tell her, Jon, to take more care with my shirts, particularly the collars. Or they'll have to go to the laundry.'

Why am I making this fuss? Flushed and baffled Jon was relieved to see him go. Would she be relieved if he was to go for good? Loosening the grip of resentment and refocusing the situation, she felt she'd been put in the position of eavesdropper. The day wore on and her raggedy mixture of indignation and affront turned to curiousness. She picked up the telephone.

'Her Majesty's? Have you one ticket? A single for the evening performance of the 18th. Yes, Wednesday. Dress Circle please. No, not too near the front. Row F or G. Centre if you have it. G25? Yes, yes. To be collected in advance. Thank you.'

'What a bloody silly thing to do,' scolded Lola. She couldn't approve. 'I'm surprised at you.'

'I'm surprised at myself.'

'But why?' Lola persisted. 'Do you care?'

Jon had asked herself a dozen times. Perhaps it boiled down simply to the fact that she'd come to recognise that while everything about her life was far from second best, Gilbert was a second-best husband. But her husband! Her husband of seven years, nearly eight. It will concern her less in the future.

Lola, never having cluttered her life with matrimony, could believe that when you marry you take on a husband according to his income, ability to provide, his friends, his needs, his, his, his. And subordinate yourself to the life he leads. If you care for him, she supposed, you'd accept the degradations offered. Rarely had Lola felt the need for a full time husband. And never a pompous ass like Gilbert.

'Do you care?' Lola repeated.

'Yes and no. But mainly no, I think,' she answered as she put her hands on things in doubt, a plea for support and understanding.

Lola would not hear of Jon laying herself open to the indignity of a seat behind Gilbert and fancy friend.

'Fancy friend?' Jon wanted to know why, her head feverish, explosive.

'Got to be fancy,' Lola's chuckle throaty, 'sitting up in the theatre dressed to kill no doubt, then spread on the bed naked to receive, no doubt. If you must get a look this is what we'll do. This'll be better than your crazy plan. Tell me how you'd handle it if they saw you.'

'If they saw me? I don't know. I hadn't thought.'

'Well think. Could be very messy,' Lola disapproved, determined to dissuade Jon.

'What would you do?'

'Not me. Us.'

'Us?'

'Yes, us. You're behaving plain stupid for a clever woman.'

'Me. Clever?'

Lola tilted back in a chair, raised eyebrows to give a twisted grin. 'In most ways, but not all. Now cheer up, it's not the end of the world,' and thought privately that Jon would need to muster more gaiety in the coming years.

The lights that spelt out 'Her Majesty's' mustered a gaudy gaiety as Jon and Lola sat in a taxi opposite the foyer, the façade covered with posters like heraldic shields, the driver told to keep the meter ticking till given the word to move off.

Lola wondering if she had failed her, Jon sat hunched up and withdrawn in the farthest corner of the back seat, brimmed hat pulled down to her eyes, cheeks flushed like pink geraniums.

'I feel quite schizophrenic,' Jon leant forward and made the claim. 'Laughing and crying,' she giggled uncertainly as the theatre crowd thickened, unnatural in the neon glow. Lola in a state of watchfulness was beginning to doubt the soundness of her plan. So many people it would be easy for a couple to slip in unnoticed.

'Want me to move on, lady?' the driver asked. This was money for jam. A finned car slid in front and two ageing mermaids, long hair swishing, were dropped.

'No,' Lola was prepared to sit it out till curtain up.

Spilling out on to the pavement, smiles were flashed as friend greeted friend.

'Programmes, programmes,' droned a pretty girl inside; the voice not reaching them, only the lacklustre expression.

Circling, knotting and unknotting into groups and couples, the theatre-goers jostled, blinked uneasily in the overbright light, chittered like monkeys as they anticipated the performance. There was a general air of pleasure.

'Perhaps the tickets were meant for someone else,' Jon had the charitable thought. 'Perhaps ... '

Lola reached for her arm.

Flushed, blatantly dancing attention on the woman he held loosely, Gilbert veered into view. Dressed in floating pink, chic, the sort of female who mysteriously can be seen renewed year in and year out, inked eyes and cherry lips purring, slinking hungrily both on and off the catwalk on her model legs ...

'Laurel Thompson,' Lola bunched her mouth in disbelief. 'Move on, driver,' she hissed.

Shaken, Jon had expected Gilbert's woman to be a stage prop, not a living, breathing, known person. Her mind was humming. Laurel! What, if anything, should be done about it?

'Leave it,' was Lola's advice, who'd had misgivings on the friendship when the girls were young, principally on grounds of Laurel's vanity. There'd not been another girl she'd ever known who could so often arrange herself to gaze at herself in a mirror. And now? What a foul friend! 'Leave it alone. For the present. Don't act in haste, not on the spur of the moment,' counselled impetuous Lola.

The evidence that it was Laurel was appalling to face; her mind postponed it. 'I don't need him,' Jon was sure.

'You don't need shelter,' was Lola's answer. Gilbert, a man of some regular habits, left the house at eight-thirty each morning and paid the bills soon after they came in. If his irregularities ran to other women, and they didn't interfere with the social life he shared with his family, and if Jon felt nothing approximating to love for him ... why tremble with loss or grief?

Jon managed a watery smile. 'The future foreclosed before the mortgage.'

'A roof over your head and bills paid regular are no luxury till they're gone. When you've got to scour round in the hopes of laying your hands on a little money ... '

Jon trembled. Bewildered by Laurel's two-facedness. Gilbert for the moment was almost unrelated to such treachery. Her mind swung back to the time Ruth was born and she smelt the sickly, overpowering perfume of the flowers sent by Laurel, smelt them heavy with duality ... congratulation and self-congratulation.

'Why didn't I guess?'

'Women are either happy or unhappy; it can have nothing to do with men,' said Lola who probably would have liked to make some man happy. But marriage! Marriage might be a nice place to visit, but she wouldn't like to live there.

'Laurel!' Jon barely heard her. 'All this time!' All this time?

All this time secretly meeting with Gilbert, or all this time since they were girls of eighteen Laurel must have coveted him. What had been her first description of Gilbert Jamieson? Yes, Jon remembered, 'Yummy scrumptious.' There would be different words now, harshly acquired en route back to Gilbert. Laurel loomed in her mind's eye. Chubby Laurel. Rounded Laurel. Well-covered Laurel. Slender Laurel. Bony Laurel. Laurel the unknown whore. Laurel the known whore.

During the week at the beach with Dorothy, her brood Ruth and Paul, she began to see the irony of the situation.

Dorothy ... broad-bottomed, low-waisted Dorothy who paddled in the shallow water with the children like a stout ship, the skin on her nose leathered, hair unmanageable ...was scandalised.

'Jon!' She pulled Ruth on to her knee, hugging the little girl as if to protect her from such sin, covering the small ears. 'Do you mean ... adultery!'

The violence of the heat had gone from the day, along the fish-hook of the beach children played and swam, beyond them breakers foamed white and beyond again the skeins of the currents wove out to sea.

The jaws of hell couldn't have widened further when Jon said: 'Yes.' Gilbert had made little effort to cover his tracks; a few enquiries had been enough.

'Jon. How terrible! One of your best, your closest friends.' Dorothy was a fervent believer in the sanctity of marriage. Friendship ran a close second. Something must be done; Dorothy still believed in action. But what action? Should Jon send her marriage down the plughole like the bathwater or should Laurel be proclaimed the pollutant?

'She must have felt something for him all these years absorbed in her own boxed life.' Jon's eyes fixed on the amiably lethargic waves pasted to the edge of the sky, rolling, swelling with the power to become brutal, pounding. Strange how few connections she'd made between now and then.

'Something must be done,' Dorothy in a punishing mood, helplessly had little to suggest.

'I'll think of something.'

'Of course you will,' nodding in a definite way Dorothy mistakenly sensed that things as bad as they could be and was reassured. 'Things can only get better, Jon.'

Jon's eyes searched the horizon. A ship slid along it, painfully, slowly, like a white snail.

'I think I'll talk to Laurel.'

'What! What about Gilbert?'

'Not yet.'

'Would you like me to come with you?' Dorothy did not relish the idea but ...

'No.' Jon bent to pick up one of the babies, narrow hips thrust sideways instinctively providing a saddle for the child, and Indian file they all scuffed through the sand, the sun soft on the prawn-pink little limbs.

Gilbert collected them at the end of the week, slap-dash gusto as usual, his teeth yellow in a too-wide grin. Stubbornly quiet, with difficulty Dorothy made polite conversation.

Jon tried not to look too piercingly at him, read significance into casual words, but couldn't resist believing he wore a new skin, tauter, shinier and coarse-grained around the nose. Tyrannical about leaving promptly at midday, she wondered if he had an assignation. No, he simply wanted to avoid traffic.

When Jon phoned Laurel, Laurel edited her speech with scrupulous care.

'Come to lunch?' pause, 'Love to,' pause, 'Though an evening would suit better,' pause, 'Love to, but,' pause, 'I'm frantically busy,' pause, 'The new collections,' pause, 'Oh,' pause, 'Yes, most of my work for them has finished, but,' pause, 'All right. Lunch.'

'Why ask her?' Dorothy when worried made jam or batches of cakes. Jon, having married with full rites of the church, should not stand on the edge of such a yawning precipice.

'There's something I want to tell her.' Jon, once so nervous, was so calm.

'Does Gilbert know?'

'Yes. But I've not discussed it with him.'

'Oh,' Dorothy mystified had a strong wish to be more helpful, but marital problems were out of her range. Neither she nor her husband had destructive tendencies. 'What will you give her?'

'Give her?'

'To eat.'

Jon hadn't considered food. 'Laurel has a minute appetite these days,' and remembered greedy Laurel Thompson. 'Don't worry, Dorothy, I won't poison her.'

Laurel, smooth hair, smooth skin, smooth body, walked confidently into Jon's material world, manicured nails, the painted, regular features of her face swathed in the fixed smile of experience. Laurel at twenty-eight would move more carefully towards thirty than Jon, and her tendency towards haggardness hadn't yet begun to show.

'Just a glass of water, darling,' she instructed Jon the light drinker, bottle poised and glass tilted to pour herself a strong whisky. 'And, darling, I hope you haven't gone to trouble with food. A crumb would choke me.' The pink tip of her tongue licked its way around her heavily pinkened lips.

Jon scaled these slippery heights, poured the whisky.

'Don't you think you should have something a little stronger?' Was her voice a touch sour?

Alerted, Laurel thought she might and her long, thin fingers twitched about the glass. Jon, hearing Mrs Leonard with the children in another part of the house, was doubly fortified.

'Lovely to see you,' Laurel raising her glass was on the brink of saying it was just like old times, girls' talk: but recollected the topic of so many of those talks. Nothing was so irksome as the self one once was.

Jon went to fetch a tray and Laurel, left alone, was relieved to have spoken to Gilbert earlier, assured that Jon had no knowledge of the relationship.

'I'd like to talk to you about Gil,' Jon settled herself, arched her back slightly. It wasn't as difficult as she'd thought. The whisky hit her stomach and she was pleasantly jolted.

'Gil?' Laurel wide-eyed fluttered perceptibly. She began to laugh but it wasn't convincing. 'Why me?'

'You're an old friend.'

Laurel was bold. 'Jon, trouble me not with domestic squabbles.'

'You're an old friend,' Jon repeated, wondering at the genial aloofness she maintained. She paused delicately, went on, 'It's not easy to discuss,' no, it wasn't easy, 'but I feel you're more worldly, more ... another drink?'

Laurel held out the glass automatically.

Jon plunged in. 'Gilbert is keeping a young woman. Has been for nearly six months.'

'What!' the fixed smile gone, face contorted Laurel jerked her head having buried it in the drink, her neck white, marbled by the little bruises Gilbert had made.

Jon repeated the statement to find she was relishing it, an avidly interested observer, Laurel toying obsessionally with an inky sapphire on the index finger of her right hand.

'Who?' Laurel was bitter in self-revelation.

'Her name?' she would let Laurel insist.

'Who?'

'Does it make any difference?'

'Who?'

Jon made a small play of reluctance. 'Well ... Janet Webb. Very young. Nineteen. Worked as his nurse part of last year.' Jon restrained herself, she had a thumb-nail sketch. Blonde, fluffy, curvaceous, little education, loved musicals, aspired to be a dancer, Gilbert paying for the lessons ... tap and Spanish ... Jon posed her question. 'What would you do?'

'Me? Do?' Garrulous Laurel had become monosyllabic. She gaped in crimson disbelief.

'If you'd married Gil?' Jon took a long breath, then spoke very deliberately. 'Instead of me?'

Laurel found her voice. 'Chance is the name of the game,' her words rose piercingly.

'What am I to do? My first impulse was to have it out with him. But that would have catapulted our lives into chaos.

Arguments,' she could almost hear them rustling like snakes in clogged undergrowth. 'There would have been ugly scenes, accusations, denials, recriminations: then decisions to take ... '

'What decisions?' Laurel whined.

'Well, I suppose, divorce. That sort of thing.'

'Will you divorce him?'

'No.'

'No! You must be mad if he dares to treat you like this. If a man makes an absolute fool of you ... '

'Or a fool of himself?'

'You actually mean to tell me you don't mind?'

'Of course I mind. I mind a great deal. But I undertook something when I married him,' Jon sucked in air. 'Marriage must become a serious matter, or it must to me, with children.'

Laurel seemed to wake from some sort of trance; the words spiteful, venomous. 'If you', emphasis heavy on 'you', 'leave a good husband lying around unattended, what do you expect to happen? Someone will pick him up. And serves you right. You've been lukewarm to Gillie for years, why he told me only last night ... '

Jon had drunk enough to have the courage of her resentments. 'Laurel! You mean to sit there and tell me he's been confiding in you about Janet Webb!'

Cool, collected Laurel lost all poise. She hurled it at Jon. 'Go to buggery.'

Mrs Leonard stood in the doorway, Paul parcelled under one arm, Ruth trailing at her skirt. Sucking solemnly at a strand of her dark hair the little girl faced them with her mother's eyes. They might have been trundled in on cue.

'Coffee, Mrs Jamieson? Do you need it yet?'

Chapter Eight

To the left is a park; a small park where an arc of yellow light bulbs gives an impression of curried moonlight. Nothing moves, what wind there was has died. The air is morose, silent as it waits for the slow filtering sun.

'I must sit,' the arches of her feet ache, limbs leaden. She's come a distance. Limping to the closest bench she sinks thankfully down, to sink head to knees. A twig snaps. Is somebody there?

Bolt upright, I'm mad, she tells herself, here in a park at night. Alone. She tugs at her skirt. All sorts of people ...

The diseased, the deaf and the dumb, the blind, the halt and the maimed since time began inch down the path, tittering together in some twisted joke. She edges forward tense in her front row bench.

'Your condition is hopeless,' she speaks out ... and they evaporate like the apparitions they are. There are no interlopers.

Her eyes circle the unnatural landscape of a place familiar by day. A small park with trees and benches, beyond the wall of darkness, swings and a slippery-dip. Heaving herself to stand, she follows the path to the swings and the slippery-dip she knows to be there. The dark outlines of the swings might be gallows posts, a pair set side by side; the rungs to the top of the slippery-dip to be climbed before a brief descent to ... Where? Only solid well-packed earth.

She sees Ruth in fire-engine red whoosh down the slope of the slide, exuberant, fearless, dark hair streaming, her little back stiffened to leap off like a grasshopper before galloping round to climb up again, her infant plumpness gone, lengthening out, soon to be lissome, always lovely. Ruth ... loving, lovable, daring, demanding; a splendid little girl given to crying and beating the ground with rage and frustration when unable to achieve or captivate. Gusty, beautiful, surviving Ruth, bent on tearing the old order down, but with style.

'Ruth,' she says with the tenderest of smiles.

She catches the chain of one of the swings, twirls it and ... there is Paul, a pocket-sized edition of her father, Fred, but she can't remember him and must take Betty's word for it. Betty, her mother, who grew to adore Paul, who no longer believed in inflexible routines, whose head was turned by the relaxed charms of her grandson, a victim at last to love.

'Paul,' she says and her heart turns.

A deepened darkness gathers. The moon with two faces, cold and aloof, fragments as she moves away to find another bench below a thickly leaved tree. From high on the shadowy boughs come the twitterings of a bird. She stills every movement, every muscle to listen. Ears attuned to the slightest sound she hears the tree fidgety with birds, restive as they settle and resettle above her head. A frail cord with her childhood remains uncut. Her thoughts wing back to birds ... and she yearns to shelter in cupped hands the Melanesian pygmy love-birds given on her fifth birthday, the rosy-faced short-tails on her sixth.

'*Birds of Australia*, from the lithographs of John Gould,' she whispers, and the words kick into her head.

'*Birds of Australia*,' ten-year-old Paul, voice bright, high, was entertaining one of his friends. 'It's a fantastic book.' There was a clatter of a bat and the softer thud of a ball thrown down.

'Ever seen a black-breasted buzzard?'

'Nah. But look at this; the frigate-bird. I spotted one in the holidays I think. Listen to this.' He began to read:

'"John Gould tells of Captain Ince who shot a pair of birds in one of the breeding grounds. When he went back there some days later he found that the chick was being cared for from a neighbouring nest. This was the only nest to contain two young." Usually there's only a single egg,' he explained unnecessarily, talking with his whole body.

'You couldn't have.' With the rivalry automatic to young boys, Paul's friend, Geoffrey, rocked back on heels, thumbs in the pockets of his shorts. Over Paul's shoulder he'd read the frigate-bird, a sea bird, was seen off the north-west, north-east and south of Australia. 'Not on the east coast.'

'They're also seen in the Galapagos. And Hawaii. And South Trinidad,' Paul grave and absorbed was not to be deflected. 'Mine could have been migrating.'

Paul had had two obsessions as long as Jon could remember. Birds and water. Unlike Ruth who'd had to be coaxed every summer to paddle then swim, Paul put up no barrier. Listening to the pull and tug of their voices, Jon heard Paul launch in on another sea bird, the noddy tern. She pictured him scowling in concentration, describing in compulsive detail.

'They glide over the water, sometimes for hours on the look-out for fish. Then they swoop down to the water ... '

Why was he so fascinated by water? Lola had shocked Gilbert telling loud and long over dinner one night that Paul's preoccupation with water had sexual overtones, which were extremely healthy, and good on him ...

'What!' Gilbert had blithered, ready as usual to resist anything from Lola. 'Nonsense!' Must she be so operatic!

When Dorothy had expressed something of the same view, Gilbert briefly considered a psychologist, but had diverted from the idea. He liked to be proud of, not alarmed by his family, his attention span low on details of their daily lives. The children were Jon's concern. Into the schedule of his life he allotted them time, gave them attention according to time-table. Breakfast ten minutes lengthened to twenty at weekends provided there was no hangover to nurse; another ten minutes should they be up still on his return each evening. Sundays he could be counted on for a full hour. He loved them dutifully but not lengthily. He'd been given to catching them up unexpectedly when very young, tossing them in the air which unfailingly caused Ruth to laugh with the shock of it, Paul to cry. So much for infantile behaviour, Ruth was to continue laughing when shocked for the rest of her life.

Gilbert when moved by good humour would bring the children educational toys, and Jon could be counted on to feign pleasure if not the children. Neither had liked the hammer with square pegs to be beaten into a square-holed board. Never overlooking his dependants' birthdays, ever, but with the changing influx of dependants, Gilbert enjoyed indulging his women more. Their appreciation was demonstrated in a more predictable fashion. He no longer had a mistress in the strict meaning of the word; little sense in keeping a second, if tiny establishment. Hotel rooms readily available, he attended all dental conferences. Janet Webb long since had joined a chorus line.

Jon, another limb to her children to do their bidding for their infant years, fought for her rights, but privately. Ruth, furious when the other limb showed reluctance, would scream hard and long until she willed her mother to work for her. Paul, all gurgles and gentle temperament, was a cause for continual rejoicing. What had she done to deserve him? When school claimed them both she began to paint again, freed for part of each day from the disproportionate expectations of others. Painting itself didn't loom so large it blotted out perspective but she enjoyed it, the training, the development, the coaxing forth. And equally she enjoyed a sense of being given back to herself.

Closing the door on the boys the raucous voices sawed through. Why couldn't children speak instead of letting it all out at a shout. Paul used to whisper; she dislodged a memory from her subconscious. Odd the fragments that glued themselves there. Half his age then, five, snaggle-toothed like a rabbit, they were visiting friends high in a block of flats from the windows of which lay a dizzying sweep of water, the slow blue currents snaked with foam. Paul, palms and nose flattened to the glass, had turned to her, pressed close, peered into the holes of her ear then put a soft mouth to whisper moistly.

'When I die, let me go to heaven.' Sunday School was a new event. 'But can I have a little window to look down on the water?'

Later repeating his request to Betty, Betty who could deny him nothing matched his solemnity and nodded that it would be arranged.

The boys burst in on her.

'Mum, Mum,' his voice excited, 'can Geoffrey come with us to Grandma's Saturday picnic?'

'Yes,' said Jon smiling into her son's brown eyes flecked by thickened honey. 'Why not?'

It was Betty's birthday and she'd let Paul choose the celebration.

'A picnic! At Farley Beach!' Gilbert begged off. It was to be a large party, nearly twenty, he wouldn't be missed. 'Blast,' he'd protested, 'the date conflicts with Oral Hygiene.'

Saturday began radiant, glittering, the sky almost chemically blue. They settled themselves on the grass edging the beach, a family herd; adults, fluttering babies and the children, picnic baskets, bottles, rugs and Ruth's puppy she'd refused to leave at home. 'If Bumps isn't going neither am I,' she laid down the ultimatum and Jon hadn't been in battle mood. Ruth, anyway, could usually outmanoeuvre her. No, she happily anticipated a good day, a gregarious extroverted ritual of a day, uncomplicated in the blades of heat and the haze of the sea.

Drowsy with sun and food, when Paul gathering up binoculars and Geoffrey told her, 'Just going to see what we can spot, Mum,' she'd nodded moronically.

'Be careful.' Automatically Betty inclined a hatted head towards the boys as purposefully they dug heels into the sand, each of their single shadows stretched out long and gangling. 'Don't go out of sight,' her voice bright and practical. 'Not too far.'

'No, Gran.'

Quickly out of sight the boys began to climb. The cliff left the beach like a fire-escape and their probing toes found the rungs. The going tougher, steeper, stumbling on knees, clawing at rocks and tufts of grass, they slipped and scrambled on. Higher.

Puffing hard, Geoffrey called to Paul just above: 'Hang on. Let's have a rest.'

Inching on to a ledge, deep but barely providing width for them to sit side by side, the sea plunged away below. With a prickling of the skin between his shoulder blades: 'Isn't this far enough?' Geoffrey asked.

Shafts of sun needled into his eyelids as Paul looked upwards and pointed. 'Up there, that's where we're going. Could be a nest there in those cracks; might be eggs.'

'Have a look from here,' Geoffrey's hand touched to the binocular case.

'Couldn't see,' Paul replied, 'too much shadow. Come on.'

Geoffrey's reluctance dissolved as glancing down he experienced a feeling of vertigo. What looked like mis-shapen lumps of sugar below was the sea, breaking white on the treacherous rocks to re-form a milky blue. Paul had said they'd be able to climb right to the top.

The cliff, high, bare and grey as an old rabbit; at the top it levelled on to a shelf, then a kind of platform. Stunted trees grew here and there bending like cripples towards the land, loosely rooted in crevices, some lightly draped in stranded cobwebs. Gulls, slowly revolving white plates, circled above them.

The breath whistled through their mouths with the effort of climbing. Narrow chest heaving, Geoffrey felt something watery on his leg, unprotected by khaki shorts. A thread of blood meandered to his foot. Quickly he looked away.

'Keep your head up,' Paul cautioned. 'Come on.'

Patches of rocks blackened like a broken frieze, darkened. Below, the starched blue of the sea greyed imperceptibly as clouds began to swing across the sky. Geoffrey seeking assurance from Paul's company called: 'How much further?'

But Paul, well ahead, didn't hear. Leaning into the cliff he braced himself to reach for the binoculars bumping comfortingly on his hips. The light had rinsed from the earlier brilliance of the day. The air was no longer still. A wind swathed about him, chill, cold. Pressing his foot deeper into its hold in an effort to pinion himself to the sloping rock, the small foothold crumbled like stale bread.

The arrangement of cliff and sea reversed as he fell, tumbling clownishly, all sense of direction lost. He bumped against a sun-warmed outcrop, fingers clawing to take a hold, one shoulder sharp with pain. The sky plunged. Suddenly it was dark, shafts of light shot at his eyeballs, then darkness again. Distance, direction, movement and balance tumbled together. Then he was still. Drowsy, disembodied, he had been caught on a ledge much the size of the one where he'd rested with Geoffrey. Weathered by the winds of a million years, pitted by a million storms, the ledge had caught him miraculously, one arm dangling down towards the hostile rocks below which in the changed light looked like sweepings of broken glass.

'Paul,' Geoffrey's whisper strangled. He knuckled one hand into his teeth, breaking the skin in terror. His eyes puckered, melting with slow tears, pants wet and sticky. 'Paul,' he pulled hand from mouth and tried to call, 'Paul.' It was one high, trembling note. Curling himself up to become a ball of survival, what was he to do? Time passed. He clung where he was. All strength lost from the sun, the great sweep of the sea lay below shot by a purpling light.

Cold, unlike Paul below him and hidden from sight who was in the delirious warmth of a coma, Geoffrey shivered in a frenzy of fear and uncertainty. The little boy knew he must move or perish, that much was clear, and gradually the knowledge crept over him that help must be brought to find Paul. Dirty tears dripping down his face his paralysis inched away and shakily he began to climb, every movement a sickening ordeal of fear. Unsteadily he climbed up and up, to the levelled shelf and uttering little grunts and cries of exhaustion, finally to the platform and the track snaking down through tussocky grass.

Saturday with its radiant promise was nearly spent, the sky and the ocean remaining alive in the darkness which was nearly Sunday, broken by a hum of voices and the penetration of lights and lanterns.

'It'll be necessary to abandon the search till first light,' the voice was official.

'No. Please don't send them away,' Jon, dishevelled, ingrained by dirt and a sickening despair, had managed to send Betty away with Lola. Young Tom would not leave her, had scrambled blindly down to the shelf before the Rescue Squad had arrived to be confronted by the impossibility of going further without light. They had not been able to contact Gilbert.

'I'm sorry, madam, but ... '

'If a little ten-year-old boy could get up, couldn't one of your men get down?'

'It's not a matter of getting down ... '

'But he's down there, he's got to be.' Please, please don't let them say things I don't want to hear.

'We can't see him. We can't be sure.'

'What do you mean?' Is it possible to be more confused. Fighting a mounting giddiness she struggled to focus.

Large, substantial with his team, he didn't want to tell her, but it had to be said. He hoped she could take it. Filling lungs he exhaled the awful words, Who'd be a parent? and almost crossed himself to think of his own sons safe in their beds.

'He might have gone right down. To the rocks ... '

'You could rescue him from the rocks.'

He admired her control. 'If he fell to the rocks ... '

'Yes, yes.'

'The tide is in. The body would have been swept away.'

The body! Surely this man wasn't talking about Paul. Her skimming mind refused to settle.

'That couldn't be the situation,' her voice was that of a hostess bent on preventing the shambles of a dinner party. 'Geoffrey would have seen him if that had been the case, I'm sorry but ... I can't accept that, I'm sure ... '

She's going to crack, he thought. Where the hell was the husband? And wanted to be relieved of her emotional stress. There was work to be done, no room to afford sentimental considerations. A voice crackled over the radio from head-quarters and allowed him to free himself. She'd do better to go, or at least take something from the hospital kit to blunt the pain of waiting.

Despite the earlier heat of the day it was bitterly cold. Jon, in a thick sweater of Tom's, shivered uncontrollably.

'Let me take you home, Jon,' Tom tried again knowing she'd refuse. Fear and fatigue fused to weld her to the cliff top, flecked by the heavy shadows of the men who moved about, the outline of the truck and its equipment. She had looked closely at the paraphernalia of official rescue hours ago it seemed, the faces about her set stern in concentration, the situation edgy as the light drew in.

The jagged coastline was dim, a giant unlit ruin, the battlements ancient, unfeeling. The sea, black as charcoal, its runnels of movement lost until the first streaking light of dawn revealed them, skulked below unseen.

'How old are you, Jon?' Tom asked without explanation.

'Thirty-seven,' her answer flat.

He cleared his throat. 'Wonder what'll have happened to me by the time I'm thirty-seven.' Death had been so remote, it was other people, never anyone you knew. Never a boy of ten. A near-hysteria entwined him which he tamped back into a corner of his mind. Out of sight. Out of loyalty to Jon whom he loved he must be neither hysterical nor pitying. Is it a social or a moral code he wondered, demanding he did not burden her with pity?

'My life is half way through,' she said, sickened with the thought, and wasn't interested in the other half. She didn't relay this to Tom, too young to see the point.

'Let's have a cup of coffee,' firmly Tom took her elbow and steered her towards the truck.

Far below where they stood as the sun rose like a butcher to cut into the little boy's consciousness, a thin wisp of wiry grass bent with the air and Paul, mouth and throat parched, licked painfully at lips covered by a ghostly film of salt. Thirsty, so thirsty. Had his blood dried up? All his juices vanished? Trying to raise an enormous head he found it unmovable. Streaks agitated before his eyes in a variety of patterns. There was a sudden blur as he tried to move, wanting to bring a hand to shield his eyes; heavy so heavy, then his vision peppered again. His skull tight and bursting, a repetitive boom, boom, boom, urged him to escape. He fainted. It was still there later. When he moved from a deep languor it threatened to annihilate him. Deliriums of thirst made him sense the sea. Water; if there was a gallon of water he'd slop it down in a gulp.

Then he was frightened as he'd never been frightened before. 'Mum,' he tried to yell through his sour mouth. Mum! He was forsaken. M-uu-m!

Below the milky blue waves swept steadily away. Precariously balanced, had he been able to move he would have plunged, to slew through the water with the fish, to drown as he soaked up the water like a deep-sea sponge.

Mum! He needed her to snatch him to safety from these perils; he was swamped with the longing to be tight in her arms. His eyes slatted sleepily like the eyes of a bat. He felt the heat of the sun on his face then a brief cascade of thorned stars and it was night.

Reactivated with first light, ropes, climbing irons, winches were tested, the cage-like, metal-framed stretcher positioned at the cliff edge.

'We'll send a man over to see if he's been caught somehow. On the cliff face.'

Somehow! It was not a word Jon could accept. Not yet. He must be down there. Her anguish both eased and accelerated as the young man expertly went over the top and descended from sight. The sun flashing mirror-like on the sea hurt her eyes. Thank God it had dawned clear, no cloud to delay operations.

A small flock of birds, six perhaps, came to clamour over a sandwich tossed away by one of the men. One bird, the leader, hopped out in front to make an inspection of the contents. How they would have delighted Paul, rarely to be seen on cliff tops. Choughs, they made a mournful whistling sound and Jon turned her back, hating them.

The signal came up from below. The boy was located, injured.

'How badly?'

They were all sympathetic ... but busy. Tom drew her back from the edge. Over the top went the stretcher.

Dear God, prayed Jon, don't let him be too broken.

Time stood still. It couldn't have been long, perhaps twenty minutes, but she felt she was clawing through a hundred hours before she became aware that the winch was coughing as it leapt into life, slowly at first then regularly as it pulled up the burden.

He looks like an Egyptian mummy, Tom thought, shrouded and bound by straps and ropes, the small face drained of any colour but darkening bruises and the rusty ribbons of dried blood.

Weeping for the first time, Jon flung her arms about the cage that held him, and smelt the nutty skin of the policeman who bent to steady the stretcher.

'Dislocated collar-bone, maybe a break in one leg.' She heard the report in precise terms. 'Could be something internal, injured spleen, something like that.'

'He'll live,' she breathed. The tissue around her eyes began to redden.

'Young bones heal quick. Now take it easy.'

Chapter Nine

She leaves the park. It's hoarded with the simple sensations of many children's physical pleasures. Running, skipping, chasing, swinging, sliding, gulping at life as they throw balls, bread for the birds, water at each other, words, tantrums, sulks and smiles. Where does it all go? Evaporated, forgotten, warm bits of life snatched into the dark. Wasted? She would like to see messages pinned to the trees.

Here:

Billie Gilroy wanted to carve his name but broke the blade of his penknife.

Evelyn Wood was nearly bitten by an irascible old dog with mange.

Keith Albert lost his green taw; it was marbled with blue and his favourite.

Heather Watson cut her fourth birthday cake and cried because she had to give one of the candles away.

Guy Mackay was stung by a wasp and his ear swelled up like an air cushion.

Lesley Jorgenson's father tried to teach her to kick a football but she couldn't become the boy he wanted.

'Flares and flashes of lives,' she shrugs, her voice a quiet reproach and thinks they'd make better records than the statistics which clog up the cupboards of the world. These tiny beacons might be more enlightening than:

Infant Mortality Rates for Selected Nations

COUNTRY	YEAR	DEATHS PER 1,000 LIVE BIRTHS
Chile	1964	114·2
Italy	1964	36·1
Australia	1965	18·5
Sweden	1965	13·3

Estimated Population of Selected Regions

REGION	POPULATION IN MILLIONS	
	1980	2000
East Asia	966–1,171	1,118–1,1623
Latin America	362–383	532–686
Western Europe	148–156	157–179
Oceania	22–23	29–35

Primly they fill the archives; flat, bloodless, dry as wafers and tailored to meet a requirement.

'Another statistic,' Jon nods knowingly and crosses the steely ribbon of the street to stand at a bus stop, the beam of electricity above it shedding a pale spotlight. 'School bus between 8 a.m. and 8.45 a.m.,' she reads, voice controlled, and the uniformed figures gather in greys, navy blues, bottle-greens, brimmed hats and caps, the badges proclaiming them privileged. 'Pretend' adults, speaking a jolly hockey-stick language. Cricket bats, chums and bullies, swarming about, chanting rhymes; by the time they return on the afternoon bus ankles thick with fallen socks, laddered stockings inked in for fun.

Except for lovely Ruth with her black hair, her mother's fine skin but creamier, and her mother's beautiful eyes. At fifteen she was tall, slender, her chatter never still.

'Ruth,' she smiles and listens to the silence. Something stirs in the slate-dark night, moody but not malevolent.

'A cat,' she says and thinks she hears it scratch amongst a jagged waste of piled stones, a small pile, waiting to be trimmed to a garden path. She's never liked cats; the way they knowingly move, claw and bite. A quivering paw runs the length of her spine.

The world has sharp teeth.

'Cleaned your teeth?' automatically Gilbert put the question each and every day, rarely lifting his head from breakfast or paper as Ruth and Paul entered and exited on his morning scene. He had developed a double ability; both to speak to them and not see them.

'Teeth, teeth, teeth,' Paul muttered occasionally.

'Good teeth are a fine asset,' Gilbert mechanically stated another of his truisms, crunching toast and marmalade along with the words.

'If we were meant to clean our teeth we'd have bristles instead of fingers,' Ruth said precisely, amiably.

'Do sit down. Eat,' Jon never enjoyed the first meal of the day.

'No time, I'm late,' unhurriedly Ruth peeled an orange at the sink.

'Paul. Your tomatoes are ready.'

'Tomatoes and bacon for him again! You spoil that brat, Mum.'

Perhaps she did.

'And you watch over him like a hawk,' Ruth made her voice anxious, churned to the surface by memories impacted in her mind three years ago.

Jon sighed. 'You really should try to eat a proper breakfast, Ruth …'

'She'd have to get up earlier,' interrupted Paul.

'I need my sleep,' Ruth yawned.

'Beauty sleep?' Paul sniggered into a hand. 'Or have you given up?'

Ruth turned from him, some of her beauty in the way her head was set upon the long throat, in the lines of cheek-bone and jaw. 'What about a television breakfast, Mum?'

'And what is that?'

Eyes circling the kitchen, roping in her audience, Ruth started to act it out. 'Well first, the entire family is assembled, the table is beautifully set,' she pointed at the milk bottle. 'Trippingly we've come in one by one from luxury Slumberland beds, fresh as daisies, clothes sparkling white, fresh, so fresh, bodies deodorised. We greet each other with sunny smiles, the children having kissed each parent.' Ruth kissed Jon, ignored Gilbert. She'd learnt from him too. 'Mother has squeezed fresh orange juice,' she extended the half-peeled orange towards Jon, 'and joyously we choose from king-sized boxes of enticing cereals, each package containing a plastic treasure for a lucky someone.'

Paul reached for the offending milk bottle.

'Then, finishing, but never scraping our plates,' she frowned towards Paul, 'we converse brightly on the coming events of the day.' She looked from one to the other. 'School, surgery and home.' Loving Jon deeply but bent on concealing it most of the time, Ruth bestowed ... 'And studio.'

Jon suppressed a smile.

'Next, the free-range eggs, timed to perfection,' she looked accusingly, 'never soft as butter, never hard as bullets. The toast pops up invitingly, a warm brown, not your usual charcoal black. And for the coffee addicts, only occasionally are there forty-three beans. This household filters freshly roasted grounds.' She lowered the curtain of her fixed smile. 'Mum, why do you drink so much coffee?'

Jon shrugged.

'You'll brew yourself a heart attack. Maureen Sterling's father had one.'

Paul looked to Gilbert interestingly.

'Mr Sterling was in intensive care, plugged in to beeps and machines. When they went to see him he was wearing an oxygen mask like a snorkel ... '

'What do you mean, like a snorkel?' Paul wanted to know.
'I don't know, stupid.'

'Well, if you don't know you're the stupid,' Paul presented his logic, eyes sober and certain.

'Oh, do be quiet, child,' Ruth spread hands elegantly in dismissal. 'Is there no low cal. cottage cheese?'

'You'll give yourself anorexia. And fade away.' Paul savoured the idea.

'Anorexia Nervosa! What a child you are. You couldn't even spell it, let alone understand the underlying difficulties of girls who … '

'A.n.n … ' Paul began, bragging tone at the use of the word gone.

'It makes me sick to listen to children who don't make any sense.' Ruth pushed two fingers in her ears then took them out.

'Do you know,' Paul was saying, 'right now will never come again. There,' he looked to the clock and watched the minute hand circle. 'It's gone.'

'It's time you were gone. You'll both miss the bus,' Jon wished them to kingdom come. When the house had been extended a studio was added. This beckoned, never more tantalising than when the shambles that was breakfast drew to an end. It was the meal that betrayed her most. Family life? She'd read a pert little comment somewhere. What was it? Yes, family life … making the best of what there was.

'It will never come again,' Paul was saying solemnly. 'She'll never pretend not to hear me spell … a.n.n … ' he began until he saw his mother's expression. 'You'll never scrape that same piece of toast made from that same flour grown in that same field … '

'Paul … '

'It will never come again,' stubbornly he repeated, 'when it's gone it's gone. If you could stop it, time that is, for a whole day, Mum, which day would you choose?'

'Wednesday,' she said absently. To her surprise he seemed satisfied. I'm a twisted cynic, she thought. Though she valued much that she had, she was not ready to allow them to sap her energies, not totally. She wasn't without aspirations, had her own small ambitions. 'Now get going. Move.' She could hear the edge in her voice, but could not control it, and sensed a fleeting shame. She wanted them gone, after all, who wouldn't? But she was lucky. So many women groped for an escape from the reality of everyday life ... looking under such diverse bushes as psychotherapy, pottery, fantasy, macramé, romantic love, gambling, sex groups, or just reading the newspapers. Marriage could be neat, purposeful, rarely heroic.

'What am I?' Ruth had asked recently, spreading herself across her mother's bed. If Ruth was after universal truths Jon would be found wanting.

'Do you think I'm going mad?' Ruth pursued, her natural outlook dramatic. 'One minute I want something, the next it's the last thing I want. Sometimes I mean to behave in a certain way, and then ... I'm doing it all opposite. Am I living my life in reverse? Am I going mad? Insane?'

Jon pitied the daughter she couldn't help more. Why must one's children be so vulnerable, why can't they learn from us? From our mistakes. Learn to put fears and doubts to one side. She said ... 'You're growing up.'

'Oh, Mother.' It was a cry of irritation tinged with alarm.

'You don't,' said Jon, longing to smooth the dark hair but never sure when affection was welcome, 'you don't have to be anything or anyone but yourself.'

'I haven't got a self,' Ruth broke off, concentrated on the knuckles of her hand, then punched into the bed. Tears welled and rolled. She took her mother's extended hand. 'I change every minute,' she sniffed. It was a time of intense self-examination, and she was in love with the maths coach. Very agonisingly, very satisfactorily for he was a married man to make it tragically hopeless ... perfect.

'It'll come right. Believe me,' she told Ruth, so demandingly beautiful, so extravagant with her emotions, suspecting that at fifteen no one else in the world understood about truth, beauty, brotherhood and pain. What was it Lola said of her? Yes, that lights will always turn green for Ruth, see if they don't. 'It'll come right,' she said again. 'We're born this way or that and we don't know why.'

'Do you really understand?'

'No,' Jon replied and wondered whether she should have said yes. 'Not fully and absolutely.' Only the absolute would satisfy Ruth, anything less intolerable. You stir old shadows I thought were gone, Jon wanted to say.

Ruth nested into the bedcovers and Jon prepared herself for another discussion on 'Life'. There may not be anymore required of me as a mother than my ears, Jon thought, for Ruth had an insatiable desire to talk with steam and intensity about her actions, reactions, religion, friends, foes, phobias, apartheid, contraception, the bomb ... Jon knew never to instigate these exchanges, tried to be receptive always, but Ruth chose time and place on whim, following her from bathroom to garage, basement to attic, wherever she led. Thank heavens, she thought, no one is required to solve the riddles of the world.

'What is love?' Ruth asked and Jon, having asked herself often, had her answer.

'Caring for someone more than oneself.'

'Oh.' She framed the question Jon had dreaded would some day rear a head for reckoning. 'Did you love Gilbert?'

The past tense! 'Yes,' Jon lied, and in the same breath prayed Ruth wouldn't hunt her down. Not too much probing, not too many critical questions. Please.

'He scares me sometimes.'

'Your father?'

'He's sleep-walking with his eyes open ... '

'Ruth,' she sat up startled. Lola had once used identical words. Lola had said ... 'He does it by believing that everything that doesn't touch him, well, it doesn't count.' 'Ruth,' Jon quizzed, 'What do you mean?'

'Hard to explain. You won't tell him?'

'Of course not.'

'He seems ... ' she took a minute to consider, 'numb. Dumb, if you like. Out of touch with anything important.

He ... he never says anything to me, he only moves his mouth.'

'We're all different,' Jon, astonished to find she was apologising for him, couldn't say more.

'Thank God,' Ruth shouted vehemently, shooting the words from the catapult of her mouth. 'I don't want him to know anything, not one detail of my life.'

There was a detail of her life they both went to pains to conceal from Gilbert. Ruth had formed a friendship of sorts with Sarah, Dorothy's daughter nearly twelve months her senior. Strange, both Jon and Dorothy choosing biblical names for their offspring. Dorothy's brood: Sarah, Rachel, Aaron, Daniel and Joel. Only Paul was New Testament.

Sarah, finding her parents plain and boring people, in retaliation made trouble. She made trouble at school, she made trouble by not going to school and then signing notes from her mother to explain why. She liked to see the films her parents expressly stated unsuitable, she liked to wear unsuitable clothes pulled tightly over a bursting figure, skirts riding high on plump thighs. She was a tough sullen young lady with criminal hobbies a possible development.

'Some exhibitionist,' Ruth condemned if she heard of Sarah's latest escapade, none of which led yet on the primrose path to full-time dalliance. Nevertheless Ruth, popular but haughty Ruth, could be flattered by Sarah's attention and during school holidays could be persuaded to spend time in her company.

'Do let her come,' Dorothy would beg, 'she could be a civilising influence.' Every family went through an adolescent crisis, she accepted, and secretly thought Jon was well on the way if remaining as overprotective of Paul as she'd become since the accident.

'She and Betty between them will smother that boy. They don't let him out of their cotton-wool wrappings,' she told Lola.

'Understandable,' Lola reasoned and Dorothy who agreed decided to say no more. Easy enough to solve other parents' mistakes. Sarah, the cuckoo in her nest; distress, frustration and despair were still well in the future. Dorothy will think of something though she's beginning to doubt the intercession of prayer. Ruth was more accessible.

'Life', said Sarah's father, 'isn't holding good cards but playing a poor hand well,' something lurking from his earlier days.

Forbidden to cake her face with make-up, Sarah did just that. Unskilfully, she'd look a clown, so ridiculous Ruth with unerring taste was reluctant to use even lipstick. Sometimes just being with Sarah made her feel conspicuous.

Sarah's eyes, circled like a seagull's in a chalky white face, made a ludicrous sight. Such a sight she alerted one of the shop detectives in David Jones's main store as the girls strolled sniffing and examining the brands displayed, a sultan's treasure to Sarah.

'Which suits me best?' she circled a finger over colour charts. 'Am I "Apricot Witch", "Soft Centre Pink" or "Bamboo Peach"?'

'"Cinnamon Toast."'

'You sure?'

Ruth's boredom was showing. 'Come on, Sarah, I want to get to the library.'

'Not yet, not yet,' Sarah pleaded and wished she hadn't spent so much on sooty mascara. She had only a few dollars left and her father, lenient on many things these days, was strict about pocket money. He would help out in a real emergency, nothing less, unmoved by her needs. 'Ruth, come here. No, closer. Don't move away. Stand here. Near my elbow. Closer,' the instructions snapped out.

'What for?'

'Just do as I say,' Sarah's reddened lips wore the blood of a kill. 'Stay where you are,' she snarled between clenched teeth.

Ruth realised she was trapped by lumpy, sulky Sarah who waited no longer, seeing that she, Ruth, hesitated, and could move aside any moment. The drawers of Sarah's dressing table full of lotions and creams, cosmetics enough for a troupe of showgirls, she was enflamed by a compulsive urge for more. Deftly she manoeuvred a bottle of rouge, flat pancake make-up and eyebrow liner to the edge of the counter. With skilled practice she scooped them down to the open bag.

'Sarah!'

'Shut up.'

'I'm going.'

'You can NOW,' Sarah purred, 'but don't be mad enough to make yourself conspicuous.'

'Me?' Ruth shot her a glance of outraged disbelief.

'If I'm caught, you're in it too.'

'But … '

'Who shielded me from sight? Who pressed up against me to be sure I wouldn't drop anything?'

'Sarah.'

'Oh, shut up and stop gawping like a fish.'

Ruth, alarmed, jerked away seared by a thousand eyes. Wounded by Sarah's deceit, she was more wounded to be such a dupe. How dare she, how dare she? She'd tell Dorothy, that's what she'd do. The rotten little sneak.

'If you breathe a word about this,' Sarah anticipated the move, 'you'll live to regret it.'

The imprecision of the threat menaced Ruth more than a direct blow. What did she mean? What could she do?

'Come down here,' Sarah flushed with victory pulled her along the shopping aisles. She rather fancied a silk scarf. She had a rayon one, but a silk scarf! Despite her poor taste Sarah was after one of those French ones, a careless 'Givenchy' or 'Christian Dior' scrawled by hand across one corner. That'd be something to show Deirdre Dodgson with her prissy airs and graces when back to school. Deirdre stole too, but her father took business trips to Paris and her scarf said 'Courrèges'. She'd settle for 'Champs-Élysées' if nothing better was accessible.

Ruth's face was already red, eyes fearful before talon-like fingers gripped her arm. She felt she'd swallowed a stone.

'You girls. Come with me.' The shop detective restrainedly

but fashionably dressed spoke with a clicking tongue. 'You'll draw more attention to yourselves if you make a fuss.'

'Run for it,' Sarah's voice slurred, but held in pincer-grip, she couldn't have gone far.

The office to which they were taken had none of the glitter of the department store. Partitioned by a thin wall, they were worlds apart; the outer inviting, seductive, the inner a few bare coathangers, desk piled with cardboard boxes and a battery of phones.

'How much does it cost? We'll pay for it,' Sarah tried to brazen it out.

'It? "Them" you mean, my girl.'

'We can pay.' Sarah looked entreatingly towards Ruth, who nodded stupefied. She couldn't have answered if she'd tried, tongue made of thick felt clogging her mouth.

'Sit down,' the woman nodded to chairs. With the docility of a lamb Sarah sat. 'Sit down,' the woman barked at Ruth.

'What ... what's going to happen?' Bewildered, Ruth found herself stammering. 'W..will we b.be sent to p.prison?'

'That depends.'

'D.d.depends?'

'Just sit down and be quiet,' the woman took a seat and folded neat legs. Somehow the posture was patronising.

Terrified Ruth inched closer to Sarah. 'What are we waiting for? Why do we have to stay here?'

'Dunno,' Sarah twisting a handkerchief corner, had not been caught before.

Ten minutes later a solid man, ill-cut suit and felt hat, sidled through the door. 'These the two?' he snapped at the woman, their warder.

'Yes, sir.' Nodding she recited the facts as observed.

'Empty your bags. And any pockets.'

Ruth had nothing but small purse, brush, handkerchief and a paperback. He handled the book, examined it, saw it wasn't new, then demanded the same of Sarah. The stolen goods clattered on to the desk.

'Got a record?'

Sarah, understanding, decided to play it dumb.

'Have you been caught before?' She didn't like the way he framed it but there was no proof. 'Name and address,' he opened a large ruled ledger.

The Doomsday Book, thought Ruth and wanted desperately to convince herself she was not afraid of the end of the world. Head cocked to one side she willed herself to hear the groans of a battlefield, to be cramped by the gnawing hunger of famine. It didn't work; she was a fifteen-year-old girl in a stringy back room of a plushy department store, unsuspecting accessory to shop-lifting, petty crime. There was sweat on her palms, she was frightened by this bulky man intent on accusing her of what she had not done. Innocent, but who'd believe her? She looked the image of detected guilt.

'Name and address,' he repeated impatiently. 'Oh, ho. So we're going to play it that way, are we?' his tone ugly, mocking. 'Won't do you any good. Once your fathers are informed ... ' sadistically guessing they held that parent in more awe than their mothers, most of them, experience had taught him, silly creatures. The girls' expressions confirmed the belief.

'Please, please. Don't tell my father,' Sarah disintegrated, the colours on her face merging as she knuckled hands into eyes. 'I'll do anything ... '

'Pull yourself together,' said the woman who sat witness, knees crossed still, legs like matched hockey sticks.

'My mother,' voice tight Ruth gulped, 'my mother is the one to get in touch with. You can ring her.'

'Good. That's better,' he rubbed large hands and reopened the book. 'Name and address? Telephone number?'

Ruth as she gave it desperately tried to outstare him, eyes tense like glass ... but was unsuccessful.

Detained for more than another hour until Jon arrived, Sarah relieved sat docile, Ruth more and more inwardly agitated, was jolted by a rush of blood when Jon appeared.

'They're good girls,' said Jon stoutly, and felt ashamed that she doubted it of Sarah. I suppose they have a job to do, she thought, but found the man and woman distasteful, aware of the unspoken condemnation ... 'no such thing as a bad child only bad parents' ... they appeared to dislike the human race irrespective of age. She wondered if either qualified as parents, whether they'd ever stolen as children. 'This will not happen again, I can assure you of that,' and wondered who could guarantee Sarah, as they were released with a caution.

'Next time it'll be Central Police Court ... '

Ruth heard a police van scream to a stop, saw herself, the poor arrested criminal thrown in and carried off to gaol. She tasted the sub-standard food, saw the iron bars. The man's voice broke through. 'And a record.'

Parents are not always the best judges of their own children. Dorothy, convinced Sarah had had a bad fright, confiscated her daughter's cache of cosmetics.

'She must have rubbed every cent she had together to buy all this,' she told Jon, neither meeting nor avoiding her gaze. 'No wonder she's upset. Losing the lot.'

How are you going to keep her from losing her virginity? Jon wanted to ask Dorothy, but couldn't bear to see the hurt that would surface in those unflinching pale eyes.

What was she to do about Ruth? By the time they arrived home Ruth was sick. Everything she'd eaten that day came up from an uneasy stomach, rucked and rumpled by the experience, but mainly by her mother's composure in putting everything right.

'You're the best friend I've ever had,' said Ruth, a pasty sandpaper white. 'Nobody I know can depend on their mothers the way I depend on you,' she gulped out. 'Most of them never tell their mothers when they're in trouble,' and stared at her knees. 'Their mothers would be the last to know. And only then if threatened by God.'

Valiantly Jon kept the smile from her lips, raked her mind for wise advice. Why God? Would Ruth always be so dramatic?

'And as for that Sarah. I hope she roasts in hell.'

She'll singe, Jon thought. We all do.

Chapter Ten

Mornings are a miracle of renewal, what are the nights? Mornings bubble blue, nights are draped black with an eerie sense of the jungle. The jungle is near-impenetrable, a state of primordial confusion: snuffling, huffing, panting, attacking, retreating.

'Tigers,' she says, 'in India ... only three in a thousand eat people. They say. The king of the jungle is in no hurry for prey; it's not in his nature to panic. They say.'

They?

She feels her hands, cold like the skin of a frog; then a sour panic, the unease to be felt arriving at night in an unknown place.

'Pull yourself together, Jon,' she directs. 'Ours isn't an urgent society ... but we all have our stock of private fears.'

How loud does she say it? She often talks to herself. Is she eccentric, or losing touch?

'Everyone talks to themselves.'

A car approaches, driven cautiously. Lights anoint the roadway, then as she watches, pass, the tail-light a glowing red eye diminishes to a pinpoint ... is gone.

Drawn on by nothing more than the urge to walk again, up ahead is a rough, high barrier, behind which builders' tools are locked into a shed beside a bulldozer. More construction under way. On the planks of this hoarding, which declare 'Post no bills', bills have been posted. So transitory, these commercial declarations. How the hounds of disappointment yap at the heels of hordes of hopeful business ventures. Small enterprises where hard work and determination, owners dreamily believe, will rescue them from never-ending hard work. Small dreams which empty themselves into vacated premises, slackened purses, no further credit. What takes you to the top of the heap? What's to be found there but the temples of new houses pulsating electrically, choked with new equipment? And where from there? Make your pile, travel. Sup to the full ... wine, coconut milk, Coca-Cola ... in charming corners of the world where poverty can be camouflaged if not altogether bleached off the streets. Travelling, tourists, building up a fourth world neither home nor abroad. But the more we travel the more we seek a home: mass-produced handicrafts triumphantly borne back to decorate so many sterile rooms.

Sweep the rooms, spring-clean and diet the bodies, flush out the minds with your choice in pop psychology to become worry-free, guilt-free, no longer burdened by what the Joneses own, say or do.

The Joneses were fulsome when she won her first art prize. Her lips curl. She snickers to think of their empty eyes as they pass her painting, nod a witless approval to nod an emphatic 'yes', relieved as wine comes circulating their way.

'Post no bills'. She bends to pick over a pile of rubble; from it extracts a chalky stone. Between a handbill for manchester at sale prices and a fast-shredding poster extolling transcendental meditation, childlike and perverse she prints as best she can:

'Water-colours. Water-colours. Roll up and see the work of Jon Jamieson, wife, mother, fraud.'

What's the line? Who draws it?

At first she tried to evoke the little, likeable things.

'Very nice,' Gilbert would water them away with tepid praise.

Jon didn't show him her work, indifferent to whether he saw it or not, indifferent to early remarks like:

'You'd get me picking up a brush at the double if you worked with real models.' Yes, he would have liked that; naked women, white and blowzy. His pupils dilated as he pictured them changing pose, wriggling. Soon he gave up noticing what she did, how she spent her time in studios, art classes, or how she worked at home. 'The wife's little hobby,' he would say dismissively. Didn't all wives cultivate hobbies or essay good works? This one threatened him not at all.

Jon harboured no smouldering ambition to be fanned to the volcano of outstanding talent. She simply wanted to paint; expecting neither rewards nor recognition, didn't yearn for the company of artists, though would have preferred it to dentists.

'Bill wants one or two of your little pieces,' Gilbert was surprised. He always felt 'art' was man's work, woman's work a decorative footnote; fluffy, light, domestic. 'Willing to buy, he says. How about it?' He gave a mirthless laugh.

'Laurel too?' Laurel, she knew, had a half-interest in a chic little gallery, a converted stone house where a brace of coach lamps glowed above stable doors.

Gilbert finding fault wherever he could with her lately snapped like an agitated terrier. 'No need to keep harping on the past.' If Jon was silent she was sulking, if she rose quickly from a meal she was restless, if she sat long over coffee she was lazy. It was Ruth who grew sulky, Paul silent with him. They didn't appreciate him.

'Bill's welcome to one if he really wants it.'

'Generous of you,' Gilbert purred. He must say she'd taken a sensible view of the Laurel affair. Alerted by Laurel, he'd confessed, Jon had forgiven and he'd dozed off into a heavy sleep, healed the next morning of any guilt. Laurel had tried to force the issue, but after all she'd known he was a married man. Who better? Laurel anyway had become far too brittle and he'd been seeing that pretty little thing at the same time. What was her name? With her long legs, golden hair and cleft chin? Like buses, Gilbert smiled towards his wife, miss one and there's always another. 'Perhaps ... '

'Yes?'

'Perhaps I should hang a few in the waiting room? Hey? Good advertising.'

'I'm not painting to sell.' She spoke very clearly to shut out his voice.

'Why then?'

She couldn't have answered. How to get through to him it wasn't exploitation but an act of tenderness. She seemed to pour a bucket of tenderness into her painting; there was an abundance of it, and while she worked entertained no thought of self-destruction, no spattering of her life on to a canvas, no vast or depraved expressions of truth but an intricate activity of yearning; butterflies fluttering under her fingertips, elusive, delicate. Doomed?

'Don't give me any spiderwebs.' Ignorant and nervous about painting generally, contemporary work Gilbert thought trash painted by madmen. Most of them nutty attempts to rid themselves of obsessional dreams of sexual behaviour. If he liked anything it was the decorous little pastiches of the traditionalist. No right-thinking person could feel anything but embarrassment at most modern art.

'What?' She heaved attention back to him.

'Spiderwebs. Your spiderwebs. Not suitable for the surgery.'

'Oh. No. Wouldn't be.' She'd recently done a series un-connected but connected to a thread in her mind; spiderwebs in which a colony of spiders shared a vast web. Sometimes dusty, sometimes flimsy, partly transparent, sometimes dis-gorging mosquitoes and flies or insects whose pale wings could no longer spiral them into the light, despairing of aid or rescue. Sometimes she'd drawn it like a stiffly wired bouquet of flowers, the spider flowering at its heart, sometimes heavy with rain, or rose-coloured by the sun or drowsing in a bundle of trumpety gold. Or cold icicles as complex as a star. Or time remembered from long ago.

'If Bill wants one,' Gilbert afforded her faint praise, though he'd backed Bill's enthusiasm for Jon's work keenly. Bill had been shaping up a collection over the last five years, knew what he liked and while amenable to the flattery of gallery owners, valued as well as exploited their expertise. Bill, with his amorous adventures, was not fool enough to follow in a father's footsteps. He intended in old age to be more than a façade, planned to be rich and stay rich. If ever landed with a paternity suit he'd have the means to settle and smile. He lived an unrelenting life of ordinariness, supporting it with all the things money could buy. Jon, he'd heard, had talent so why not get in on the ground floor.

Her lecturer at the art school had persuaded Jon to enter the competition. 'You could win,' he'd raised wispy eyebrows and let his expression beetle into hers.

'No.' Jon was amused. 'No,' she denied the possibility again. 'You're wonderfully encouraging but, well ... ' she paused, 'I don't specially want to win.'

'Why not? A feather in your cap.'

'A tiny one.'

'Yes, but a start.' He was grateful to have found her; her approach intelligent, intricate, subtle. So few of them painted sensitively, most of his students brash, inharmonious, unthinking.

'I've no real ambitions to ... ' she broke off abruptly and shrugged.

'But you want to paint well?' He liked the flickering rhythmical concavity of her skies, the image of sunlight had a new lease of light in her work.

'I do like to paint ... it's as if I'm allowed to think my own thoughts.' She laughed like a person indecently displaying too much feeling.

'Yes.' He stated again, 'But you could win.'

Must that lie side by side with success? she countered silently. Puzzled by what might constitute success, she mistrusted it. And mistrusted herself. Should she try to declare herself, one moment one of a hopeful crowd, the next nakedly apart. 'And such a tiny success.'

When a letter arrived saying she'd won the prize Jon thrust it into a drawer. She told no one before the announcement appeared in newspapers.

'All that money for that little painting,' Gilbert was taken aback, astonished more than pleased.

The children were thrilled; she'd not only won but been photographed and interviewed, and Ruth was jubilant, Paul reflecting his sister's mood like a seismograph.

'They're treating me like Rembrandt,' Jon was amused to relate to Lola.

'You should be more pleased with yourself.' Lola was tempted to say more.

Jon smiled, shrugged careless shoulders as they sat in the studio. The sun slanted in from the windows crossed by frames like the bars of a bright, strange gaol.

'You've sealed off a little bit here, haven't you, Jon?' she asked instead and tapped at her breast. Since it was more a matter of feelings than words or facts, Lola found a difficulty in expression.

Jon began to murmur a protest to find she was crumpling. Wildly she reached out for Lola's hand, eyes brimming. 'Oh, Lola, Lola. There are certain places, times, you leave never expecting to return. It was all so long ago. Why does it still matter?'

'We all visit the worlds of might-have-been and might-be-yets. As long as the sizzle's there ... you never forget.'

'But I can. I do,' she said after a while. 'Sometimes for months, almost years ... '

'You've got a burning in the blood, and that proves you want more than you can get,' Lola lamented and stroked the hands in hers. 'Who knows,' she added without confidence, 'maybe it's better to want rather than have.'

'I want you to think about an exhibition of your own.' It was Gilbert's belief she needed managing. Collectors were asking to see her work, galleries contacting her, two of them desirous of putting her under contract, vying for consent.

Jon pictured an exhibition, so many of the same people in

different clothes; the women screaming and cooing as they postured, the men, pinpoints of dandruff on well-groomed shoulders or speckled into the weave of denim. Anointed or naked eyelids sheltering the straying eyes, rooms congested, air thick with smoke, skittishness, squeals and suggestion. Catalogues flapping like agitated moths, smiles to protect against the violation of their bankbooks, few but the occasional brutally lined old couple serious about what hung on the walls.

'I don't want an exhibition.' Her voice was absent.

He gave her a long uncomprehending stare. 'Now Jon,' his tone was arch, 'let's not take that tack,' as if she was a sullen and resistant sixteen-year-old.

'I don't want an exhibition.'

Gilbert broke wind. Why did she have to upset him? Did she design her every move just to thwart him? When he'd married her he'd married money. She'd been a good and uncomplaining wife. Unexciting, reliable. Not very bright but restful. Nearly twenty years later the fact had emerged that she was talented. And here she was intent on dispossessing him. Some men would never have lent such encouragement; he'd not only provided her with a base from which to face the world but his unqualified support. He'd never told her not to paint. If she'd accept proper responsibilities she'd see she owed it to him to accept public acclaim.

'Look at it this way, Jon ... ' his voice took on a lecturing sound. She must be in what he could only suppose was one of her moods.

She broke in. 'What do you want?'

'Let us just clarify the basic issues ... ' The words whirred like the whine of his high-speed drill.

'Clarify the basic issues,' she heard her voice echo, harsh and ugly. 'Ha! Do you want to lend me to any passing guests the way an Eskimo lends his wife?'

A vein in his temple throbbed. 'What on earth do you mean?' If she was morbidly monogamous, well, that was her affair. Close to exasperation he snapped, 'Who'd want you anyway?'

The world immobilised. She was all the wronged women down the ages, then indifferent to what may follow flung out, 'You do, though it's as perfunctory as cleaning your teeth. Damned teeth. Mouldy, yellow, damned teeth!' She stammered hurt and bitter. 'What am I? A toy to be wound up at bedtime to perform when other engagements are unavailable? But with no feelings, no opinions of my own.' She swelled with self-pity.

'Damned teeth? You're making a damned fool of yourself,' he shouted in a different voice, to turn aside and make a noise like spitting. Reference to his work he found always an unprovoked attack. He moved towards her, hands red and knuckly. 'You never refuse.'

'Do you imagine my needs were ever properly met.' She was more pained than angry; the words chiselling the stone between them. She veered backwards in time to his wooing behaviour ... much kissing, much petting and the desire to marry money.

'You never complained,' his pitch increased. 'And you never complained about my other women. Never wanted to know ... '

She felt hollow, empty; inert for centuries.

'Why do you suppose I never question what you do? And with whom? Because I don't want to know. How can you be so obtuse, so stupid? Has it never occurred to you that I don't care? Have you ever thought of that?' I've jogged through life in an iron mask, she thought. If only he'd leave. If he'd go I'd lose little.

Gilbert had not adjusted to hear her last words. Had she really been indifferent to him, his body? He'd never noticed a coldness in her eyes as she'd lain beneath him. He should have looked. Naturally the marital bed was less exciting than the illicit, any fool knew that. After all it's an imperfect world, and busy elsewhere he made few demands on her. For the first time it struck him there was no occasion in all their years together when she'd ever made any overture, any suggestion that ... Not once. He'd put it down to her upbringing. A spasm of fear hit home; her function was to run the house, care for the children and cook. No Cordon Bleu cook, meals were adequate, good in fact, he couldn't fault her on the domestic front, how could he, there'd always been help. What if suddenly she took it into her head to leave? This painting lark; her recent success might spark the idea.

'Don't be silly,' he said shocked at the thought.

'Don't be silly! Is that all you can say?' her voice less rasping.

Was there a fugitive gleam of light ahead? Gilbert fumbled for the switch. 'I'm sorry, er, er … darling. If you think I've behaved badly, if … '

It was a mindless comment that led nowhere. Her misery drifted with his words. Unhappy marriages so resemble one another, she sighed, why especially try to chart the course of this one.

But it was hers, her marriage and it intruded, eating into the years of her life. What held her? What prevented her cutting loose? Despite all inner protestations why couldn't she look to an immediate severance other than expectantly, fearfully? What prevented her leaving? Had she absorbed some rigid sense of duty during her growing years with Betty, impossible to cast aside?

'I did my duty to your father. I never failed him.'

Her mother's words flushed like a tap from the past washing away time. At child's eye level she saw the box of the coffin, the black and grey of the mourners' skirts and the legs of well-creased trousers. And she remembered marble cake with whorls of cochineal pink, muddy chocolate, awkward kissing and much patting of her head, unrhythmical, unsure, inexperienced in the role of consolers. Auntie Doris, dead years ago, who had questioned insistently 'When was a clever woman ever happy?' rose up again with her pursed-up old woman's lips and the faint smell of lavender. Or was it vanilla?

By what accident did I become me? she asked wordlessly. Age, weight, status, distinguishing marks, distresses, complaints … my thoughts mixing in the blender of my head?

Resentment, fear, the urge to hurt, the craving to be hurt,

what in God's name kept her shackled to this man? Her eyes, she suspected, stared reproachfully from deep sockets. She had every intention of separating, divorcing herself from him. And before she was worn out, fit for nothing. When Paul leaves school; in two years' time. She'd been considering it, reasonably, rationally for some time. She'd work towards that, would accept no permanent truce. She would not permanently cut her losses, sever all hope to resign herself to Gilbert. Two years' time ... Ruth would have her degree, Paul would have decided on a future, zoology, oceanography, something like that. Two years' breathing space, time to consolidate, get her house in order. Two years, in two years' time ...

'Er ... sorry,' distantly she heard him repeat. What could it mean anyway? Jon refused to acknowledge his apology.

Gilbert had no intention of mentioning an exhibition again, no matter how clamorous the offers, though it was beyond him why she wouldn't ride in with a cresting wave. He would not provoke an upheaval in domestic arrangements, wanted no structural alterations to his way of life. After all what had he ever wanted but a loose knot? Reasonable. Right now he was all for forgiveness, acceptance and reconciliation.

'Nothing is drastically changed,' was all she said, and sprung the trap. 'All right, Gilbert ... ' In a world full of humdrum little people living out tedious lives, I'm no superstar. She had no aptitude for organised resentment. But ... 'If it would please you ... '

Please him? What did she mean? She left no doubt.

'I will hold an exhibition. I've nearly enough things ready. You arrange it. Time, place and the terms.' She could almost see the hot gravied kiss of greed touch his lips. Gilbert was speechless. She went on, weighting each word, 'I'll ring Cyril. First thing tomorrow. He's the best framer for my sort of work. That should give about six months to prepare properly.'

'But, Jon ... ' he bleated.

'Yes?'

'You were so positive you didn't want to ... '

'With your experience of women, Gilbert,' she paused, abruptly exhausted, 'you should know how the silly creatures are given to changing their minds.'

Gilbert's indigestion had begun to worry him more. His rages had begun to worry Jon less. Again they found themselves an entity united by resentment.

Chapter Eleven

Stars mass above her; she's at the harbour edge. Reflected lights lurch drunkenly in the black molasses of the water. The path takes her right to the margin where earth becomes sloppy, sticky. There's a pungent smell, something rotting, death skulking in the air. She moves on. The city, dirty, unforgiving yet promising still, is surprisingly close. Here it's so quiet she should be able to hear the fish. Her toes strike a stone. She bends easily from the waist, gropes, finds it, half scaly the underside slimed and with fouled fingers heaves it away like a roosting bird to nest in an instant, deep and submerged.

'Everything will eventually be accounted for,' she says. 'Or will vanish.' Living men and women? What do they represent? Who is superfluous?

The silence seemed to be waiting.

'It's all a romantic haze,' she murmurs. 'You start travelling north, south, it doesn't matter. And the taste grows bitter.'

Somewhere, unseen across the water, on it perhaps, a scream hatchets her ears. Inhuman, metallic, it protests from the throat of an engine, chews into the night, screams again before resolved in throbbing action.

Unnerved, she's cold. The water looks velvety, warm and enfolding. Her mouth's dry. Which of her senses would be met first should she drown? She's read it's an easy way to go, but who knows for certain; when inexhaustible jets of fountains stream in to clog your nose and banish smell, block your ears and erase sound, fill your mouth and wash away words, blur your eyes and extinguish all sight. Would you be able to walk into water, wade deep and pull it voluptuously over your head, turn in its folds, step to its rhythm, run free ... and drown? Then nothing, nothing but pure terrible darkness.

'I'd give my life for a cigarette,' she says, who rarely smokes, and turns. Stinking worms of mud ooze about her feet, no longer sucking the sharp lemon of self-destruction but spitting it out with every step she takes from the water, quivering with distaste. Shunting these thoughts into a siding, she longs for a tangible gaiety ... a circus, side-shows, dancing in the streets, childish pleasures which we never totally outgrow, where we mix cruelty with acts of kindness.

This street too is deserted, bare, and she steps slowly in solitude. What if an earthquake suddenly dimpled the ground, cracked the land to its bones, would someone appear?

Someone will appear. A winking light darts jerkily towards her, dit-dit-dit-dotting a message she can't read. Her feet baulk, fear swarms over her, she's so idiotically equipped for any encounter. Weaponless. Despite the cold her armpits are moist, a thin sweat dampens the backs of her knees. She hasn't encountered an actual person in hours. The picking light comes closer. Closer. She wants to crouch behind cover. She listens. There's nothing more than approaching footsteps, irregular, pausing now, faltering, marching again. Towards her.

With a lifting of pressure she makes out the shape of a coated figure. Man or woman? Whoever, dark and shrunken by the night, tied by a lead to ... a dog.

Thin as a weathered pole, the man approaches, coat flapping, a long scarf wrapped about the neck like a plastic tube. In the meagre light Jon sees his beard, extravagantly bushy and white. Benign.

'Come along, come along,' he speaks to the dog good-naturedly; they're obvious friends. 'Evenin',' he nods to her and she's relieved by the normality. 'Chilly out tonight.'

She gulps. 'Yes.'

He's glad to exchange a few words as if his world's lightly peopled. 'We come this way most nights. But we're late tonight. I dozed off, then he,' he jerks the lead ever-so-slightly, 'he gives me the nudge. "Don't forget my walk," he tells me, and I say, "Oh dear, s'pose it's not all that late." But it is.' He touches to where a watch must press at his wrist. 'It was going on one when we started out. One a.m. Still he must get out and I like my little constitutional ... '

'Yes.'

'Pardon the liberty, but ... but are you all right?' Keenly he looks at her as if she's been handed a ticket for another place. 'Well, what I mean to say is ... You're not wrapped up. For such a night. No coat. Are you ... are you all right?'

'Yes. Thank you.' She feels obliged to say more. 'You're kind to ask.'

'Well, if you're sure.'

'Quite sure. Thank you.'

'Right.' He peers into the heavy darkness about their feet. The dog, a patchy little thing of indeterminate breed, has tangled paws in the lead. He bends slowly to the dog, voice muffled. 'There, Max, there. Keep still a sec, keep still. Ah,' he straightens. 'Funny he didn't bark. At you. Usually makes a racket with anyone strange,' he laughs lightly. 'But I trust his judgment; he knows who to start hollering at ... '

Jon backs away to let them pass.

'Good night then. Good night. Come on Max, we're not going far tonight,' he croons, 'Max. Come along, Max.'

Max!

Loneliness before had been being alone. She feels cut adrift from mankind. Max! Paul's dachshund, his dog, Maximilian Otto. Max.

Dorothy had thought it the strongest of the litter when she chose the dachshund pup for Paul after the stay in hospital. Seven years ago.

'Jon,' she continued to caution when discreetly able to inject the suggestion, 'try to let him have more freedom. He has to take risks again. Will anyway without asking leave.'

Jon understood Dorothy was right, but recognition and reconciliation were not easy.

Paul; he was magnificently involved in whatever he did, with his broadening shoulders and friendly eyes. He dealt with her affectionately, had close friends, no enemies and to his father tried to show a respectful deference, though often failed. Unlike Ruth, whose approach to Gilbert was tinged with mockery, Paul attempted to keep a distance between them. Gilbert made him jumpy, his eyes darkening with fury at opinions Gilbert voiced; out of his reach was calmer, happier, his face unshuttered. Where Ruth would inject tactless remarks to nettle her father, Paul afforded remoteness instead.

'Education's supposed to create analysis and enquiry,' Gilbert pompously would precede dinner discussions. 'What do you have to say, Paul? Eh?'

Paul, one year to go at school, would say as little as possible, offer abstractions if pressed, his mind veering from the particular for he distrusted Gilbert's arguments; his father convinced he was stupid.

'The ability to think does have its occasional uses,' Gilbert prodded each word unnecessarily.

Paul glanced uneasily towards Jon.

'From Mickey Mouse to Einstein,' Ruth came to Paul's defence, trying not to involve him, her chin jutting, teeth lightly clenched. Paul hadn't developed her sense of self-preservation. Food he let take up the slack in the conversation, appetite larger with Gilbert present.

'What am I educating him for?' Gilbert, a fist slammed to the table, would toss about in his platitudes like a child in autumn leaves, throwing up Paul's limitations, Ruth's lavish exaggerations, scornful.

He's being educated to free himself. And free me, Jon would smile. One more year.

'Not so much to smile about,' Gilbert off again on well-worn tracks would push back from the table, soon to make an excuse and leave them. When he sat these days there was a minor landslide, stomach rolling down; when he stood up it jellied into place, plumply upholstering his frame.

'You really should exercise, father,' Ruth's capacity for dedication was immense.

'Don't tell me that again.'

'What do you measure? Around the waist?' she persisted.

'Excuse me,' he was heavy with overstatement. 'Jon,' his digestion was permanently tortured. 'Where's the antacid?'

Jon efficient, lapsed into a vague clumsiness when Paul took to canoeing.

'Safe as houses, Mum,' he was reassuring, doggedly overriding doubts she expressed. Unconfirmed worries triggered in Jon's head ... the flimsiness of the craft, the necessary balance, the currents, the snags, the hidden dangers in the rivers.

As his enthusiasm increased – the isolation of the waters he and his friends were keen to paddle, their supportive base could be miles away, a rough track over which they carried canoes and equipment, inaccessible by vehicle – she found out all she could about buoyancy bags, had advice to offer on the best jackets.

'Mum.' He was pleased by her interest, indulgent about her concern. Facts he felt could dispel fears. 'The way I see it ... ' any and everything could at his age be cured by common sense, his brand of common sense. 'I'm not off to paddle the English Channel. Lots of people have, and twice across the Atlantic. Wow! 1928 and 1957. What do you think of that?'

Her thoughts; only glad it wasn't her son attempting it, she tried to think of something non-committal.

'Now if you think that's risky ... ' Tall, he rearranged a limb.

'I do,' she said, but he wasn't listening.

'During the war enemy coasts were reconnoitred from canoes. They operated from submarines, were used in masses of commando raids.'

She had to allay fears, trample them into neutrality. 'I'm convinced,' she said unconvinced. Irrationally she hoped it was a passing phase. Last year it had been astronomy.

'Good on you, Mum. After all I'm no wild-water racer. Not yet.' Her expression alarmed, he added, 'Doubt I'll get to be a wild-water man.'

'Of course he must go,' Ruth, Lola, Dorothy, even Betty agreed, when finals over and the long summer holidays about to begin, Paul made his arrangements.

'Canoe safari, you do get your terms mixed,' Ruth ruffled the sandy hair.

Paul grinned and the grin stretched like new elastic. If he had to have a sister, who better than Ruth? There was an aura about her, an invisible spice. On the person to person level he knew no one like her. Apart from being such a good looker, she could be pacifying, protecting, yet who could stir a hornets' nest quicker with her swimming way of looking and her furry voice? When he found his girl he hoped there'd be something of Ruth about her.

'Got everything you need?' Jon was struggling not to fuss.

'Yep.'

Paul made up six when the truck arrived, the three canoes serried on some sort of structure under the tarpaulin, his particular friend, Hugh Renfed, sitting up front with the older Renfed boys. It was hot; heat slumped in the air.

'Hi, Mrs Jamieson. Hi, Ruth.'

'Hello, Mark. Hello, Hamish. You look colourful, Dick.' Dick Blaze wore emerald shorts, shirt striped yellow and a royal purple.

'Off in a blaze of glory,' Hamish Austin, the youngest of the party, should have resisted. Groans all round.

Paul stowed his gear, jumped down to fling a careless arm about Jon's shoulders. His face blurred against hers as his breath skimmed her cheek. She felt there was something she must say to him, but what were the words?

'See you on the 20th, Mrs Jamies'n ... ' Owen Renfed called, 'Mum's got the exact location for the rendezvous.' Jon was going to drive the hundred kilometres with Vera Renfed and further supplies; they were looking forward to it. 'If you can talk Ruthie into coming ... '

Howls from the back of the truck.

'Goodbye. Have fun.'

The truck revved. 'Say goodbye to the old man,' Paul winked, raking fingers through his mop of hair. 'Bye Mum.'

She raised a hand to shade her eyes. 'Goodbye, Paul.'

The light was coppery with heat. Shudders of warmed wind kicked back in the wake of the truck, swam troublesomely round her as she made her way indoors.

'Ruth,' she called, her throat congested. 'Ruth.'

But Ruth had disappeared upstairs.

Unseasonable, the violence of the heat seemed to bruise everything. The sun daggered from all directions; upwards, sideways and down when she stepped from the sheltering house. Ruth lay about full of drift rather than rebellion.

'Nothing takes some doing today,' she would sigh as she sat away three-quarters of the day. She'd passed exams, was luxuriating in a spell of futility with the world, THE world, not simply her part of it, her boundaries; smoked in moderation and suggested Jon should try. Jon tried, didn't like it.

'Victim of your era, Mum. And your upbringing.'

'Perhaps.'

'Gilbert has his booze, don't you need a prop?'

'I don't know. Doubtless you find my attitude negative, but truly ... I don't know. I can't seem to categorise my needs.'

'I don't need it; I just like it now and again. It's my phase of non-commitment.'

'Ruth, do you need a prop?'

'Hell no. Let me put it this way, Mum. Corny as it may sound, you know I'm hooked on life.' She flung her arms. 'I'm just a privileged drop-out till next term, so it's necessary to suffer a smart ennui. I'm going to be slovenly, aggressive in a deadpan, guarded sort of way,' she grinned as wide as Paul and a rare resemblance flashed to Jon. 'I'm going to be socially uncooperative and keep clear of the mess called Them.' It was reassuring to have something stable to reject.

'Including me?'

'Yes. And no.'

'I'm relieved to hear it. Just the denim, not the full commitment?'

'You could put it that way,' said Ruth. 'The parties are all flat, the guests from all over the jungle. I want to keep out of the scrum for a while. I don't want to pass from darkness into darkness. And I won't. I don't want to be desiccated by the time I'm twenty.' Voice definite, her twentieth birthday was looming.

'You won't,' Jon said it with all the emphasis she could muster, the heat enervating.

When Hugh and Vera Renfed brought the news the message was jumbled. Anchored in silence she could not unravel their meaning. When the sudden sharp thin cries rose to loop round her heart she could only deny them.

'No. No, no.'

'Jon,' Hugh, tall, bald with a braying laugh was swallowing hard. He took her in his arms to hold her woodenly. Vera's arms encompassed them both.

So much happens by mistake. Why do we get off at the wrong station, marry the wrong man? What makes an accident happen?

Ruth sent to Betty, Gilbert summonsed, the four of them set out on the withering journey.

The Colo River was a hundred kilometres north. Hugh drove, tense and shaky, Gilbert uneasy beside him working an imaginary brake with his foot, eyes constantly flickering sideways, insisting that before long he take over the wheel. They were in this together.

The heat was searing; tar on patches of the road heaved and undulated, grass edgings a brutally blistered brown. Garden sprays valiantly circled to preserve flower beds and lawns. By the time they'd cleared the city it was after midday and fingers of open land began to probe deeper into the suburban sprawl.

Listless in the back of the car the women swayed uncaringly with the motion, Vera from time to time nickering softly like a lost puppy, forlorn, waiting for moral sustenance. Anxiously her husband straightened periodically to glimpse her in the

146

rear-vision mirror, fearful for her, willing to bear her burden in addition to his own but unacquainted with the means of transference. So, manfully he tried to choose cheerful phrases which were not his own.

'It could be a different kettle of fish by the time we arrive.' Then: 'Let's look on the bright side until ... ' the words suspended awkwardly in the tone kept for children.

'I could do with a drink,' Gilbert interrupted suggestively. Silence. 'How about you girls?'

Hugh spoke for them. 'We must keep on.'

'You're right. Of course. Righty-ho.' Gilbert strained the words through his teeth, squeezed out agreement. A ten-minute halt wouldn't make much difference. Mouth aching with dryness, a beer would do. He saw a lacy foam lining an empty glass. 'On we go,' he smiled tightly, though they hadn't stopped.

'Try to get a bit of sleep.' Hugh desperate to protect Vera from the violent disturbance of possibilities, panic, sighed for the inadequacy of words. She was very dear to him; they'd shared a good life together with their three boys, uneventful, unexciting but stable, satisfying to their needs. 'Try to get a bit of sleep,' he repeated. 'Both of you.'

I want to wake up so I can sleep, Jon's head was heavy, banded by a rope of burning light. She coveted some weight-less dream, unaware of strain, no friction. She looked to Vera's pathetic face, pretty though the skin had begun to break up round the eyes into a fine mesh of lines. She still had a thin flower-stalk of a neck; fragile face and throat now red and blotchy. Jon slid a hand of dubious comfort to cup Vera's agitatedly spastic in her lap. Swung together as the car took a corner Vera whispered:

'Do you think it's foolish to pray?'

Sideways, thought Jon, that's how I'd pray. Too hard, too fiercely, too fervently and an implacable fate turns on you. To conceive if you don't want children, to forget if you want memory sharp and defined, to starve if you're hungry, to remain stationary if you want to advance. Always for a random destination if you know where you want to alight. Prayer? Luck must play a considerable part in everyone's life, but did luck come only to those ready to receive? To sneer and double back on the unready?

'Of course it's not foolish,' she said. 'If anyone's prayers deserve answering yours do,' and dropped her eyes unsure whether Vera's lips moved by design or trembled beyond control.

The hot near-empty road was indifferent offering little resistance to the rate at which Hugh drove. Bulldozed for speed it cut the landscape to pieces. Gilbert, his voice somewhere up the scale from loud, tried to interest them in the extravagant quality of being free on a week-day. Not that it applied to today, certainly not today.

'Abstractly, of course,' he petered out meeting no response, 'certainly not under present circs ... '

They drove in silence.

Picking over her bits and pieces like a tramp, Jon rationed her energies. She would be drawn into no union of tearful complicity. Shrunk into her corner, she shrank even further into the light clothes she wore. 'Take a pair of heavy shoes, sandals could slow you down on the track.' Who had said it? What track? Where would it lead? Her feet fumbled on two lumps, the walking shoes, two-toned navy and white. What was that silly old joke? Co-respondent's footwear, brothel sneakers? A central preoccupation rooted in her mind. When they were home again, all of them, she'd try to interest Paul in painting. Of course wouldn't rush it, but would break open to him if she could the soothing pleasure of connecting mind to hand, use art to ritualise a meaning into life and the events of living, open what is real beyond muscle, bone and blood. Yes, when they were all home again.

The sunlight sharpened gorging itself on her flesh through the glass of the window. Open paddocks stepped away then a ridge of abrupt hills dappled and dancing swung into view, the peaks battered salt cellars as they simmered in the heat. Next a little weatherboard township thrown together so casually it might have blown off the landscape if a strong wind rose.

Hugh, driving again, slowed at the crossroads. Morbidly Jon thought of a gibbet ... conjured the figure of a cloaked crone directing ... 'Right to heaven,' the voice cackled in her mind, 'left, my beauties, to damnation and hell.' Her sticky fingers tore such nonsense away pressing hard at her eyeballs.

'Which way?' Hugh asked.

Gilbert consulted their sheet of directions, economically said: 'Left.' He'd lapsed into near silence after they'd first crossed the Colo. 'Twelve kilometres down here and we should strike the farmhouse.'

As they rumbled over the cattle grid the house came into sight. A tethered dog barked and a woman emerged from the deep verandah, two children shy at her skirt. She stood like a snorting horse as Hugh, Jon and Gilbert swung open doors, then pushing back a ragged mane with the bones of her wrist folded fingers into a spreading waist.

'G'dday,' she said, 'What can I do for yers?' Their stress must have communicated to her. 'Gees,' she came forward, 'yer not ... ? Didn't reckon ye'd git 'ere so quick. Blue,' she yelled over a shoulder towards a shed half collapsed under a heavy vine. 'They're 'ere.'

A freckled man in shorts, singlet and working boots emerged, advanced towards them through a panic of poultry. Formally he shook hands with the men, then, the occasion demanding it, proffered a hand to Jon.

'Any further word?' her voice was husky.

He shook a slow head.

The woman joined them. 'The kettle's on; a cuppa tea in a few ticks.'

'Shouldn't we ... '

''Ave a cuppa tea,' the man advised and started to lead the way to the house. 'I can fill yers in on what I know.'

It had been just on dusk the previous night when Owen had stumbled out of the bush by their lower gate. The day had started well, conditions perfect. When the third canoe with Paul and young Hugh had failed to meet up with the others, they weren't uneasy. Midday and an eternity of hours began to set in when lounging under trees on the bank, a paddle slowly, rhythmically eddied towards shore. Roused from the shade where he lay, Dick, wading in to retrieve it, had given the alarm.

Owen and Mark, unofficial leaders, the strongest the eldest, had taken the decision to paddle back upstream as far as they could till they met the shallow water tumbling fast between rocks and shore. There'd been a good, long stretch of it, exciting, testing, one of the reasons they'd come. The water was high from heavy rains the previous week, the currents deceptive. It was only when they'd found the capsized canoe in a side pool they'd admitted the possibility of an accident an actuality. Mark, after searching with Owen, set off downstream again for Dick and Hamish and on their return, for ever it seemed to Owen scrambling and calling along the bank, it was settled that someone should go for help. It was just on dusk when Owen had stumbled out of the bush at the lower gate.

In the dim, low-ceilinged kitchen, the heat aggravated by a fuel stove, they sipped tea, Hugh and Vera close on a bench drawn up to the table, Gilbert, mouth folded in, continually wiping at his neck with a handkerchief, but seeming to find no relief. Jon, winding deeper into herself as she listened on a low stool, came back abruptly to the present as the younger of the two small children laid a cheek on her knee. Her hand patted out to the damp curls. Outside the dog whined.

'Frank Brady, 'e's the sergeant, and Jock, that's Jock McCarthy, the constable, come out in the four wheel.' Blue Picard splintered out his words. 'With the young fella … '

'Owen,' Vera breathed.

'Yeah, with the young fella, they would have took it about a mile down the track. No further, ya can't get wheels no further. After that ya gotta 'oof it.'

'How far?' Hugh wanted to know.

''Ard to tell. After me cow paddock she falls away steep for a while. S'ppose it's a good five mile till she 'its the Colo.'

Hugh wanted the women to stay at the farm.

'No.'

'But Jon ... '

'I'm sorry Hugh, but I must come. Vera, dear, you stay.'

Vera looked to her husband. 'I'd like to come.'

While Blue Picard hooked a trailer to the tractor, his wife packed a haversack with food, a battered thermos. She included a flagon of cooking sherry, had nothing stronger. God knows, she thought, they might need it. Blue had told her to throw in a couple of blankets.

The faint road led before them past a stretch of dry land covered with shaggy grass, a fence dividing from grazing cattle until it came to narrow to a bush track bristling with burned stumps where its owner was trying to clear, expand his holding. The four-wheel was parked in meagre shade. The throbbing heat cooled marginally, a breeze welled occasionally out towards them. It was relatively easy walking until suddenly the track plunged down, rocks irregular on each side which sent them scrambling for a foothold, hands grasping wildly for any support.

'Not much of this,' Blue ahead called back. 'She flattens out real soon.'

Tough trees self-sewn in rocky crevices grew tall, the leaves a sour green throwing a shifting shade, some of the trunks silvery smooth where the bark peeled back like scabs. Touching at one for balance Jon felt a gummy wound, suppurating.

Shadows began to fold down; when evening came moths and buzzing mosquitoes would replace the flies.

'Could git a bit of rain later,' Blue tried to make conversation. 'But not much.'

God, I could use a drink, thought Gilbert, and half raised a hand to the pattern of flies between Jon's shoulder blades, sprinkled like tacky dark chocolate. His gummed-up throat, sweat pouring through the hat on his head, veins practically bursting from his flushed skin, let alone pinched feet and punishing calves made him ache to lay the blame fairly and squarely at someone's door. Jon halted momentarily and he collided into her.

'What the hell!'

'Sorry.'

Sorry, sorry, sorry. The whole damn mess was her fault. It was true; if she hadn't always been so indulgent with the boy, she was giddy with love for him, lavishing him right and left with ... well ... with ... with whatever he wanted. And when the tune was called, the piper to be paid ... here he was stumbling like a clumsy handmaiden to pay the price for her whims. Bitch, bitch, bitch, he wanted to scream at her purposeful, fly-blown back.

She slowed to squeeze beside him on the narrow path, one hand switching a length of bracken like a fan.

'Gil ... '

'What?'

She shrugged. 'Nothing,' and screwing up her eyes, closed them to prevent him looking into them even by chance.

The track opened out to a clearing, and the sun soon to drop was a bar of blood across the sky, bleeding down to the horizon. Blue led off to the right, brown sluggish water lay to the left. Another track soon forked from theirs, showing some signs of recent use, tall grasses trampled, fern fronds broken. There was a pungent smell of summer vegetation, the resinous smell of the bush, small birds flickered through leaves. Pale scars showed in the sides of trees where branches had been wrenched off in past storms or broken under their own weight.

Blue leading, still with a regular gait, the rest of them tired, confused, came to a stop as soon as the river was fully in sight. Jon dipped down to rest under a tree, fine maidenhair near the water, strips of wet weeds licking her ankles. A bitter oiliness mixed in her nose to itch with the peppery dust.

''Ang on, I'll give a shout,' said Blue and his voice jumbled over to an answering shout. 'Found 'em,' he announced.

A crawing magpie screamed a fiendish welcome. Constable Jock McCarthy came filtering through the bushes, shredded looking, brown-faced, heavy-shouldered, solemn. 'How do, m'am. M'am,' he nodded to each of the women, anxious to speak only to the men.

Hugh detached himself from Vera's arm. 'Have you got any news? Are they found?'

'Yes.'

How do you stay afloat, what are the mechanics of survival? Jon felt shapeless, grey, her knees feathers as she tried to remember how to stand. She looked out on a world for which she had no words.

Hugh found the words. 'Are they all right? For God's sake, man ... '

The constable gulped. 'One. One of 'em's okay. Will be; nasty gash on the head, lacerations, a few superficial scratches ... '

'The other?'

'The other one's ... the other one's drowned.'

Vera began to cry; a subdued and pain-filled sound. Jon found her feathered knees jointed by steel. Running, fleet-footed, she tore past the young man facing her, over the dappled ground, awkwardly hurdling a fallen log, following on till she found them, the clearing where he lay under two spray jackets flooded with oppressive shadows, the last of the light catching a flowering gum which foamed with blossom.

A receptive cell in her brain registered finality. Paul lay like a ruffled bird, arms partially spread as if in an attempt to dry wet wings.

Then Gilbert was beside her, words clicking, hiccuping out from between his dry lips.

'But ... but. It c.can't be. P.Paul, Paul. Paul. Sit up. Sit up lad. Do .. do you hear m.me? Paul?'

Hugh's hands were firm on his shoulders when he began to screech like a demented parakeet. 'Come along, old man, drink this,' his voice caressive.

I can't help him, Jon knew. Not now.

The five boys, a broken little army walking away from battle, cheeks sunken, eyes red with fatigue, tangled with the scene. Young Hugh, a pulpy wound on his temple, head bandaged inexpertly, limped shakily towards her, legs moving heavily, slowly as if in a dream. Tears jetted from his eyes the colour of river pebbles as he clung ferociously to her, his face a mottled grey.

At a small distance Blue with the sergeant and constable set about felling saplings ... the blanket to make a rough stretcher.

She had to get away from the savagery of this place, the dead blue dusk dragging this terrible day with it. A primitive instinct forced her to leave the others, Gilbert, and she began to climb the slope above them which rose wild and silent. Half way up she found a rough little hollow, fell down on a bed of stones gasping, out of their sight, a cornered beast. Her landscape rolled desolately away; her life past and present severed. She wanted to plunge into some escape, fall into an all-enveloping oblivion.

Summer lightning lit up the sky soundlessly like the ripples of fire to douse itself in the encroaching night. A thin wind ran round the world. When the quick summer storm slid against the hillside like a few sheets of dirty water, Owen, who had watched her go, climbed up to claim her again for the living.

The track back seemed interminable, all else abandoned but the need to force one foot after another. Exhaustion when it came had a voluptuous quality, sleep deep like oil.

Chapter Twelve

Her heart sinks, what's left of it and she retells herself a legend. Robert the Bruce, King of the Scots, so inspired men that when he died his heart was extracted, embalmed and deposited in Melrose Monastery. Divided from the rest of his body. Her mind hums.

How do you extract a heart? When does it shrivel?

Cold rises from the ground and recalls quieter melancholies; needles into her eyelids and stings. The towering blocks of darkened flats make it a place of alpine silence and sniffing what should be pure air, she wrinkles her nose in distaste. The facts are too palpable, useless to ignore them. The air's unclean.

She looks to the monkey-puzzle of the stars and envies the purity with which each tiny tinselly point shines down on a blistered world where man is no more than a tenant. To understand the stars would lessen their appearance, but ...

'What do I understand?'

'How do you accommodate to life's changes?'

'Is nothing we do truly moral unless we're free to do otherwise?'

'What makes a defence a defiance?'

Silence is the answer as she stands juggling the questions. Eerily quiet her voice seems to address the air or anyone who cares to stop and listen. But there's no one; only an uncluttered bareness about the place though a hundred people must be within earshot.

She glides like a waxen swan on the river of roads polished and flecked by the lights of the night. The gulf of silence scoops her along, steals away her identity and she rides the surfaces like a bird on the sea.

She rounds another corner. And another and another. Suddenly the silence breaks. Thin, high music whines into the night; grieving it keens out to her through the tobacco smoke and alcohol of a party. The lighted house seems a haven for exiles. Her spirits rise. She's cold and alone and longs to peer through the steamed-up windows. Inside? Warm, welcoming faces, hands raised to hers and the stumbling words of greetings encouraging her to join them. A glass thrust into her hand, easy chatter from mobile throats, self-possessed women, engaging men. Or eyes cold like ashes? Mouths fixed on mechanical smiles? Is it beyond the bounds of possibility to talk with these men and women who speak her own tongue? Surely whatever was said would begin to break up and detach into comprehensible words and phrases.

She moves through the open gate and sits on a step, knees drawn to chin. Once she might have buried face in arms and begun to sob, but not now, not now. The tempo of the music changes. She taps a toe, gay, carefree as it spills on the air. Unexpectedly the door opens. A lumbering figure staggers out burdened by clinking bottles to deposit them only feet away.

'Close the door, it's bloody freezing,' comes a shout slurred from inside and she winces at the crude answering voice as an altercation erupts.

Above the shouting men a woman giggles, whinnies. Someone turns the volume up, but above it, trembling like a racehorse, she hears glass shattering, drunken yelps of pain. She draws fingers around her neck as if sealing an envelope and continues to sit on the step.

The door explodes; two wrestling figures tumble through, the punches clumsy off target, as they jab and bruise the darkness. One drops to the gravel.

'You rotten drunken sod,' the other mutters, teeters

precariously but manages to swivel back, spit contemptuously and lurch in through the still open door. Someone bangs against it. It closes, sucking up the shed light.

On her feet panting she looks towards the body, undecided, self-conscious. The man rolls on to his back, rattles breath through his throat, opens one eye, closes it again and slurping at words begins a sort of song.

'Tra, lalala. Gagah … '

Accustomed to the light she rocks his way and a sickening contempt assails her. The sound hurts her ears. With his bulging neck, coarsened face split between nose and mouth by a short moustache he bears an uncanny resemblance to Gilbert.

Dying, with all its certainty, is a very uncertain event. Weeds riot over the flower bed of a life and it no longer exists. Gilbert, who had only acknowledged Paul in life, never known him, bound by the rigidity of his death, which no argument could ever change, now saw him with no equal, above the crowd. The relationship hesitant and troubled, came to be one of companionship, love and trust in his eyes. Paul, the model of growing manhood, his achievements would have been great.

'That boy could have done anything, gone anywhere,' his voice would rise hot and loud.

Those terrible days had somehow been eaten away and the world had moved somnambulantly before Jon; everything seen through a watery glass. Gilbert, storm centre of the scene, had lain alternatively sobbing and moaning on the bed in Paul's room, his eyes a mad haze as he breathed in painful gasps corroded by misery.

'Sedate him,' Lola demanded of the doctor and it was done.

Dorothy, voice low, questioned Lola. 'What's reduced him to this? He must have cared more for Paul than any of us ever suspected. He's reduced to … '

'A gibbering idiot.' Lola who'd never had much time for Gilbert swelled with pity for him. She could not mourn in order to exhaust sorrow herself and grief had angered her.

Who was responsible? God? A compassionless God, who could tell, for we're not used to the young dying. Young men in war, yes, and if there's any accommodating to that waste at least there was the enormity of the expectation. But Paul ... senseless, horrible.

Dorothy, drained by the effort to understand, made a small gesture of protest and leaned back in her chair, half collapsed. People, she believed, tried to rise to the occasion however distressing, stirred by an inner strength, some courage in adversity, a stoicism. She tried to curb a critical tongue, but... 'It's so ... excessive. He's got no thought for Jon. Lola, don't think me uncharitable,' she drew a deep breath, 'but it's, well ... downright unmanly.'

Lola nodded a slight assent, the blue of her eyes ringed with ash-grey circles, hands opening loose in her lap. Life had become more complicated than Gilbert – a sad spectacle – had ever supposed. Death had forced him to wake from the slumber of his life; his selfish, sulky, superficial life. He'd opened his eyes and was afraid. Cringing back groaning, he'd given off the stench that fear can produce, frightened that the father might have to follow the son, his paroxysms of fear kept him noisily alive. Not for Gilbert a wholly destructive folly.

'Poor shuffling soul,' Lola said to Dorothy, 'but resilient. He'll come through.'

'Jon?' Dorothy wanted confirmation.

'It'll just take time.'

Jon, terrified to close her eyes and see the water-logged body of her son, endeavoured to comfort Ruth in her bewilderment, Betty in a crumbling desolation. Stretched upon her own rack, blearily she recognised she must not allow the fragile alliance between heart and reason to snap. The reasonable world had turned inside out but continued to turn. Day followed day to sink tracelessly in the past. When she fell asleep it was as if her eyes stayed open. She was claimed by plaguing images and a plaguing dread, the inside view of a nightmare. If it had to be, had his death been instantaneous, the price nature demanded?

There must be a vantage point called Later; she longed to

believe in it, something. Later. Later the pain would ease. A little. Later. But when was Later? Would it never come?

Gilbert aged five years in as many months; his mind snapped and gashed in turmoil, the chocks of reason close to rolling away. With partial recovery he looked to the social form, the family, the clan, his wife for support. And they gave it. Shocked by his breakdown and fearful a malevolent fate could render him permanently impaired they united in efforts to help. Young Tom, Jon always thought of him as young Tom though now more than thirty, was an incredible support, willing to spend hours with Gilbert, comforting Ruth, desperately trying to cushion them all, intervening where possible between Jon and well-meaning friends who had great trouble with the word 'death', understanding her need for isolation.

Gilbert's depressions were terrible and involving. His sleepless, agitated nights left Jon sleepless, agitated, Ruth distraught.

'You can't go on like this,' Lola warned.

'It's all wrong for Ruth.'

'All wrong for everyone. What can we do?'

What could she do? People living in intolerable conditions looked to ways to ease these conditions. If things fell apart the centre was rotten. Gouge it out, attempt a rebuild.

'I can't leave him,' she spoke by rote. 'Not now.'

Lola hesitated. 'No.'

'Then it's got to be made to work. At least in part. Ruth must leave us soon ... ' When Ruth left she feared it would become a tight, silent place.

'But ... '

'I know, Lola, Lola, I dread it. But she must.'

'Yes.'

Day in day out Gilbert sat morosely in a silk Paisley dressing gown, sweat glistening in the thinning hair, by night his face a pale, pale green in the soft light, eyes red-rimmed, his gaze distracted. The seasons changed. Gradually he began to question the movements of the household, began to show a little interest in his practice, the locum who was running it with great efficiency. Skin doughy, open-pored, his moustache turned grey, he sat for lengthy periods on the lavatory or in a closed room and there was little left for Jon to recognise in the man she'd married.

'Help me, Jon, help me,' he whimpered from time to time and the only help to offer was her continuing presence. She couldn't help him salvage the energies of youth, didn't know if there was anything else he wanted. She didn't know him, never had. For more than twenty years they'd stood numbly apart and for most of those years she'd thought his inadequacies had tipped their boat. Occasionally she felt a blind gesture of fury for the waste of it all, wanted to brandish a two-edged sword against fate, wondered why they'd condemned themselves to such luckless indifference like pock-marked effigies mute on the walls of an unused church.

When Betty, unable to cope, went into a nursing home he was solemn, understanding and kind; his eyes tearful. He cried easily these days.

She'd cried too, eyes dry, when Betty's collapse offered no alternative. Betty who seemed separated by a greyness as dense as concrete, the weird and unsettling questions she formed, unsupportable. Wearily Jon experienced a strange sense of guilt. She should have been able to buffer the blow for Betty somehow. But how? Desperate in her own loss, indignant, no, far more, bitter that Gilbert could offer no support, she dredged deep for energy to make the necessary arrangements to install her mother as best she could, Lola and Tom by her side. Jon felt enfeebled by a spiteful fate, helplessly unable to fulfil some filial duty to ease her mother's lot.

'Jon,' she heard Gilbert, his voice awkward, 'if I hadn't had you,' he sniffed as he groped for a handkerchief, muffled the words, 'if ... I might have ... '

What is a breakdown, she questioned. A piece of property acquired, the owner ever ready to talk about it, demand, blackmail?

So he bound her to his side; by a frail and tormenting

thread. Was his need sufficient for her to endure, forgive? Was this the price for the girlish indiscretion of inexpertly choosing a husband? When you're a lightweight creature of eighteen, twenty, with what miraculous insight do you probe an unknown future, lope into the right lane, shutter emotional needs against the wrong partner, sexual needs against the conspiring body? How is the delicate game played; do you bounce on neat little feet, banter with steel-tipped tongue to succumb to a crooked grin, a head of curly hair, a slow enslaving smile to join your life with pastry-maker, flautist, gambler, ornithologist, home breaker, stock-broker, degenerate, butcher, bigamist, architect, anarchist?

Stop, she counselled herself, this way lies madness. Many relationships between people didn't fall into prescribed categories to survive. Was it too late?

She looked at the wreck that was Gilbert and tried to assess salvage costs. She took his hand plaiting it into hers.

'You're kind,' he tried to murmur, 'so kind,' but had difficulty gathering words. At this moment in her life it was a seductive argument. Kind. He looked strangely frivolous for a moment as he drew his lips back to smile, eyes glittering between creepered brows, his complexion a tinted map of patches and vein tributaries, eyes vague, chin stubbled. With her free hand she smoothed at his hair surprised to feel it so spare and limp, to see the skin of the skull etched against the dark strands.

'I'll get lunch,' was all she said.

'Yes, but ... ' he held her hand puckering at the skin with his white fingers. 'Jon ... ' He twisted the wedding ring, rotating it slowly, half-heartedly hinting at some kind of ownership.

'Yes?'

'If ... if I try. To be here more.' It didn't make a lot of sense, it was a limp plea as he'd been incapable of leaving the house for months. 'We could ... well,' a peculiar expression scattered from his eyes, 'we could get things in order. A bit. That any good to you?' the question a plea.

She withdrew her hand, plumped at the pillows and with tired eyes looked out through the window to the indolent blur that made the sunless day.

'Yes. I think so. Yes.' She heard him hiccup mournfully as she left the room.

In the kitchen she found she was trembling; he'd pierced the veneer of her composure. So much time had been taken up in arriving at the reality of loss, more than half a year had passed yet the numbness remained, the shock. It was time to take other decisions, she supposed, little locks that had to be turned in the mind. The house was so drab; everything barnacled, rotting like weed washed up by an abnormally high tide. She'd pick some greenery, arrange it carelessly, the roses in the garden too formally remote. They'd requested 'No flowers' but so many people ... and the pitying tones of friends had rasped her nerves, well meant, fumbling for the words of comfort. Wandering from room to room, startled by a kind of wry surprise, she looked at the furniture that must for so many years have furnished her life. She'd get the painters in, alter the colours, immerse herself in change. Yet part of her screamed to keep it as it was, the way he'd known it. No. She owed it to Ruth, friends, herself. To Gilbert?

There had been no promises given her, no defined guide-lines. Gilbert lived up to his improved image for twelve months before the chains of habit reasserted themselves and with a two-day working week – and why shouldn't he reap the rewards of all those years of hard work? – the rest of the week divided indiscriminately into two-day seducer, three-day drunk.

Hopefully Jon displayed no characteristic to him but patience, tried to sound cordial, took refuge in work but felt as hollow and as empty as the space between the stars.

'I see my life as essentially scripted,' she told Lola with a twisting smile.

'What do you mean? Exactly?'

'I can't think or act independently. Everything seems to lead to the next scene, the next curtain. The next dissolve.'

'The play goes on, love.' Lola, philosophical in her clichés grinned, disturbed at Jon's pale aged face, dark rings smudged under the eyes, her features seeming to bear a double burden of time.

'What would I do without you? What would any of us do without you? Ruth feels the same.'

'You see,' Lola squeezed Jon's sagging shoulders, 'I've got a part in your play. Little ray of sunshine, that's me,' eyes swimming as she saw Jon's pain. Silently Lola prayed there was a right part in which Jon could be cast; that she wouldn't leap up on the stage from the audience, wild, impulsive, in a role never written for her, never planned.

'Lola, tell me, am I mourning now for myself or for Paul drowned?' she found it difficult to speak easily of him to anyone but Lola and Ruth, shoulders hunched over her swollen heart. 'I'm close to drowning too, in a sea of demands made by someone I've never really cared for.'

'Gilbert.'

'Yes.'

'Can't you try to talk to him? Talk it out.' She hesitated. 'Like me to speak to him. It's nothing to me.' Lola concealed the distress. 'I won't mince words.' The blue eyes slitted, challenging Jon to stop her from speaking out. The occasion demanded it. Gilbert succeeded in keeping his unpleasant habits a secret from no one.

'Dear Lola, thank you, but no.' Dismal she tried to sound valiant.

'Can't you talk to him then?'

'When he's home and when he's coherent, there's little conversation.' Enmity, she thought, is catching, I'm beginning to feel as he does.

'You mean you sit there without a word!'

Jon shrugged. 'The television sops up the silence.'

'Won't you try? Winkle him out.' Lola guessed Jon had stretched her capacity for communication to the limit.

Jon determined to try that night. What food hadn't shrivelled in the oven had congealed on the plates when finally he came home. He'd already dined on young female flesh so his tongue wasn't completely clogged. She knew the signs, his tomcat mentality. Any closer and she'd be chloroformed by the woman's perfume and the stale smell of his satisfaction.

'You're late,' she tried to smile but heard the rust creeping in. 'Why didn't you phone,' and quickly anticipating the irritated interruption, 'I would have gone ahead with mine.'

'Would have gone ahead with mine,' he mimicked and any pain she felt went underground. He seemed programmed to stifle and destroy so much. Gilbert the destroyer. Never a man who prized control.

His teeth were yellow in a too-wide grin as he sauntered towards the Scotch. By the time he'd downed two, three, tone resentful he launched the attack, scornfully emitting words like an octopus emitting clouds of ink.

'Don't just sit there. If you can't raise a laugh try propping up your mouth with a couple of matches. Have a go. Ha, ha, ha, Jon, the poor little matchstick girl. Out in the cold, cold snow. Yes snow. Miles and miles and miles of ... '

Miles! Long gone sensations buzzed in the bottom of her mind. Heavily she began to pull herself out of the chair.

'Stay where you are.'

Whether or not the threat was idle she stood up. Whether or not he struck her she knew he'd try to renegotiate their relationship in a day or two without a word of reference to any such ugly incident. His ability to forget was prodigious. Remembering had become her talent.

Drink began to knit pink blotches on his face. The vein in his temple throbbed, an easy barometer to read. She wanted him locked up, put away, dead.

'What a thoroughly objectionable woman you are. Ungrateful, surly and too well pleased with yourself. Smug.'

'Have you finished?' She knew the clock wouldn't go back to nicer times. Nothing remained but a wide humiliating silence. The room seemed to harbour the vilest air for human lungs she'd ever breathed.

Staring hard at her with egg-shell eyes, unhatched, he

opened them and the whites were raw. There was something he wanted to grind out. Grind out and grind into the carapace erected to keep him out. When they came the words were deliberate, no joke from the man who enjoyed someone else's joke in doubtful taste.

'When all else fails, Mrs Jamieson, don't fall back on your charm. You haven't any.'

Chapter Thirteen

This night between days. Is she a spirit figure, vaporous; voyaging, searching, discovering a rightful place, a rightful home? Had it been with Betty as a child or was she a changeling, some fairy infant substituted for a human immediately after birth?

She snorts amused. So many of us have fallen back on that trick, that fantasy; misunderstood, misjudged, misused, misemployed, misappropriated. She wants to accuse someone, not of something, but of everything. But no, not her mother; not the Betty of today, a shrunken paper-thin little suggestion of the indomitable woman she had been, with occasional bursts of interest like hot meteors, gone again where the eye could not follow. Blank eyed and speechless Betty had received the news of the tragedy, a double tragedy for her as she'd only loved dutifully till she'd loved Paul. He'd presented himself unknowingly as a vessel for adoration, comfort, peace and calm. When the vessel had shattered and was no longer there as the centre for love's indulgence, though the old tribal tradition of duty held, an intangible sickness took hold and squeezed her. Time drugged her, disturbing a part of the mind and where her actions and thoughts had been aggressive, resolute, today were lingeringly inept. Chambers in her mind were collapsed, never to be extended, made whole again.

Her blue-black night is a series of diminishing horizons; she walks on in semi-daze, eyes choked with pictures past and present, indigestible, blurred, the colours running. Jumpily her fingers pluck leaves from a shrub, shred them, hands acrid with the pungent odour. Flashing needles dart in and out, in and out of her head, frenzied fingers embroidering a complex pattern. She jumps, suddenly startled by the sight of her moon-thrown shadow which walks beside her.

'I'm a bleached out creature compared to you,' she tells it then gasps. Up ahead stands a rigid figure, straight and bulky, motionless in the night. She freezes in twin currents of indecision and fear. The figure motionless, she urges herself to proceed. Closer, closer then her fright evaporates. She giggles convulsively. Planted on the edge of the pavement stands a letter box, an old fashioned letter box as stolid as Queen Victoria.

'You never answer, even when you write,' wrote Ruth from Asia, loose in the world, travelling a slow route where trails led into old, old cultures, some of them rough, brutish, backward yet mysterious, compelling.

How could she write her lovely daughter on her ugly father, and her own jaded life with Gilbert? How to scratch on an unsullied sheet that she didn't want Gilbert dead or alive, with a sudden outburst of truth tell Ruth that when love or affection need bolts on the door it's non-existent, nothing to lock away.

She wraps an arm around Queen Victoria, peers into the dark chasm of her mouth, wondering if ever it's possible to recall a rashly posted letter.

'Where is Ruth?' she asks. 'Now? At this precise moment in time.'

Does Queen Victoria belch? Of course not, the metal of the box rings hollow, empty as she rests against it.

'Come to Bangkok, come and meet me there,' Ruth had written, 'come if only for a week.'

From Thailand, Ruth was going to India then overland, 'in great discomfort, I suspect', to Europe. 'I want to see you,' she elaborated on this and had managed just to squeeze the post-script: 'There's someone I want you to meet.'

The flight was silky smooth. It was after midnight when she stepped from the air-conditioned jet to be engulfed by the tepid bath of the air, sticky like damp sugar. Bused to the main airport buildings, excitement at the thought of Ruth so close twisted her pleasurably, she was like an exalted novice about to enter a religious order.

Even at this hour it was comparatively busy. Up a long escalator, formalities completed, she passed on to the outer hall, baggage to be collected, and saw her.

'Ruth. Darling.' They waved furiously grinning inanely, Jon not to be released until luggage spun into sight, hefting the suitcase off with impatience.

How beautiful she is, Jon thought, and my daughter. How had it happened? Tall, in flat sandals, jeans and skimpy top, smooth arms the colour of rosewood, hair tied back like a lick of tar. She's thinner, Jon noticed, but she'd kept up exactly with my memory of her. How I do love her.

Emotionally they clutched each other.

'You'd like a drink?' Ruth was in charge. 'Will coffee do, the bars are closed?'

Jon had the impression their roles had been exchanged. Delightedly she let Ruth guide and direct, words spilling over, 'You've come, you've come. I knew you would. It's wonderful, everything's wonderful,' and took Jon's hand as soon as they'd seated themselves. 'Don't laugh, it sounds silly,' Ruth confided, 'but I believe you made up your mind to come with help from an inner fairy godmother I was able to wake from a hundred-year sleep.'

'No need for spells or magic, believe me … '

'To leave Gilbert?' Ruth's eyes, copies of her own, bored into her mother's with awful intensity. She never could just hint around the edges of a subject.

'That,' Jon said firmly, 'we shall not discuss now.'

'No, no, of course,' and dropped her gaze to their entwined hands. Loosely encircling her own wrist were two ropes of tight white flowers, the scent heady, each small bloom patiently threaded to make the ornaments. Ruth slipped them off delicately trying not to bruise the petals. 'These are for you, I almost forgot. They're sold everywhere; as temple and shrine offerings. They're my welcome to you and ... and carry as much devotion ... Do I sound very soppy?'

'No.'

'Good.'

They sat talking on in the terminus, now deserted, no further flights in or out scheduled before six a.m.

'Only three hours,' Ruth was staggered. 'I hope we won't have trouble getting a cab. It's a long way to Bangkok proper.'

A streaky pink light flickered into the sky; dawn when they settled into the room Ruth had engaged at the Thai Hotel, a second-rate place – one star – she declared splendid.

A bathroom, plumbing spasmodic, was attached to the bare twin-bedded room, the air-conditioning alternatively freezing or non-existent, Ruth was, she said, lolling in more luxury than she'd sighted in months. High on the seventh floor, from the balcony part of the unwieldy spread that was Bangkok was beginning to stir below, the heat a blanket never rolled back to allow the millions of sleepers properly to cool. A towering Buddha as high as a small building speared up into the sky, creamy yellow in the early light of this great exploding city of the East, the bejewelled temples of its Buddhist community a façade behind which lurked slums, poverty and corruption; where meditation, murder, piety and prurience were centuries-long bedfellows.

They did little the next day but talk, Jon carefully watching what she ate, disturbed when Ruth bought food from street stalls.

'Is it safe?'

'For safety's sake I should have been kept a permanent ten-year-old,' Ruth answered. 'Don't worry, Mum.'

On her daughter's strict instruction, however, Jon drank only bottled fizz.

'We must drink regularly,' Ruth stated. 'Important not to dehydrate,' and would call for a glass each time.

'Ruth,' Jon cautioned helplessly, 'should you drink from a glass? Is it sensible? You can't know they've been properly washed ... surely a straw's better ... less risky,' she petered out.

'Use a straw, by all means,' Ruth smiled back at her, two days later to grin, 'Notice how short the straws can be?'

Jon hadn't noticed. 'What do you mean?'

'Oh nothing.' Ruth continued to grin.

'What do you mean?' Jon insisted.

'Well, my darling hygienic mother, nothing's wasted here. A straw's used. And used and used and used, until it's soggy enough to be cut down.'

'Ruth! You devil.'

'You'll survive.'

But how would she survive living with Gilbert, Ruth was determined to discuss.

'Who am I to meet?' Jon countered. 'You said in your letter ... Is it someone important? Important to you? Tell me. I won't be side-tracked.'

They had passed along the dazzling white walls of the Royal Palace and through the buttressed gateway to the temple precincts. A gluttonous feast lay spread before them.

The ridges of the steep saddle roofs tiled in orange or green undulated slightly terminating in gilt, some piled elaborately one above the other, eaves and triangular gable ends ornamented with symbolic decorations.

'What a casket of jewels! We'll be here hours and won't see even half.'

Gateways, windows and pavilions rose tier upon tier like the ceremonial umbrellas and crowns. Pillars blossomed out in capitals of lotus flowers, walls, doors and shutters covered with carvings, inlays of pearl, mosaics and lacquer work. From the eaves hung long chains of bells, chiming in any puff of breeze.

The reflected light was blinding. They'd retired to the shade of one of the covered cloisters with murals depicting the past of old Siam and India ... animated scenes from the life of Buddha complete in minute detail.

Ruth turned from Jon to examine expressions stamped with delicacy on an uninhibited group of followers of the great Lord waging war on a pack of demons.

'Just look at this brushwork ... '

'I won't be side-tracked,' Jon repeated as she knelt to an earthy depiction of everyday life in an Eastern society, raised herself and followed Ruth. 'I know you well enough to know you're dodging.'

'Me? Mother, how could you!'

'Tell me,' demanded Jon and took Ruth by the arm to sit on a shaded step.

Opposite, a huge image, half-girl, half-cockerel, glistening with glazed tiles, stood guardian to a temple; the figure bi-sexual in portent. Two saffron-robed monks, one scarcely more than a child, padded past bare-footed, the older man's shaven head splintering with new growth, the young initiate less lost in meditative calm.

Ruth, extravagantly generous with her emotions, had fallen in love, and wore the expression of an exquisite, sleepy child.

'It had a shaky beginning. I was travelling with an Italian countlet, Giotto, and Marcel, a French boy with a tricoloured face.' The flippant words were no camouflage. 'You see,' she smiled shyly, 'it was worth studying languages.'

'What does he speak? His native tongue?'

'English. And superbly, but he's a Scot. He's so, so ... I can't find the words, so ... well ... wonderful.'

'Does he have a name?' Jon asked patiently, indulgent.

'Dougal.'

'Dougal.' Jon tried it softly.

'Dougal Goderic Ivor Heriot Innes.'

'Try to describe him.'

'I'll try, but won't do him justice. I'll only manage a card-board cut-out. When you meet him ... .

He was twenty-seven, tall, strongly built. Bearded, with riotous hair reddish-black, eyes blue, an anthropologist, tender he was, sentimental he was not ... 'And everything I want.'

'Is it reciprocal? Does he love you?'

'Yes.'

'How long have you known him?' What ordinary, mothering questions I'm putting, Jon thought, when what I want to know is beyond questions, speculation. I want a crystal ball from which all shadows clear, proof against pestilence or plagues, fires, floods and the unpredictable climates of mood and age for my daughter. I want her protected from shock and outrage in the name of love, ignorance and intolerance. I want no fractured heart, no fractured marriage, if she wants marriage. I want the impossible.

'Years ago you said, I remember,' Ruth was speaking eyes directly on hers, 'you said, to love someone meant to care for someone more than yourself.'

'Did I say that? To you? Yes, that would still be my definition,' but she'd loved once where the mix was passion and despair. Love! She'd learnt not to place a magical faith in the efficacy of the word. Jon smiled to Ruth. 'I'm glad to have had a few pearls to drop.' If only there'd been more, and had a momentary flash of Paul. Recently she'd wondered if the good times were just a chance between the bad. The room of my life papered with false starts? she wondered, eyes moist.

'There have been lots of pearls. And lots of good times. You, Mum, provided them all when we were growing up.' Ruth might have read her. She swallowed. 'Paul would agree.'

Jon stood up as if anxious to meet Dougal at once, expecting to like him. Some adjustment of attitudes, of course, would be necessary, but radical adjustment clearly had to be made just to live in the world today. The structure of society was shaken by the young and simply drawing your older skirts back in distaste on the sidelines left you beached high, removed from the swim. The angry waves smoothed to ripples with the years anyway, rebels converting to pillars of communities, snarling chic expressions and clothes often exchanged for a seat on the board.

'Where is Dougal? When am I going to meet him?'

'He's in Chiang Mai. Five hundred miles north,' Ruth sighed, the sun scorching. 'Cooler there, among mountains, it's the second city of Thailand, and unbelievably,' she glanced to the close and visible signs of reverence, 'about twice as many temples. And the centre for Thai handicrafts ... silver, lacquer work, marvellous things, and if that's not enough some of the most beautiful women in the world are to be found there too.'

'Worried?' Jon teased, sure of the answer. Ruth rarely reached for a mirror or crammed to catch her reflection in plate glass. She knew who she was.

Ruth shook her head, ignorant of the full power of personal appeal. 'He'll be back on Saturday. He thought we'd like time together first.'

Milk chocolate waters burdened with sampans and small river craft balancing fruit, vegetables, flowers, fresh and dried meats, fish; the canals teemed in the early morning before the real heat of the day. From the houses on the banks, from the raft houses tied to the banks, heedlessly the river was used for swimming, bathing, washing and dumping refuse.

Jon and Ruth separate in the hired boat watched as water was scooped into cooking pots, teeth brushed, hair shampooed, women and children bathed and urinated, modesty somehow observed, privacy almost non-existent: boat vendors paddling supplies to households, the ritual of bargaining long and elaborate.

'Another fairyland of the East,' said Ruth, 'complete with smell. The stench in some of the smaller canals is too much. Revolting.'

The klongs spread into a network of waterways, banks crowded, richer shuttered houses rambling in compounds, pavilions, bell-shaped temples tapering to spires, impressive stupas, shrines, so many places of worship and religious activity.

'No more tourist delights. We've had enough for today,' Ruth announced over lunch. 'We're going to talk about you.'

Jon trembled, protested mildly there was nothing to ... She circled her fork in the plate of food.

'We both know that's not true.' Ruth, Jon saw, was gathering breath to continue talking with full knowledge you could make your own rules of thumb but you couldn't arch over and span the whole human condition. 'To put it kindly,' Ruth was trying, 'I've always had as a father a man of roving disposition.'

'When did you realise?' Gilbert, it seemed, had kept his string of women a secret from none.

'I don't know exactly. I couldn't have gone back as far as the Laurel era ... '

'Poor Laurel.'

'Why do you say that?'

'I don't know,' Jon replied.

'She was such a vapid, shallow creature, or that's how it struck me. Her only instinct seemed to be other people's goods. I bet she traded men like kids trade marbles.'

'Perhaps.' Laurel, she'd heard, was given to prowling her well-furnished life alone. She'd married again, again briefly for apparently there'd been no joy in it. And reputedly Laurel's nerves were disordered. 'But if she'd got what she'd wanted when she first wanted it ... '

'Gilbert?' Ruth anxious for her mother's future was fascinated by the past. Did everyone ache for someone as she herself ached for Dougal? But they were not jaggedly cobbled into a pattern, a futile life together because their nerves and senses interlocked. Theirs was no prize-fight, crown awarded, victory won, scoring points and knocking each other down.

'You must leave him. You must.' Ruth jumped in tenderly strict. 'You can't keep sacrificing yourself to his disgusting affairs and his drunken bouts.'

Jon wanted to explain you don't make sacrifices, you make compromises, which had seemed the only thing, the proper acceptance of reality. But, perhaps after all she'd been too easily seduced into that thinking. Had there been some guilt which had led her to muddle up cause and effect? If Paul hadn't, she would have ... Had she made it too difficult for herself? Why had she let the marriage haemorrhage on all this time, discontent as draining as the loss of blood?

'Ruth,' she said, 'try to understand it doesn't hurt as much as you think. Gilbert's behaviour. I don't like it, of course I don't. In fact I hate it, but it's years since I ... cared for him.'

Ruth looking at her shook her head slightly. 'But you just might conceivably want to share your life with someone else,' at Jon's laugh to go on, 'you're not sexually obsolescent you know.'

Sex, Jon drew in air, means being literally naked and expressing your feelings and that's terrifying to me now. Sex for her with Gilbert had seldom been more than limited to the barest politeness. Exactly what she wanted seemed an open question, bewildering.

She knew what she didn't want: she'd seen too often too many middle-aged women svelte in imported Puccis and St Laurents, faces regularly tightened by loneliness and cosmetic surgery, tanned as evidence of seasons spent in the right places, the golden tan of youth a kippered crust.

But other women seemed to have a great deal of purpose in life, made decisions, stuck to them. What was the key? Never the backward glance?

'You're hardly a pile of crumbling bones or a crumbling mind,' Ruth's voice was tinged with urgency. 'And only forty-six! So why wear an albatross round your neck?' Ruth fumbled for her hand. 'You're lonely and you weren't meant to be alone because you've so much to give. You poured it into us,' she paused, 'and as sole beneficiary now, I don't want you pulverised any more by that unfeeling bastard.'

Jon smiled. Should she click in disapproval, murmur reproof, he was her father after all, but seeing a certain erectness in Ruth's neck and shoulders realised unexpectedly, relieved, that her mothering role was at an end. She had grown out of motherhood, there was no longer the need to be watchful, Ruth could watch over herself. She, Jon, had somehow achieved the goal; they were two women, close and understanding friends.

'Leave Gilbert. Save yourself. We'll aid and abet you in any-thing you do.' Ruth's face flushed. 'Dougal and I. Anything.'

Jon was deeply touched. And a little unnerved. Dougal, she supposed, must have classified differing societies ... tribal mores of births, initiations, fertility rites, marriage and death practices, the roles of girl child, pubescent female and woman.

'And there's your painting,' Ruth was saying firmly. 'How can you work in such an atmosphere?' She understood her mother's range of lines and pictorial thought.

'Ruth. Don't overrate any talent of mine. I don't.' She had been puzzled by her success. 'I wish I was more creative. I just have disappearing experiences and interpret some of them. I recognised my limitations years ago. My work's competent, saleable in certain areas, therapeutic and I enjoy it. I don't ask for more.'

'What do you ask for?'

There didn't seem any sure ground on which this question could be met. Perhaps a child's animal sharpness of taste and smell, she thought, and like everyone she needed a degree of respect and attention, but ... 'I wish I knew.'

Jon slept relieved after meeting Dougal. She could pinpoint no fixed formula by which she felt certain he was right for Ruth. He had an air of exclusive welcome, transferred to her after he'd kissed Ruth, holding her still. There was a natural-ness which appeared to lead on to an uncomplicated desire to make people happy. It was easy to see how deeply they cared for each other.

He talked at length about his home, the hills rising round it plastered with heather; his family, he explained, busy near the tartan throne hundreds of years ago with connections irregu-larly acquired by a female forbear. Hearth and home would for him, Jon divined, never go out of fashion. There was a younger brother, a doctor in Edinburgh, and one sister living on a farm in Provence.

'I'm taking your mother to see the Emerald Buddha,' he told Ruth, 'if she'll come.'

Willingly Jon accepted, guessing he wanted to talk about Ruth. Honking like a pig the taxi wound through swarms of bicycles, unhurrying crowds of pedestrians, swaying through the chaos of the traffic, the driver trusting to no more than an amulet to keep them safe.

'Would you approve of your daughter marrying me when she's ready to marry?' he asked.

She liked his directness, the implication of depth and commitment. 'Yes.'

Ruth ... he loved her with her turbulence and her capacity for wonder, her intelligence and wanted his life to continue with hers.

Lightly he threaded an arm through Jon's. Climbing the temple steps a small girl trailing a family group tripped and lost balance. Jon's hand shot out to grip her, righted her, to be snatched quickly back by Dougal's as she reached to pat the sleek little head.

'Unwise to pat a Thai child's head,' he explained.

'Why ever not?'

'Simple. Thais are extremely sensitive about their heads.'

'But why?' Jon frowned.

'Each person possesses a spirit, a khwan, which resides in the head. Should it leave the person he may become ill, even die. If the khwan isn't able to get back into the head, you see, it may flee frightened, so most Thais resent anyone trying to touch the head, especially in what they'd consider a careless gesture.'

'I could have caused trouble?'

Dougal laughed. 'Unlikely to have provoked an international incident, but ... '

'Just as well you knew.'

The sole of the foot, she learned, was a different matter, unlike the head a degraded part of the body. In touch with the soil it may unknowingly have killed insects and other life, a violation of Buddhist teachings for all life is sacred.

How little I know, Jon thought, but knew that with Dougal Ruth had every chance. It was delighting to see the pair of them together holding hands whenever they could, thighs touching under tables, companionable, replete. And she felt strangely jealous, not directly of either of them, but jealous, savage she'd been cheated in the game of chance, losing out to spend more than a quarter century married to a husband who could drive miles under cover of darkness to dump secret litter in lonely places, a man with whom it had been necessary to learn how to make conversation by day and avoid it by night.

'There's not just one man for one woman, one woman for one man. You know that,' echoed painfully now out of the past. 'Perhaps during a lifetime there could be five, ten more whom we could love deeply.'

She struggled with an anger, destructive in intensity, unready for relegation to the role of fringe-dweller in a dangerous world pitted by traps, but obviously the only one the élite inhabited.

I will leave, Gilbert, I will, she reinforced the recognition; no world-shattering event, no national decision. Common sense. What would be lost? Who would care? As she spoke to herself the voice seemed to come out of the future, or the past, words full of the familiar. How was it she'd never said them aloud having seen a future with him black, a screaming battlefield at best a tense desert, herself a dismal link in their life together. You can keep going if you're not sure, she wanted to cry. It's the certainty that kills. There'd been no life together, yoked by common law just a few obligatory meetings in the market place of marriage. You pay your money and you take your chances. Where to seek consolation?

Money no problem, God, what a thin-blooded creature I've been, I am, trickling along my contained little veins for ever back in the department of failed dreams. The attempt to warm and comfort Gilbert, make him perhaps cosy in shared misfortune had failed. How can people vanish, she thought, and still be in the same flesh before you? The slate was wiped clean. A twinge, some impulse pushed her on. Little shocks ran through her, seesawing. She was no longer threatened by responsibility for him or to him: the scar tissue of the past was puckering at the edges, toughening up.

'I've been thinking about what you said,' she told Ruth before dinner. Taking the flight out of Bangkok the following morning, they were leaving for Burma on a visa permitting a week's stay as soon as she left.

Ruth looked up quizzically.

'I'm going to leave Gilbert,' Jon said it with firmness having rehearsed it several times, cheeks unnaturally pink. 'I've thought about it often enough, weighed it, deliberated, dismissed it, but the time's come to do it.' Strange, strangely relieved, she would wait for time to stretch itself between resolution and occasion, then painlessly into the receding patterns of the past.

'You must try to forget everything but the way ahead,' Ruth stroked her cheek, her mother a child to whom a tender lesson had to be taught, the right way demonstrated to lead her on into an acceptable future.

'It's never easy. To change the patterns of the past,' Dougal too wanted to lend support, yet neither of them with knowledge of the odd reassurance that habits of servitude can engender. To face the unknown would hurt, it must, but new experiences need not be total agony. More of the same with Gilbert would.

A sadness lay about their last evening, difficult, clumsy somehow, parting close but ten hours away.

Let death of love not enter here; Jon wondered if she dare pray as she watched them achingly, their glances lazily exchanged, handsome, jaunty, chosen. She smiled, read again the letters provocative, undulating on Ruth's T-shirt ... 'Anything Can Happen'.

'Share the joke. What so amusing?'

'Your shirt.'

'Ho, hum,' Dougal sneered, but lovingly. 'She's a victim of the cult market; that loosely defined area composed mainly of young adults waiting for the next trend.'

'You concede I'm adult.'

'Most certainly,' his expression intimate.

An old hag with a tooth like a tin-opener and the eyes of a burned-out eagle sat cross-legged on the pavement where the taxi disgorged them, soiled cards and charts spread methodically on a gaudy cloth lit by a hurricane lamp. Still almost dark, a direct light from above illuminated her cruelly. Imploring, she stretched hands seamed with lines and grime towards Ruth, who found her own hand held in the ancient claw. A grave, bulbous-shouldered little man joined them, the hag burbling, dribbling.

'Future, missie. We tell future?' He was the interpreter. 'Good life, good luck in land over many seas.'

'What powers of deduction! Remarkable,' Dougal muttered to Jon amused, and firmly took Ruth's elbow. 'No.'

'But Dougal … '

'No. I've seen enough of this sort of thing to be wary.'

Ruth wavered, but only for seconds.

'No,' he said again, but defiantly she was pushing notes into the extended hands, overpaying in aggravation.

'I can't see the harm.'

'Good luck, missie,' the cords in his neck stiff, his voice a muted falsetto he wheedled, 'we tell future … '

'No.' Dougal was adamant.

'Many fine sons … '

'But …' Ruth began again.

'Listen,' he tried to be patient, 'she'd only gibber something unintelligible in some infernal up-country dialect. Some rubbish … Look to me for your future. Okay?'

She pouted. 'Okay.'

The man who had been fawning about in hopes of further bahts drew back, nostrils snorkelling, then spat as Dougal propelled them aside from a gathering crowd.

The crumpled pewter of the sky had begun to layer with light, the oncoming day's heat sliced by the air-conditioning as they swung through glass doors. The sound of a plane thudded like a giant headache in the sky overhead.

'Flight 480. Flight 480,' particulars hammered in Jon's ears … 'Flight 480, boarding now at Gate 7 … '

'Goodbye, my darling. Be happy,' Jon's voice was strangled, Ruth's fogged with tears as they clung in farewell.

'Flight 480, boarding now at Gate 7. Passengers travelling on Flight 480, Bangkok to …'

Chapter Fourteen

She leans against a coarse bush which spills wilfully over a fence and sighs. With so many intervalled street lamps the world is filled by full moons. They don't wilt and gutter out like candles, time spent, but obey a hand to a switch, or worse still, removed from human touch react to a mechanical device.

The moon, the real moon, swings high in the sky humbled by no hand, no piece of machinery, answerable to no one, solitary, aloof. Is it perhaps covered with croaking birds or the ghosts of godless souls? Do they rustle and flap and foul up the surfaces to make it a carrion-infested place?

'Morbid,' she says, 'morbid and unnecessary.' She instructs herself: 'Think happy.' She dreams of a hundred little fountains playing, filling the air with rainbows, rilleting one into the other as they shoot high, jetting and throbbing, playfully cracking like ice.

She shivers; after all it's a winter's night and she wears no coat. Crouching, she bows her body as if to face a blizzard. She's freezing, but won't freeze to death. She's not drugged by the cold, preparing to lie down in deep, weightless drifts of snow. There's no snow. No rime of frost to coat her eyelids. No ice. Not outwardly. How she'd welcome a fire; heat bouncing up to the face, extremities oddly detached till a flood of warmth streams down the causeways of the body. But how quickly red flames whiten. How quickly it happens, like the processes of age. The day is endless to the child who wakes unburdened to play for hours, to crawl on his belly through long grass, to be caressed and fed, and like a lovely doll laid between fresh sheets as soon as the sun goes down. He grows but it's all so slow; impatiently he longs for each day to pass, aching for the years to produce the promised delights.

'When you're six. When you're ten ... an adolescent ... ' then, at last ... 'a grown person you can ... '

But can you?

Unaccountably, without warning you're an aristocrat of time and you use it with a swashbuckling lack of care, yours to exploit. But it twirls like a dervish and the nights spin round with the haste of a windmill fanned by a hurricane. And you're sealed into old age, slowed to a sedate pace where once you ran, memory patchy, and the grisly prospect of decrepitude lurks behind the blind which inevitably will be drawn. No one can tell you why, and you, the 'you' inside the shrunken frame, the decaying faculties, can be the motionless antagonist seething with passions improper for your state.

Why? you might ask, and anyone who answers will lie, not deliberately but in confusion. For the truth in itself is unendurable.

'I don't want the roses to fade from my cheeks,' tears slip down her cheeks, cheeks she knows never bloomed with roses, but creamy pale, the colour of bleached straw.

Dashing a hand to these cheeks she is surprised to find them damp, puts the hand close to her face in the charcoal of the night to examine the evidence of melancholy. Grief?

Purposefully she wipes them off hard down the length of her body, head full of sliding fantasies. She shakes them away, shrugs and walks briskly, briskly, briskly.

'Where am I?' she questions and dimly discerns an outlined signpost. She runs, and close enough to read it thinks not of roses, petals bathed in warmth, fragrant, flawless ... but Rose.

'To Westhaven Convalescent Home'. Westhaven ... a euphemism? Resthaven? Rest Haven. R.I.P.

Rose Maria Jamieson, born 1914 Rose Maria Connoon, wife of Laurence Arthur Jamieson, deceased, loving mother of an only child, Gilbert Laurence Jamieson, died ... who can predict?

Humph! Rose Maria Jamieson, born 1914 in a warring world, she battled and finally dynamited kindly Laurence Arthur Jamieson, corner-shop fruiterer who allowed his customers credit.

'Five pounds of spuds, soup veggies — carrots, a turnip, stick of celery. A jug of milk — it holds a pint and a half: not a full quart, mind. And boiled sweeties for the kids ... Can I put it on the slate, Mr J.? Until my Bert gets paid next fortnight. Yes, he's got a job. At last; brickie. I know your missus won't have it, but we're hoping our eldest, Billie, might be earning soon. Oh, bless you, Mr J. And aren't you the canny one, only having the one.'

Loving mother of an only child, Gilbert Laurence Jamieson. Smothering, jealous, critical, hypocritical, querulous, demanding mother of Gilbert Laurence ... evil mother-in-law of Jon, wife of Gilbert Laurence.

Jon's resolution wavered to find Gilbert meeting the plane. It broke her mood of holiday, freedom. But only for minutes.

I've clarified the basic issues, she longed to shout through the straight woven walkways of the airport building.

Dark suit, sober tie, his face, she thought, a shattered brick ... red, veined, deep lines bracketing the down-turned mouth struggling to hoist to a welcome, hair ridged by a comb. He looked to her, despite the expensive cut of cloth, a cushioned, pouchy-eyed walrus, thoroughly unendearing; a hulk she'd determined to abandon regardless of any plea.

How curious, she smiled and advanced towards him, how objectively we see our intimates after separation. Yet how easily we reacquaint ourselves with their dominating landmarks. Like old towns revisited, the narrow streets narrower, the cobblestones rougher under foot. Gilbert battered, worse than remembered and a short interval only had elapsed.

To what do I owe this unexpected pleasure, rose icily to her smiling lips which formed instead to say: 'Gil. What a surprise.' My smile, she felt, is too enthusiastic for credulity.

'Thought you'd like it.'

Everything changes and little appears to. Could he be serious? Genuinely surprised, she knew he'd snapped any string that could bind them, but it seemed he wanted to be liked. That was evident. And his voice, oddly confidential.

'How about a quiet dinner à deux?' It was barely asking, he seemed to take her reply for granted. 'You won't want to get back to the domestic round straight away. I've heard of a smart little place … ' He'd gone so far as to book a table.

Was this the time or place to inform him there was to be no further domestic round, the saga of their life together over? Yet the absurdity of it, the absurdity! We're living in an ever-accelerating phase of structural change and I'm fretting over one minute link.

'And I've bought a few surprises,' he was burbling in her ear. 'For you. Should make the house easier to run. The biggest, the best air-conditioning money can buy, two-way cycle hot and cold, plus a whole new range of kitchen gadgetry,' he went on like a pushy salesman.

The new gadgets switched her into a gaping silence which he interpreted as gratitude. A commercial love song played, the candle-lit restaurant discreet despite a pretentiousness Jon couldn't exactly place. Starched white cloths, napkins, the menu too extensive, the middle-European accents of manager and waitress struggling to be French. She tried to concentrate on choosing food.

'It's good to have you back,' he said, and amused she was almost shocked as he reached to pat at her hand which lay on the table. This was ludicrous and she sought to look down the dim alleys of his intent, through the sinister doorways for some kind of illumination. A couple of drinks and further signs of him becoming more fulsome! When he began to walk his fingers, the second and third of his right hand, across the table to hers, she was stunned. Evidently he anticipated she'd play along. She took refuge in a vague expression. What was he up to?

The house when they reached it was unlit. But as his key turned in the lock and she preceded him through the door, she sensed it inhabited, nose twitching to sniff out an occupant certainly contained in the darkened rooms above. Something, some whiff of another person filtered down through the floorboards, curling faintly towards her.

'Who's in the house?' she was opening her mouth to ask, advancing towards the staircase. Rounding in front of her he spread hands to prevent her passing.

'Sssh,' Gilbert was guiding her elbow, touch far from gentle as he forced her towards the sitting room.

'What?'

'Sssh.'

He closed the door behind them, snapped on a lamp, sudden and sharp after the darkness, the room familiar but different. Blinking, she looked around with a new curiosity. No longer the actor in detailed sets of airport and restaurant, he was blustering, bullying Gilbert Laurence Jamieson ... only child of Rose.

'What's this all about? Who's upstairs?' She put a hand to either side of her head as if to pat at an elaborate hairdo or remove bent hairpins of unreason she thought pierced her mind. What was this all about? Having stepped from the plane fully in control, fully determined enough was enough, she had a separate life to lead.

'Sit down, I'll get you a drink.' He was all conciliatory again, like lantern slides he was changing the frame ... now a teeming bazaar, now the Taj Mahal.

She was almost relieved at not having her question answered definitely.

'You're confused,' he said and was right.

But only in part. Out of the confusion swirled something rich, potent and alive. What was it? And clearly she knew. Freedom. That was it. Her freedom ... to plunge into work or play. Pile dishes in a sink, skip meals, take up causes, drop the lot, rage, range beyond known limits. She felt more energy than she'd felt in years. If she couldn't unlearn the ugly lessons she could dismiss them. Everyone was a victim, the world was full of injustices, but ... I'm removing myself from the battlefield. I won't lie strewn here, an arm severed, a leg crushed, head filled with sparks before the darkness falls. I'm one of the lucky ones. I don't have to fret and worry about money. Betty had done that for her. Thank you, Betty, thank you. Driven to it you enjoyed the market place.

When she thought of her mother she liked to think of her then, not now. Chasing and closing deals in what was strictly the preserve of men. I didn't like it but you were happier devoid of the strangling arms of love. Betty ... she couldn't place exactly when she lost the secret grudge and hurt she'd kept against her mother as a child. Long ago.

She thought of Betty: pictures of the old days whirling in her mind, crossing and recrossing in tangled memories of childhood. 'Green Briars', grease-proofed school lunches, grease-proofed kisses, the limp legs of the first pair of silk stockings Betty had bought her hanging to dry on a line hoisted by a clothes prop, Betty dosing her with syrup of figs, insisting on long-sleeved vests in winter and tents of towels for inhalations when she pronounced her 'chesty'.

Remembering made her sit very still. Betty had never listened even when acknowledging her daughter's world, leaning over to help with arithmetic, spelling, mouth pleated with pins for a fitting, hemming her gym tunics, lengthening little Tom's trouser legs and cutting toes out of his sandshoes.

Seasonal remembrances ... Christmas, brief summer holidays in rented cottages where stoves always tended to be antagonistic, the verandahs sleep-outs and the mattresses lumpy. Betty creaming crusty winter hands to avoid snagging soft fabric, Betty purposeful, her step buoyant as boldly she climbed from rung to rung.

After Paul's arrival the old grudges were forgotten. After Paul's death ... Jon had an instant recall ... Betty in black, her hat clinging about her tired pale face loosely like a wreath.

Betty, who now complained that the straight pictures on the walls of her supervised room lay crooked, that there were secret and dangerous bubbles in drawn baths. She barely ate, fingers fidgeting with food, peeling off bits in a dainty way but conveying no more than crumbs to her mouth. Betty so thin, bodiless, who hardly lived inside her flesh but hovered somewhere above it, a garment necessary to put on if going out in public ... but she wasn't going out.

Mothers, Jon sighed, the necessities of the human race, the collective breeding grounds. But a mother ...

'Mother,' Gilbert eased the word into the room but lost it as it fell, bumped against polished wood and was absorbed in the carpet. He rattled the ice in his glass.

'What?'

'Not what. Who.' Gilbert cracked the words, hastily, anxiously.

'Who?'

'Mother.'

'This is ridiculous, Gilbert. Stop playing your games.'

He cleared his throat, always a sign he was about to shout.

'Please don't shout, there's no need.'

'There's every need,' he shouted, 'you're such a bloody imbecile.' He swallowed hard. 'Sorry,' he muttered, about to proceed with something she saw now to be serious.

Thank God I've made up my mind. At times I'll be lonely, miserable, but there'll be none of this humiliation. Swelling with pride and trickery instantly followed by a sort of cheated discontent. She quelled a ridiculous impulse to thumb her nose at him, this shabby creature in his masterpiece of tailoring who would have been more properly outfitted with a club and a skinning knife.

'My mother', he enunciated each word with exaggerated care, any gesture of goodwill collapsed, 'is upstairs.'

'Rose?'

'Yes.'

'Is she ill?'

'No. No more than ... ' he reached again for the bottle in

defence against Rose's rheumy eyes and the long-playing record of her ailments that revolved whenever impossible to dodge the duty visit. More often than not it was Jon who made his excuses sympathising at the dismal recital of malfunctioning organs and in the old woman's healthier moments listening as Rose talked of her soul as if one of her closest friends. She had no friends. 'In my soul I'm a ... ' Rose piously seemed to see herself a minor saint, though this saintliness had never managed to blossom into active goodness. If she'd been stronger, basked in 'the blessing of good health', oh what would not have been achieved in soothing the path for the unenlightened and those who'd strayed.

'Did you invite her then?' her voice devoid of expression.

'Of course not,' the words burned out like hot chillies. 'If you must know, Miss Blackett,' the paid companion, one of a long line, but forced to stay through penury, 'Miss Blackett has a recently widowed sister who's had the gall to woo her away. Doubtless to slave unpaid.'

'You've advertised, of course?' With a mixture of obstinacy and dread Jon went on. She felt squeezed into a corner, a sharpened fear contracted her stomach muscles. 'You only had to arrange emergency help until ... ' Jon pictured Rose: clothes always gathered up in too many places, her shoes for years giving off creaky mouse-like squeaks, teeth clacking despite Gilbert's work on them. She saw the cherry-painted mouth in the powdered face with tufted moles, picking poisonously with every word. Jon recalled her mother-in-law on her last visit; huddled in an old shawl from somewhere, an ugly grey which must have been comforting in texture. In it she'd looked a badly-wrapped parcel, the big safety-pin a stamp, as she nursed a hot-water bottle, feet in ruptured felt slippers, sun and air kept at bay by drawn curtains, a single shaft of sunlight penetrating to a pattern on the carpet, the room oppressively hot and stuffy.

Gilbert, it finally transpired, who felt neither natural nor comfortable in his mother's presence had given his word that she was to live with them, Jon to take care of her.

'You'll only have to take her meals, run her bath ... '

She barely listened to this brutal assault to her reason. 'You tick off my life like a laundry list,' she said and felt swamped by a tidal wave. Incredulous, afraid, outraged, she realised he was placing yet another demand on her. How dare he? she flared, but it ran much deeper than any flash of anger. Soon she would be at the top of the queue, her turn to die and what, if anything, had been achieved? Moments only; moments when the world has been filled with a sparkling simplicity, moments when she perhaps had qualified ... but for what? To be human, to be hopeful? She began to laugh but it wasn't convincing. How little the present accords with the past and our expectations. Love, hate, lust, despair, there must be another universe to inhabit where all things are possible. Perhaps you enter by a narrow staircase slippery with oils, designed to daunt the unwilling, or a rope ladder swinging perilously between a jumble of mountains and endless sky. Maybe there was the lamp burning in the window for those to see who could see.

'Jon ... ' he was floundering on.

Dear God, she thought, where does duty reach its limits?

When Jon appeared with the breakfast tray the old woman's face flushed only with greed.

'One boiled egg, only one! No, of course, I don't want two. Is it soft? In the middle. I won't eat it if ... And pour the tea into my cup first. Before the milk ... ' the eyes sharp enough to rake the tray.

'I've brought you a pot. And milk in a jug. Good morning, Mother; slept well I hope.' She had already smiled too long.

'I never sleep well.' The chalky face dotted by shot-gun moles became agitated. 'I like honey with toast. Not marmalade muck.' Biting into a slice, butter dribbled from the stained cherry tracks at the corners of her mouth, sounds dental and guttural. 'And buttered hot. Hot, do you hear.'

The air was thick, permeated by an odour which could have been equal parts of seaweed, the drift of rotting leaves and cheap soap.

She's a domestic sadist, Jon was convinced at the end of a week, Rose faulting everything. Gilbert, well aware of her breathlessness having laboriously guided her upstairs on arrival, had assumed she'd make day quarters there too. Downstairs Rose would fume sulkily to herself, enthroned in the most comfortable chair. Fiddling elaborately with her hearing aid to ensure any civil statement from Jon did not penetrate, furrowing deeper lines into her forehead she'd complain that nobody bothered to as much as pass the time of day with her ... a poor, useless, unwanted old woman ...

When Gilbert dared to suggest that she, Jon, provoked his mother's odious behaviour, she was almost glad. It made her plans easier, but there was little chance to look for something to rent, work out her own arrangements. Having advertised for nurse/companion, hours were wasted sifting deserted wives with little experience and neurotic or rapacious spinsters with too much. Not that she blamed them; Rose would be a thankless task, enough to wilt the most dependable cabbage. What was needed was hard to find ... a combination of professional detachment and a degree of compassion, someone to smooth the rubber sheet yet be firm in a jocular way. Where to find such a paragon? Of course it must be possible to engage a suitable applicant, but was proving lengthier than anticipated, time-consuming, Rose herself quick to point out they'd cheat her darling boy and take advantage of her own easy disposition.

Weeks ran into months and nature began to plot against her. Sorry for the irascible old woman left with nothing but peevishness, her reproachful manner, twisted arthritic hands and the wasting limbs Jon saw as she helped her to dress, insidiously guilt began to undermine her intent. Some mornings she'd wake battered, tormented by outrage for something barely understood. She kept catching flashes of a recurring dream in which she was overwhelmed suddenly with trepidation and pleasure. But inexplicably a guilt shadowed her throughout the day. Yes, Rose was Gilbert's mother, but that didn't allay her responsibility. Again she was forced to ask herself where duty reached a limit.

Looking back Jon saw when it first began; the day Rose, digestion balanced and memory more reliable than usual, spoke of Paul. Jon had come to believe Rose had been born with a knife in the hand, savaging everyone who drew breath until:

'Jon,' said the old woman, 'the boy would have been nineteen on his next birthday. Yet old and useless bodies like mine creak on. Yes. Old and useless, we clutter up this earth.'

Enraged, suspecting Rose of some bid for sympathy, Jon held her tongue.

'He had charm,' Rose's words singsong, 'a quiet charm, and that's rare. Not like the girl,' she paused, 'she's a lovely humming-bird. Paul. He was like ... like a sleepy cub. I wish I could have known him.' She dabbed at her mouth, closed and opened her eyes. 'I suppose you think I'm dotty?' The old woman examined her daughter-in-law's face, and it occurred to Jon that she was trying to read her mind which made her uneasy.

'No,' she replied.

It was Gilbert who first raised the scheme for his mother's disposal.

'She's driving me mad.'

And Jon could see it was true. Why was he late? Where had he been? With whom? Why didn't he bring friends home? Who was Darleen? She'd picked up the extension and heard him talking to someone called Darleen as if his life was at stake. Three times in one week! He was drinking too much. Well, if it wasn't drink that flushed and puffed him to a red balloon, what did his doctor have to say? He must be full of bile. Why wasn't he seeing a specialist? He could afford it couldn't he? He wasted enough money, that was as clear as the nose on anyone's face!

'Mother, don't excite yourself,' he made a great effort not to shout, but could not resist raising his voice, moving lips with exaggerated care as if she was deaf, dumb or mentally defective. Curiously since Rose had come he'd felt older, much older, and as his head lolled sideways on the evenings when forced to sit with her, rocking, rocking, rocking, knowing he should help her up to her room, he'd wake fearful her unblinking gaze would be on him as she'd sit watchfully chewing with that timeless rhythm of the aged.

'Good night, Mother,' he would rise and say, neck muscles tense, intent on ignoring the cheek she thrust his way. 'See you in the morning.'

Rose, squinting up as she rocked, invariably would answer: 'God willing, dear. His will be done.'

Gilbert began to long for the old devil's removal. When it appeared after three months it would not be from immediate natural causes the future become intolerable.

'I'm getting rid of her. She's a dominating bitch,' he said to Jon warming milk in the kitchen. He puffed at his cheeks as if he wanted to be rid of them too. 'She's always upsetting you, Jon ... '

She turned on him, hatred ill-concealed. They were two hawks in the sky. Had each stooped on the same quarry, attacking, they would have found it to be two parts of themselves.

'Don't lose control of yourself again. And don't ... ' she caught up the words and was silent. There was no need to reply whatever the accusation. It came as she'd suspected.

'But you must want her out of the way. It's you I'm thinking of ... What with her bloody scalding tongue and her weak kidneys.' He gave a high, cracked laugh. 'Don't tell me you like having her here? Watching her wolf down her food, my food, wobbling every cup, slurping her tea and whining, whining, whining.'

Clarifying the basic issues? The question begged to be put. Tightening her lips she kept silent.

'I can't so much as have a phone call in private.'

She lifted shoulders and sighed. How tedious he was with this blatant interest in women's bodies.

'Is that asking too much? In my own house! Her ears plaster the walls of every room and ... ' he paced the floor and thought of Darleen; legs, thighs and frilly suspender belts. He had as much right as anyone else to continue to have a good time as long as he could. He liked them young for display as well as the other purpose. It would be many a year before he gave up his pleasures, damned if he would. 'It's snoop, snoop, snoop. Non-stop! Doesn't she have anything better to do? It's enough to drive a man from home.'

Jon ached for the old woman huddled in her bones and the belief that her son cared. If her brain or memories sharpened to absorb the shock when Gilbert delivered it, her physical health began to deteriorate and an attack of bronchitis replaced the occasional wheeze Gilbert suggested was a charade.

'You'll be far more comfortable, Mother.' The words oozed with real concern; real concern that the move be made without further hysterics. 'You'll be with people your own age.' He tried to be jolly, laughed with a backward throw of his head, and went on, 'you'll have a great time talking over the good old days ... and ... '

Bad old days, thought Jon.

'I know what they mean when they say only the good die young,' the old woman in a flash of lucidity hissed accusingly at this man, who stood looming over her. She wouldn't even care if someone bumped him off with his loud voice, his obscene sentiments, and folding her face like an old pair of gloves groped at the hearing aid.

'Mother, listen to me ... it's for your own good. Listen to me,' his voice swerved on every corner. 'You'll have a nice sunny room overlooking the garden and ... '

Dear God, is he going to top it all by promising a weekly visit? Jon reached for the tray and left the room. If only Rose would vent her spleen on Gilbert and batter him, bludgeon him with her tongue as she had his undeserving father. Submitting to Gilbert, but what choice did she have, doubtless she'd soon submit to a daily round of changing, combing and prettying before the matron's inspection. Once she'd seen a searing film with a wispy octogenarian, pink ribbons in what was left of her hair once thick, glossy and long, the wheelchair coyly drawn up between two very old toothless men topped with party caps like corks held by elastic under the remnants of chins. Well-intentioned party givers suggested the old woman — Jon even remembered her name, Mrs Gambol — should bestow favours equally upon her two beaux. Torn by loneliness, had the old woman wept silently into the pillow of her cot that night or dozed fitfully, lost in the conquests of her youth, breath whistling through her open mouth?

Jon thought she rather needed Gilbert's whisky. Unscrewing the bottle she heard him call peevishly down to her. He seemed so little worth the hearing; the future for both of them had become a thing of the past. Wanting to tear down the house on top of them, knowing it wouldn't help, she poured herself half a tumblerful, retipped the bottle to fill the glass to the brim and sank into the most comfortable chair, still warm she fancied from Rose's wasted body.

Chapter Fifteen

She pauses and with each step debates whether or not to go on. This gives her a lop-sided walk in the no-man's-land of this day between days, with a cold, pink dawn soon to flush away the night and its secretive caches of twisted riddles and whispered rules.

'I've been a carthorse, ploughing away at my own life,' she murmurs, 'but the ground get harder to break each year.'

Clip, clop, clip, clop. She starts forward again. Clip, clop, clip, clop. But the ground breaks away and she begins to float out on the sea. A large, happy crowd loudly bewails her departure from the quayside, waving and calling as the water widens, and she searches madly for something wanted that does not reside in faces before they shrink to blurred pinpoints and are gone. Gradually the land folds out of sight altogether and her senses sharpen to the smell of salt spray. She had no idea of her direction. Rolling with the swell she's weak and nauseous, tasselled tails of light flash spasmodically, but she has strict orders not to drown.

'Clip, clop,' she cries in the paling light and with frenzied effort strains in the creaking harness, and makes progress. But memories shuffle confused in time.

'Ride a cock horse to Banbury Cross

To see a fine lady upon a white horse,' she sings to baby Paul.

'Baby, baby bunting, Daddy's gone a-hunting,' she croons to little Ruth.

The weight of the harness lightens and straightening she finds the shafts of the cart no more than the first shafts of light feathering into a quiet tree-lined street.

The edges of light are the edges of life, she muses, the small kindnesses and cruelties that make you vibrate. And they reveal people.

She quivers then the raw air clawing her body, begins to tread lightly placing one foot with care, reluctant to reveal her presence, though she wonders to whom? Yet she wants no prying eyes, no straining ears listening to pick up her footfalls to follow down her labyrinthine way.

'Don't creep nervously along on tiptoe.' It's a chastising voice she uses. 'Please,' she adds, but the crypt-like street with the vaulting of trees induces a rigidity which threatens to starch her with fear, an uneasy sense of something unnameable, something that could be construed as the first step to … And cold, so cold, so cold. In the strangely muted street suddenly she stiffens, immobilised, breath catching like a fish hook in her throat. Blank and bewildered, she stares ahead certain that paced, regular steps are overtaking hers; at a distance still but distinct, approaching as inexorably as the new day. She longs to let the terror out, scream.

She screams, to cut it off as though by a knife. The world is loose and cracked and spinning at a furious rate. If she moves quickly enough can she escape this fear before it hunts her down? Shadowy, cruel, stupid, she's caught in it, a hapless victim. Is there any way out or has it been dogging her always, spying and following ever since a child when she'd stolen a few coppers from the milk money, refused to play with a little girl who stank, sneaked a look into her mother's drawers forbidden to open.

'God help me,' she whispers and reaches out to the comforting platitude for use in every disaster. 'God help me.' Where does one seek consolation? She's no plodding carthorse but a cruelly hobbled mare chained in her own ineptitudes, boxed in a valley that leads nowhere. Her head begins to throb.

Nipping the air, pinching it with tiny beaks the first chips of sound break in the trees above. The half-world she inhabits becomes fractionally cosy, the sounds of the birds laying a thin mantle of warmth on her shoulders shattering the audible darkness, calming the tottering balance of her mind.

From the half-light the apparition begins to solidify. An athlete, thick-set, muscular in running shorts, his feet beat out the threatening rat-a-tat she was convinced would take her into the world of the damned with its creatures of slime, stenches, unspeakable pits and chasms of muck.

'Good morning. Don't see many like you out,' steam hisses from his mouth with the words, 'before first light,' and his figure disappears, the slipstream almost bruising.

Goggling after him, up ahead there's another runner, this one with a jittering crate of milk bottles, and she yearns for another season when the sun shines, and another country where husky arms dip deep into pails to splash milk into waiting jugs, where toddlers stand in puddles of dew by women in shawls, woodsmoke funnelling from chimney pots. Nicer times? Certainly not; villains were hung, adulterers castigated, disease rife and rickety children sidled up to sparse tables like wasps sidling up to a pot of jam. In a world of incontrovertible events you pays your money and you takes your chance.

Don't demonstrate the futility of human life to me, she wants to cry, show me the absurd, I prefer it.

Too exhausted to mind the cold she plods on, the intrusive runner, the chinking milkman gone. Utter silence rings round her in two-way stretch, where no warning voice or even a neighbour can be heard whispering. Streets, endlessly leading, cross in haphazard geometry. Is she set on some blind course she must maintain?

'Where am I?' she asks, feeling homeless and far away, to make the discovery she's on familiar territory. Blocks of flats: Huntley, Bellevue, Shalimar, Buckley Towers, for a moment she can't take it in she feels so lost, Clareville, give way to houses with taut blinds in the cheek by jowl existence of suburbia. Well-established suburbia, maintained by executive energy, professional punch and financial acumen. She wouldn't care to assess the probable cost of upkeep. Large-bonneted Mercedes and Volvos stand beside Minis and Hondas in two-garage comfort behind Rollamatic doors.

The arches of her feet ache wretchedly. Stepping out of her shoes, she leaves them, walks on. The home stretch – familiar. Familiar gates and gardens. They run back through a projector in a crevice of her mind.

The Melis: Lena and Giorgio sleep well enough but what passionate storm will break when the truth is known that Isabella, their ripe and desirous second daughter, is overripe without blessing of church and has appointed the coming day to be aborted, unshackling herself from the centuries-old prohibition.

The Maloneys: Agnes and Brian. All as usual; Brian had yawned in vain competition through the Bette Davis re-run, sneered 'woman's rubbish', refused to make the Ovaltine, then as usual again used so much talc after showering that the big bathroom was a small snowdrift. He'd bought pork instead of veal, neglected to order the bulbs and she'd come close to refusing to accompany him on a third cruise to Fiji. And if he continued to side with the daughters-in-law over striped awning against plain ... well, he could do without her on late shopping nights. These irritations, part of the mould of thirty years of marriage, had begun to take on a desperation. Astonished to find she could have barbequed him in place of the best porterhouse he laid lovingly over the gas grill, she was shocked to find she relished the thought of his burning flesh. Brian, oblivious, breathed easily, Agnes beside him drugged by valium.

The Gillets: Keith, the accountant, satisfied his figures were beyond reproach, in sleep reproachfully turned a cool back to his wife, cold-shouldered as usual by her frigidity. She simply didn't like it, and while deploring censorship – except for children and who knew better than Gloria what children should like and should read – had found her vocal cords paralysed in shock, violated, by books Keith had once brought into the home … 'To try and turn you on,' had been his pathetic excuse. Little Tracy Gillet slept pleasurably out of her mother's sight, one thumb in her mouth, the other snug in her crotch.

The Sampsons: Timothy, barrister-at-law, twitched occasionally in the water bed. He'd pulled the plug out of the bath of his former wife with dubiously gained information. Impecunious! Humph! Why should she strut in comfort, and the children bright enough to make it unaided! Hadn't he. Was there a smile playing about Sonya's lips as she slept? Certainly: her dream his nightmare. Bobo, stretched out on his rug, twitched involuntarily like Timothy.

The last of the stars has been wiped out of the sky. The ghostly silver light beaten out by an antique moon is gone. The sky different now, high, wide, will be opening soon to a wintery sun of little warmth but welcome as a cup of wine.

An over-pervasive melancholy takes her hand and lifts it to open the latch of the gate of the house where she's lived for the last twelve years. Fragile memories accompany her to the door. The house seems to be waiting. Inside the early light seeps into the rooms like water.

In the sitting room she begins to move things, tidy as if divorced from her own hands, then from a low table lifts a worn bulky book, the spine buckling.

Birds of Australia. She looks distractedly at the faded cover for a moment, weighs it in both hands, allows it to fall open. Peering close in the half light …

'"The Prince Albert Lyrebird,"' she barely moves lips and swivels her eyes from the page. '"These are timid birds which run away when alarmed with their tails erect … or … or fly to the nearest tree where, with great hops in and out of the branches, they seek a safe place."'

Slowly replacing the book on the table she circles the room

and sits down. Her heart hurts. Crossing arms over it, she rocks a little and pivots on the chair to find she's facing the wall which backs on to the dining room. Abstracted, she looks into one of her own paintings and as she looks it withdraws leaving only the rectangular frame. Voices intrude; she listens as they demand her attention.

JON: Do let us try to make this an agreeable meal. It's among the last we'll have together.

GILBERT: What do you mean?

JON: You know precisely what I mean. I refuse to go into it all again. I'm leaving and ...

GILBERT: You can't I won't let you.

JON: There's nothing you can do to prevent me.

From her chair in the sitting room she smiles wryly at this badly scripted domestic scene, the dialogue so familiar it drains the imagination, blocks the will. Wife of twenty-seven years finally can take no more of the suburban tyrant. Plans a bold, new life in a bold, if not new, world. It continues: her tones resigned, his rinsing the last grain of sugar out with his words. Breath harsh and shallow, taunting, determinedly he tries to provoke her in an effort to justify ... To justify what?

GILBERT: Getting in first, eh? Making your little stand before I walk out on you. Fucking bitch.

JON: Please ...

GILBERT: You misunderstand the delicacy of the phrase. Fucking bitch! Ha, ha, ha. That's the joke of the century. Non-fucking bitch.

JON: And you can't see why I'm leaving?

GILBERT: Leaving! Everyone leaves you. Your snooty daughter, your precious son. Everyone wants to be away from you. Even my mother. You drove her away and that was no mean achievement.

Jon exits with soup plates, to return and place bowl of mushrooms, salad, on table, exits again quickly to return with two plates with steaks. Places one before Gilbert, sits opposite him with other. Gilbert eyes the food.

GILBERT: You'd probably like to poison me. But you're gutless. Ruth, she's a peacock to your ... your sparrow. Grey and inconspicuous, that's you, a twittering sparrow. Ruth's a girl with my spirit. Yes, Ruth could do it, but you!

JON: I suggest you eat. You're too drunk for any coherent conversation and I'm not interested in your sodden self-pity.

GILBERT: Eat! This leathery muck.

He hurls the plate at her. It misses, splatters the wall behind.

JON: Gilbert ...

GILBERT: *Mimics.* Gilbert.

Grabbing clumsily across the table he hurls the mushrooms, the salad, aim inaccurate.

JON: Stop it. For God's sake ...

GILBERT: God! Even He stepped in to take a hand. Inter ... Intervened, as they say.

JON: What …

GILBERT: Didn't think you were even fit enough to watch over that poor bastard, Paul.

JON: Paul?

GILBERT: You heard me. Paul. That namby-pamby you gave birth to. I didn't father him. You must have done it all by your clever little self. *Belches.* Who'd help you? Who'd want you, not even Blind Freddie. Your son. A miracle, eh? Ha, ha, ha. Another … What's it called? Another immaculate conception. St Blessed Jon.

JON: Stop it. Stop it do you hear me.

Gilbert about to hurl the bottle of wine after the food reconsiders, attempts to pour a glass, but aim unsteady raises bottle to his lips. Then bottle in hand staggers to his feet to advance on Jon.

GILBERT: Paul. That lily-livered son of a pathetic, feeble, cringing bitch. Would have been just like you. *He searches for each weapon.* Anaemic. Soft. Helpless. Watery. What a lucky thing for him he died. What a lucky thing for all of us.

Lurching, almost on her, the empty bottle slips from his grasp. He extends spread hands towards her, reaching for her throat.

JON: Stay where you are. Don't come any closer.

He leers close, the cells of his skin like grains of wheat. Eyes on his, Jon stands. Her hands scrabble over the table in futile protest, steady the end of a handle against her palm, then curl about the handle of a knife, the blade sharp and long.

GILBERT: Don't tell me what to do.

JON: I'm warning you don't ...

GILBERT: Don't you tell me ...

JON: Come any closer and ... and I'll kill you.

GILBERT: Don't you ...

Swaying he reels and loses balance ... to fall ... the knife unmoving in her clenched hand.

The raised voices recede. In the sitting room she hears nothing more than the rhythm of her own breathing. This sound is intoxicating because as slowly she stands, objects she knows as well as the palm of her hand ... but who really knows the intricate lines of the palm of a hand as we claim? ... swim in double focus, distractedly refuse to be still. Hammer strokes pound her head.

Twittering pecks of sound snap and reverberate. The pitch augments and from it a clearly audible but unknown voice asks with severity of light needling into darkened cracks ...

'Who killed cock robin?'

She responds. Everyone knows the answer.

'I,' said the sparrow,

'With my bow and arrow.

I killed cock robin.'

She felt something hovering, ghost grey.

'Who saw him die?' the inquisitor's boom becomes a lulling voice for children.

She responds ... after all it's a traditional rhyme, isn't it?

'I,' said the fly,

'With my little eye.

I saw him die.'

She's impelled to move to the window, the light the colour of a shallow wave, but her limbs hang limp, her feet concreted where she stands.

'Jon,' she entreats and words bulge in her mind but won't emerge. She feels a great fuse had blown. A cathartic sob escapes; she doubles in speechless panic. It passes.

Now she's a small ketch swinging gently at anchor, riding sleepily on the water in pale sunshine. No. The anchor weighs. She's a fish, the indigo shadows shafted by light, and it's easy to dodge the long, bobbing line of the net paid out in attempt to catch her. She won't join the heap of silver to die smothering on a shore of sand.

'I'm so tired,' she says. 'So tired of remembering.'

Her mind cranes. She remembers certain times but not the proper sequence. Perhaps she's stayed too long everywhere.

Steadily, with unexpected serenity after the crumpling night she moves to the dining room. Curtained, it's darker, unrippled by the advancing light and ... somehow heavy, crowded, the table unnaturally burdened.

Outside the sky will be a blank hard blue if it fulfils the early promise. Bread has been baked, news printed, trains will run on time. She touches the heavy body which can never be eased back into life.

'I am a stranger in my own head.'

There's an inability to remember. It all seems like a time that happened long ago, she muses, and turning her back on the room leaves it.

Adam's rib run amok? What a phrase to invade her mind!

She climbs a short, steep brutish path and upstairs fills the bathroom basin. She lifts her eyes to see a face reflected. Her face. The hair about it is wiry, faded. What could be done with such a face?

Lines can be removed from skin, gaps from teeth, down from lips, crimps and curls from hair, hooks from noses and psyches. But mutilations don't always show; not like hunger, greed or ignorance.

Etc. etc. etc., she demurs and drops her gaze, eyes welling.

She raises, then, with slow deliberation lowers her hands and washing away the blood sees it curl then melt pink in the water.